A SPECIAL INTEREST IN MURDER

Also by Mette Ivie Harrison

The Linda Wallheim Mysteries

THE BISHOP'S WIFE
HIS RIGHT HAND
FOR TIME AND ALL ETERNITIES
NOT OF THIS FOLD
THE PRODIGAL DAUGHTER

The Vampires in the Temple Series

VAMPIRES IN THE TEMPLE
GENEALOGY OF WEREWOLVES
RESURRECTION RITES

The Princess Series

THE PRINCESS AND THE HOUND
THE PRINCESS AND THE BEAR
THE PRINCESS AND THE SNOWBIRD
THE PRINCESS AND THE HORSE
THE PRINCESS AND THE WOLF

Other Novels

THE MONSTER IN ME
MIRA, MIRROR
TRIS AND IZZIE
THE ROSE THRONE
RHINE HIGH

A SPECIAL INTEREST IN MURDER

Mette Ivie Harrison

SEVERN HOUSE

First world edition published in Great Britain and the USA in 2025
by Severn House, an imprint of Canongate Books Ltd,
14 High Street, Edinburgh EH1 1TE.

severnhouse.com

Copyright © Mette Ivie Harrison, 2025

Cover and jacket design by Nick May at bluegecko22.com

All rights reserved including the right of reproduction in whole or in part in any form. The right of Mette Ivie Harrison to be identified as the author of this work has been asserted in accordance with the Copyright, Designs & Patents Act 1988.

British Library Cataloguing-in-Publication Data
A CIP catalogue record for this title is available from the British Library.

ISBN-13: 978-1-4483-1643-4 (cased)
ISBN-13: 978-1-4483-1644-1 (e-book)

This is a work of fiction. Names, characters, places and incidents are either the product of the author's imagination or are used fictitiously. Except where actual historical events and characters are being described for the storyline of this novel, all situations in this publication are fictitious and any resemblance to actual persons, living or dead, business establishments, events or locales is purely coincidental.

No part of this book may be used or reproduced in any manner for the purpose of training artificial intelligence technologies or systems. This work is reserved from text and data mining (Article 4(3) Directive (EU) 2019/790).

All Severn House titles are printed on acid-free paper.

Typeset by Palimpsest Book Production Ltd., Falkirk,
Stirlingshire, Scotland.
Printed and bound in Great Britain by TJ Books,
Padstow, Cornwall.

The manufacturer's authorised representative in the EU for product safety is Authorised Rep Compliance Ltd, 71 Lower Baggot Street, Dublin D02 P593 Ireland (arccompliance.com)

Praise for the Linda Wallheim Mysteries

"Has good reason to draw a large readership"
The New York Times

"Linda has an engrossing voice"
USA Today

"Suspenseful . . . Those looking for a nuanced character study will be well rewarded"
Publishers Weekly Starred Review

"Highly recommended"
Library Journal

"An extremely smart and refreshingly imperfect series lead"
Booklist

About the author

Mette Marie Ivie, who writes as **Mette Ivie Harrison**, is the award-winning, national bestselling, *New York Times* Notable author of the Linda Wallheim mystery series, featuring an amateur sleuth who is a Mormon bishop's wife. She is also the author of numerous young adult fantasies, including *The Princess and the Hound*. Mette was formally diagnosed with autism in 2017, which inspired her new series featuring autistic amateur sleuth Ada Latia and FBI agent Henry Bloodstone.

Mette holds a PhD from Princeton University, and works at a financial firm as a licensed security trader. A divorced mother of six children, she lives in Utah and enjoys triathlon, knitting and crochet.

www.metteivieharrison.com

Dedicated to Michael Austin, friend, editor and beta reader who saw this book first in infancy and encouraged me to continue to write it into a series.

ONE

Ada Latia stared at an incoming phone call. It was from Rex Friendly. Her ex-husband.

He had called her twice since their divorce eight months, two weeks, and three days ago.

The first time had been to ask her for a password for the company that he'd taken in the divorce, Good Cosmetics, based on non-petroleum oils and with no free plastics to ruin the environment. Early on, Ada had invented an entirely new lipstick formula that stayed on until it was removed, and the formula had worked for her other products, as well. It was non-permanent permanent makeup, or that was the tagline that had made her (or at least her company) very wealthy.

She'd given the password to him, ignoring the impulse to refuse and tell him that he could use the income from the company she'd built from the ground up to get an IT guy in to break into the systems that he wasn't smart enough to hack himself.

The second time had been when he had told her, two months, one week, and one day after the divorce was finalized, that he was marrying Tomi, her former best friend and vice president of the company. At one point, Tomi had told Ada that she should be careful that her husband wasn't cheating on her, that he wasn't going to take the company right out from under her with the help of the board.

Tomi had been right, but Ada didn't exactly give her special credit for the information.

Ada tapped the screen to answer, trying to breathe in a rhythm of four counts in, then four long counts out.

Rex appeared on the screen. He looked very much as he had when she had fallen in love with him three years, four months, and sixteen days ago.

He had a bit of a scruffy beard. His hair was perfectly coiffed, blond, and his chin was very square. His eyes were an arresting shade somewhere between green and blue. He could have been a Norse god.

She'd thought she would have been more affected by the sight of him now, but she felt only a twinge of embarrassment. How could she have so easily been distracted by the mere appearance of a handsome, symmetrical face? There was little else to recommend Rex. Besides the fact that he had that stupidly ironic last name and a set of skills that were useful for a neurotypical person who had turned out to be selfish and possibly narcissistic.

'Ada,' Rex said. 'Good to see you.'

She got out a sound that she supposed sounded moderately affirmative.

'You look— What in God's name is that outfit you're wearing?' Rex asked. 'You look god-awful.'

Ada looked down at the purple-and-green plaid jumpsuit and orange T-shirt. It was quite bright in color. She rather liked it. It did something she liked for what had been called a weak chin and coloring that was bland and almost invisible. She had good eyes, but that was her only moderately good feature, and they were a plain, dark brown.

'It's comfortable,' she said, though she wished immediately she hadn't answered so defensively to Rex. He had a gift for making her react that way, as if she had to apologize for herself in every way.

She put a hand down to smooth the nicely soft fabric. The jumpsuit had only seams that were sewn over, so that they didn't have any sharp edging next to her skin. In high school, Ada had sometimes worn her clothes inside out. Not because she couldn't figure out which way was the 'right way.' She could, absolutely, though she never understood why most people liked to wear seams next to their skin when it felt so much better reversed, with seams on the outside.

Rex had encouraged her to wear things in darker colors. As camouflage, she supposed. So that he could be the one to stand out. Right now, he was wearing a black suit with a fine gray line down it, a dark red shirt, and a tie that was almost as loud as her jumpsuit – except that it was so much smaller.

She smiled to herself at the idea of Rex's size being so small.

'Well, if that's all that you care about now,' Rex said.

'I don't run a cosmetics company anymore,' Ada said.

'True. But you're going to have to get a job at some point. You really should take better care of yourself. You don't want to give up entirely. You're too young for that.'

Ada was keenly aware of the fact that she was only twenty-four years old. She'd been the youngest millionaire in the cosmetics industry, at least for a little while. And then she'd been out of that industry.

'I'm sure you didn't call to offer me advice on the next step in my career path, Rex,' Ada said. 'What can I do for you? I'm sure it must have been important for you to take time from your busy schedule to talk to me.' She wasn't important. Not to him. Not anymore.

'Ah, yes. Straight to the point. No small talk for you, Ms. Autistic,' Rex said, smiling back at her.

Ada tensed, trying to figure out if he was making a joke about her autism. He had done that often when they were together, and she had tried to be good-natured about it. She'd also tried to ask him not to make fun of her because it was painful to feel left out like that, as if she were on a stage and he were part of the audience laughing at her. But he'd always insisted that she just needed to 'learn to have a better sense of humor about herself.'

She never had.

She waited, arms crossed, silent, for Rex to spit it out. Silence had been a useful tool for her in her relationship with Rex. He'd called it a weapon, but she'd never been the one attacking with it. She had only used it to try to protect herself against his attacks.

'I have a link I'm sending to you via email. I think you'll be very interested in it,' Rex said, clicking on a keyboard behind the screen. 'There, it's sent. You should take a look at it.'

'I will do that, Rex. I'll get back to you as soon as I can,' she said blandly. This was a phrase she'd learned from Rex himself, and he knew exactly what it meant. She hated saying it because it was a lie, but she'd practiced it over and over again. It meant she had no intention of looking at it or ever getting back to him because he didn't deserve her time or attention.

'You're really going to want to look at this story. It's all over the internet,' Rex said, his eyes very intent.

Don't do it, don't do it, Ada warned herself. Whatever it was that Rex had sent her would be designed to hurt her. She should stay away from it. He was an expert only in making sure that he got what he wanted and no one else did.

'It's about a couple of autistic children at a special autism school near where you live now. It's Idaho, right?' he said.

'Utah,' she found herself saying automatically.

He waved a hand dismissively.

At least she knew what that gesture meant, though so many others were so impenetrable to her.

'Utah, Idaho,' he said. 'Same place out there in the Midwest.'

Neither Utah nor Idaho was technically in the Midwest, and Ada struggled not to correct him. Her teachers in elementary school had never liked it when she did that, and she'd eventually learned to just write her correction down on a piece of paper rather than saying it out loud. In this case, she just told it to herself silently.

'I'll take a look at it when I've got time,' Ada said, trying again to use one of Rex's own trite and false phrases back to him.

She hated that he had taught her so much about the neurotypical world that was useful. She hated that he had been so right about so many other people, and even, in the end, about himself "slumming with her" as he'd said, pretending it was a joke though it had turned out not to be.

'You kept telling me that autistic people weren't monsters, but this looks very much like they are. Even the younger ones. They aren't really human, you know? You look human, but you aren't, not underneath. You've got no emotions inside of that skin sack of yours. It's all just numbers and schedules and rules inside there,' Rex said.

She felt as if the top of her head had popped off and some vital part of her was floating above the rest of her. She never felt entirely connected to her body, not really. It always felt like it was an annoying encumbrance more than actually her. But this was worse than most times.

'What is it you said you were going to do now? Study extraterrestrial worlds? So you could find a planet where humans could go in case we destroy this one?' Rex said mockingly.

'I'm studying ways to communicate with aliens who come

here,' Ada found herself saying, though she was aware that Rex wasn't listening to her now any more than he had before, when she had told him her plans for the future.

Aliens could not possibly be more cruel or more deceitful than other humans. She looked forward to actually communicating with them in a plain and honest way. In her opinion, a coming alien invasion was the only hope the rest of humanity had to be saved from their own worst inclinations. There weren't enough autistic people to really make a difference, and they didn't have any power, of course, not in the neurotypical-dominated world of politics and business.

'Well, one autistic kid is dead because another autistic kid murdered her. They're saying it's an accidental death, but I don't see what difference that makes. No normal kid holds another kid down until she isn't breathing anymore. That's a subhuman monster. That's the kind of kid who should be put in jail. Like all autistic people. Keep them away from the rest of us, so we're safe.' Rex cut the call then.

Ada was briefly relieved that she didn't have to think of some calm way to respond to him. She let out a long, low scream. It felt good to hear herself make a noise. It felt good to feel her throat get painfully sore.

Then she heard a thump from upstairs, and she remembered she lived in an apartment building now and she had to think of other people. Which she did. Because whatever Rex said, she did have empathy. She cared about other people. She didn't just pretend to with planned facial expressions that looked as if she had emotions that she didn't actually have.

Ada went through another round of her breathing exercises. Count four, hold for eight, let out for four.

Ada opened her email and clicked on the link Rex had sent. It wasn't a reputable news source. It was from a distorted social media site that invited comments and got advertisers based on the number of responses. Designed to gin up outrage, like most sites designed by neurotypical people were.

The original post was titled 'Autistic Kid Kills Other Autistic Kid at Fake Autistic School.' There were claims that autism wasn't real, that parents were simply refusing to properly 'parent difficult children,' that ridiculous diagnoses were proliferating now that insurance companies paid supposed experts to explain why those who had no 'discipline' acted badly, and that all of this was a result of 'woke liberalism.'

Ada might once have been hurt by these claims. Not anymore. She didn't enjoy the internet generally and avoided most social media as the worst possible outcome of neurotypical people who were unchecked in their privilege. But she had also heard all of these insults over and over again, many of them from her own parents when she was diagnosed, some from her own husband. They didn't really hurt her anymore.

What drew her attention was the graphic photograph of a young girl, dead, posted underneath the screed against the rise in autism diagnoses. This was not the kind of photograph that she thought she would ever become inured to, but it was also true that she had never before seen the photograph of a dead autistic child. Immediately, she was sure that this girl was autistic, though she wasn't able to explain the reasons to herself why she was sure. There was simply something about the girl that reminded her of herself at that same age, the plump cheeks, the badly cut hair, the clothing that was some strange combination of things her parents wanted her to wear and things that she herself chose to wear – not at all fashionable and not quite comfortable, either.

She did her breathing again, but she didn't look away from the photograph.

The young autistic girl hadn't been given the dignity of a name, but Ada tried to focus on the objective details of the photograph in the hope that doing so might provide some kind of shield against the wave of sorrow that she felt rising inside of her. She hated emotions. She never knew how to deal with them. Crying was supposed to be the right response, but she tended toward something neurotypical people considered unacceptable: either a complete repression of emotion or an overexaggerated throwing of objects and screaming until she was hoarse.

Focus. Focus.

The girl had thick, dark hair, which was like a rain cloud around her head in the photograph. It didn't look natural. It looked . . . well, fake or posed or something. The girl's bangs were unevenly cut, but someone seemed to have tried to make them look better by combing through them, possibly even spraying something on them to keep them in place.

That part was wrong. But there were more wrong things.

She had to keep looking, making notes in her head.

Ada guessed that the autistic girl was not yet in her teens. She hadn't developed any breasts, and the clothes, presumably chosen by her parents, didn't seem to emphasize feminine body shape. Ada remembered her own parents insisting suddenly when she had her first menses that she had to wear different clothing, even more uncomfortable than before. Tighter skirts, more feminine blouses, shoes that made her fall over.

This wasn't a crime scene photograph taken by an expert, Ada thought with certainty. She went back to the top of the post and read through it again. Nothing that indicated anything about an official police investigation. No names of police officers or jurisdictions mentioned. No official statements by the police or by the school. Though that didn't necessarily mean that there had been none. She would have to look that up in a little while. She made another note to herself to do that next.

Look at the photo again.

The dead autistic girl's small hands were carefully placed, one at her left side, the other above the right side of her head. That also indicated posing. An official crime scene photographer would have been careful not to contaminate the scene, surely. Even if they felt sorry for the girl. So who had done it? Someone else, someone who wanted to make sure that the girl looked . . . not her normal self. Not autistic, even. Which was strange, since the whole point of the blog post was that the autistic girl wasn't really human, and the autistic kid who had killed her accidentally was also not human.

How soon after the death had the photograph been taken? The face didn't have that grayish tone that Ada had seen when her mother had died, just an hour or so later, when Ada had let go of her hand and left her there. Had the photograph been taken immediately after death? Wouldn't someone who was there immediately have been more concerned with trying to revive her? CPR or something?

Ada looked more carefully and then knew why Rex had sent

the photograph to her. The little autistic girl was wearing makeup that Ada herself had created and that Good Cosmetics as a company had marketed and manufactured and sold. It wasn't anything from the new line that Tomi and Rex had worked on together. This was Ada's own line, and someone had put it on a little autistic girl to make her look better. Was that irony? Or just a terrible and sick neurotypical need to contain everything autistic and make it 'better'? Ada couldn't believe that the little girl had purchased and applied the makeup herself. For one thing, it hadn't been smudged at all. It was all too perfect.

Ada's brain revved up into 'hot brain mode,' a kind of hyperfocus she couldn't control. It wasn't just the girl in the photograph that was wrong. The room around her was combed free of toys, and the carpet had been vacuumed so that lines showed up clearly behind her head. If this was truly an accidental death, then why had someone gone to such lengths to make the photograph of the girl look so perfect? Who would want to manipulate the image of the girl? Who would want to make her death look more benign?

Someone who was involved in a murder, Ada thought, and who wanted to cover it up by claiming that it was just an accident. Someone who blamed an autistic child for a murder they hadn't committed. Someone who wasn't autistic at all, but neurotypical – the kind of person who was always concerned about appearances, who was always manipulating, always lying. Just like Rex.

Now Ada turned away from the photograph and began to look at other information in the blog post and in the comments below. The name of the autistic school was NAVITEK, which stood for Neurodiversity and Variation in Teaching Exceptional Kids. She found the website, which said that it had been running for three years under the direction of Soledad Sanchez, who took over from the previous director. It was in rural Idaho a few hours north of where she lived in Utah now. There was a brief statement on the website asking for 'privacy in a difficult time for the staff and students of NAVITEK.' That was the only reference to the death that she could find publicly, other than the original blog post that Rex had sent to her, and various other related social media that all seemed linked back to that post.

No one was investigating this as a murder. Rex hadn't wanted her to investigate it, either, Ada was convinced. He'd just wanted her to be hurt by the accusations about autistic children being monsters. And he'd wanted her to see that her makeup had been used by an autistic child who had supposedly been killed after using it. Rex wasn't particularly intelligent or inventive – one reason why he'd needed Tomi when he took over Good Cosmetics in the first place, damn him.

But her personal feelings about the man who had directed her to this injustice really had nothing to do with what she was going to do now. It had nothing to do with the fact that she might have been that dead autistic girl, if her life had gone slightly differently, if her parents had decided that she needed more assistance and had believed her diagnosis. Her first therapist had warned her back in middle school that, as an autistic person, she had an 'unusually rigid and unapologetic view of justice' that might sometimes make her stand out and set her at odds with society in general. At the moment, she didn't care. This little girl, whatever her name was, deserved justice, and Ada was going to get that for her.

TWO

Ada made a list of the problems she saw in the photograph.

1. The room around the girl's body was meticulously clean, without a single object on the floor around the body. There were even vacuuming marks visible on the carpet. Who would have rearranged the room after the child's death and then taken a photograph without concern for law enforcement complaining that evidence had been tainted or completely destroyed?

2. The girl was lying on the ground with her hands one at the left side, one at the right above her head, which Ada felt sure was not how she would have fallen if she had been strangled or suffocated, in the way the blog post said was how her death had been reported as accidental. If it was accidental, she would have been in distress, and that would have shown somehow in her body position and probably in her expression, even if it had relaxed in death. Almost as if the person who had taken the photograph had known that it would be circulated online and hadn't wanted it to be as graphic as it might otherwise have been.

3. The girl's bangs were uneven, probably a sign she had cut them herself, but they had been pulled away from her forehead just enough that it was less noticeable, and the rest of her thick, dark hair fell around her face in a way that couldn't possibly be natural. Someone had combed it and arranged it like that. Ada remembered her own mother trying to style her hair over and over again, and it never lasted for more than a few minutes. A girl at an autistic school would never have done that herself, and it wouldn't have stayed that way anyway.

4. The girl's lipstick was Nuclear Pink, a color that Ada had created when she'd first founded Good Cosmetics. She also wore foundation from that same original pallet, the one Ada had called Pink Cosmos, because she thought of it as the colors of the natural universe. Someone had applied that makeup after she had died, Ada was sure. It wasn't the kind of makeup a girl experimenting with color would choose. It was makeup that an adult who was trying to manipulate and deceive would use – a neurotypical adult.

5. The girl's top had feminine lace around the collar that was somehow untouched by any sign of violence – no wet stains or blood. On her torso, she wore a knit skirt that was pulled the wrong way. The effect was a strange combination of child and fashion. Ada didn't know if the top had been replaced and the skirt hadn't, but it bothered her. If someone had a top on hand that fit a girl that size, it was suspicious, surely, that they had replaced it for this photograph in death.

6. The shoes were still on her feet, and they were delicate Mary Janes with a strap still closed, something that Ada felt sure was impossible. A girl who had been struggling for her life would not have kept her shoes on, and somehow Ada did not think that those shoes had been chosen by the autistic girl with that haircut.

7. The photograph had not been taken by anyone official, not a mortician or anyone involved in law enforcement. It wasn't marked with a time stamp or any other details, and the body was posed directly in the center, cutting off the chair in the background that might or might not have had anything to do with her death.

8. The girl's eyes were open in the photograph, which wasn't necessarily proof she had been posed that way, but it felt invasive to Ada. She would have wanted her eyes closed if people on the internet were to see her. The eyes open made her seem more naked, and that made Ada have a more protective response. It made her angrier on the girl's behalf,

and more certain that whatever had caused her death, her body had been used by someone who might have been the murderer to obfuscate the truth.

The case hadn't been picked up by any wider news sources, and Ada admitted to herself that the whole thing could be fake news, the photograph AI-generated, based on a real photo of a dead girl, perhaps. The blogger could have passed it along as intentional misinformation to increase traffic so that parents of autistic children were more likely to see it, and to increase fear of vaccines. It had become a familiar feedback loop: scare parents about the horrors of autism, then convince them that the solution was to stop vaccinating children. Or any number of other ridiculous quack cures. When the real solution – acceptance of autism – was never suggested.

Ada went back to the blog post and forced herself to read some of the hundreds of comments already there:

That school should be sued to the last penny for allowing anything like this. What is the state of our public school system when teachers leave kids alone and then are surprised they get hurt?

What kind of money are we pouring into that school? Millions of dollars of public spending that is taken out of the system for normal children, who are the ones who deserve education. The ones who are useless should go to institutions where they can bang their heads against the wall in peace.

Why are autistic girls the ugliest creatures on the planet? Good thing this one is out of the gene pool and will never reproduce.

You can tell she isn't dead. Her eyes are about to blink. She's just a stupid girl trying to get attention.

That's not a human. That's clearly an alien.

This last comment was one that Ada itched to comment back on. But as soon as she started to write about aliens not looking anything like humans, the commenter posted a second note:

They're taking possession of humans so that they can control our government. They tried to take me. They took me up into their spaceship and kept me there for days so they could scan me and get all the information they needed to infiltrate our society.

Ada sighed. If aliens really had that much information about humans, they could just create their own clones. They wouldn't need to possess human bodies. Not that they would do that, either. There was no logical reason to assume that aliens would want to take over humans. Or even the planet. It wasn't as if Earth had any important resources left.

She went back to the document with the list of problems and added a list of attributes she thought would be likely for the murderer, because it was clear to her this was murder, not an accidental death. It hadn't been done by an autistic boy or by any autistic person. There was too much manipulation, too clear an understanding of the audience who would be looking at the photograph and the distraction that the photo was meant to create – talk about autism, not about a possible murder.

Ada thought it was most likely someone on staff at the school. That was obvious, just based on opportunity. But who? She didn't think she could know until she met them, but somehow she was sure that she would have an immediate and instinctive response to that person. Not that she would be disgusted. She wished she was good at guessing at the minds of other people. She was not. She was often easily fooled, at first. It would take her time to see the lies and deceit. But she wanted a chance to do that. For the sake of that autistic girl. For the sake of young Ada, who might have been that girl.

Ada stared again at the photo of the dead autistic girl. It was a mystery, and she had never learned to let a mystery go. She needed to understand the way everything fit together. She needed for the world to make sense.

It didn't make sense, as long as humans were in it, at least. She knew that on some intellectual level, but she hated it. It was like a tag on her shirt that she cut off, but which still bothered her because there was a seam that wasn't quite tucked down, and then a thread that had to be pulled out, and on and on, until she had to cut the shirt into pieces and reassemble it herself, the proper way, so that it all fit together.

Ada wrote up a bit more along with her list about the problem with the photograph, then attached the photo and sent it to a local news station. She wanted some attention on the case. She was sure that no police had been called as yet, or else there would be more online about it, not just the one blog on a social media site.

Two hours later, Ada hadn't gotten any response from the news station. She realized she shouldn't have started there anyway. She looked up the contact information for the police station local to the Idaho school, which was in an unincorporated township with a sheriff rather than a traditional police chief. She called the number listed online.

'I'm calling to report a murder,' Ada said.

'Who has been murdered?' the woman on the other end of the phone asked her.

'I don't know her name. She's a young girl at an autistic school.' Ada explained about the photograph she'd seen online.

Even to Ada, it was obvious from the woman's response that she was simply being kind when she said, 'I see. How troubling.'

'If you would look at the photograph,' Ada insisted, and told the woman how to bring it up online.

'All right, I'm looking at it. What makes you think it's a murder? It says it was an accidental death. She looks like she's just asleep, poor thing.'

'A girl who had been accidentally killed by suffocation by another child would not look like that.' Ada tried to explain how she knew the photo was faked. She was sure that the woman was going to tell her that she was seeing things that weren't there. Rex had told her that frequently.

Instead, the woman took a sharp breath in and asked, 'Are you a professional medical examiner?'

'No,' Ada responded directly. 'I am a high-functioning adult autistic woman. And I can promise you, there's something wrong with that photo of a dead autistic girl. She wouldn't look like that if it was an accident.'

The woman said, 'Hmm,' and there was a bit of a pause before she said, 'All right, honey. I'll ask the sheriff to look into it. Do you want him to call you back if he decides that he wants to pursue it?'

'Yes, please,' Ada said.

The woman on the other end took her information, but once she hung up, Ada had no confidence she would help – even if she did believe her. She didn't have any power either.

Ada did her breathing again, but her limbic system was too far past normal functioning. She was going to feel accelerated heart rate, sweating, and pressure on her chest until she got to sleep that night. If she got to sleep that night.

It was painful for her to come up against situations that she was not an expert in. She preferred dealing with data, with numbers, with spreadsheets and products. She knew how to deal with those.

Humans, on the other hand, were much more difficult. They were so unpredictable, so unknowable. People were always erupting in emotions that made no sense, and then they insisted that she, Ada, made no sense.

She checked the internet, but there was no change as far as she could tell. Still the only place the photograph was available was on the blogger's website. No one had demanded he take it down because it was evidence in an investigation. The comments continued to come in, but they were all the same as before.

Ada looked at the photo of the girl again.

The dead child was about ten years old, but was small in stature, possibly due to malnutrition, though, of course, Ada couldn't know that without more information. Some autistic children simply did not like the process of chewing and swallowing food. Some had so many aversions to texture and flavor that it was difficult to get them to eat any kind of variety. Many autistic children liked to eat only what was familiar so that they could avoid the kind of unpleasant scene that unfolded when presented with a food in a social situation that they could not chew and swallow.

Ada herself had struggled to eat when she was in the midst of puberty. This had been one of the reasons that she had been sent for a diagnosis. The school nurse was concerned with her weight percentage on the chart for her age (it had been below one percent).

'Do your parents allow you to eat whatever you want?' the nurse had asked.

'No. They like me to eat healthy food,' Ada had explained.

That had led to a visit to her house by Child Protective Services. They had found nothing to complain about. The house was neat as a pin, everything in its place, the carpet vacuum lines always clearly laid out because her mother cleaned every morning before she began her own work. In fact, her mother found it impossible to get her brain to focus on work before she had the house entirely clean.

That photograph was like something her mother might have staged. Not that her mother would have ever murdered her. That would have been too messy. But there had been more than one occasion when her mother had made it clear that she wished Ada had never been born.

'I will warn you that should you ever decide to have a child, you should think twice. It is never what you think it will be. There are few rewards, despite what they say, and the disadvantages are enormous,' her mother had said.

'The cost-benefit analysis of a child is never a positive figure,' her mother had said another time, when Ada was working on her statistics assignment in high school.

Her mother felt Ada should be grateful for every scrap of attention given her, that she should be trying to pay back the initial investment.

It was nearly five hours after she'd seen the original blog post, and past midnight, when Ada called the FBI public number and left a message on a recorded line. That was surely all she could do for the little girl. She needed to let this go. She wasn't a trained investigator, and she didn't know anyone in law enforcement. She didn't have control of the human universe, or any other universe. There were no aliens here to take over the government of all the countries on Earth and to make sure that all humans were treated equally, and that wealth and resources were distributed fairly to all. What she could do was continue to work on her deep space probe and the communication device within it. That was where her attention should be best used for the good of humanity.

THREE

Ada wasn't able to sleep that night. Instead, she got up at three a.m. to look more carefully at the NAVITEK website.

There was a list of teachers with credentials that seemed mostly legitimate, though Ada was always skeptical about what neurotypical people said, especially on the internet. *Don't trust and definitely verify* was her rule, and she planned to follow it here. She noticed there were no photos of any of the children at the school – probably a privacy issue. Fine. Ada stared at the photos and brief information about each teacher.

Madeleine Lynch, communication specialist, had dark hair and dark eyes. She listed as credentials several autism training programs at schools Ada had never heard of. She also was completely unsmiling in the photo, which made Ada like her more.

She'd always been told she should smile in photos to make herself look more approachable. People would sometimes comment to her about whether 'this smile' or 'that smile' looked more authentic, but Ada never understood those sorts of comments. All smiles were fake, all were a performance. Ada never smiled when she was by herself, only when she was with other people. It was a social response, not a natural one, for all that other people insisted the opposite.

Tina Abrams was listed as the friendship facilitator, whatever that meant. She looked very thin in the photo, and her arms and hands seemed to indicate height. She had a psychology degree from Brown University and a Master's of Social Work from NYU. Or said she did. Ada tried to look up to find any online confirmation, and while she did see photos of Abrams at Brown, there was nothing from NYU. Hmm. Might not mean anything.

Nora Glock was the math tutor. At least that was clear and useful. Many autistic children were good at math. Though many were also not good at math. That was a stereotype that wasn't particularly useful. The tutor had bucked teeth in her wide smile in the photo, and very freckled skin, but somehow she seemed very pretty even so.

Jennifer Langham was the manners specialist. Her photo was of her at the finish line of a running race of some kind, though she looked as if she'd just stepped into the race without any of the usual sweating or hair mussing that happened with most athletes. She even had makeup on.

Maybe it was some of the makeup that Ada herself had invented. But no, probably not. None of the colors were right. She didn't list any credentials at all. Interesting.

Indira Johnston was the nurse, and she had trained at the University of Utah. She looked trim and had a white jacket and white shirt on, as if it were some uniform. But she didn't have a typical nametag 'Nurse Johnston.' Ada checked to see if she could find proof she'd gone to the university she said she had. On her Facebook page, she had more than twenty friends who listed the same university and their major as nursing. She also had a résumé of other nursing jobs she'd had. Probably wasn't lying, then.

Dr Lorraine Berling was the final staff member listed – a reading specialist. She claimed to have a PhD in special education from Utah State University. She had glasses in the photo and a book in her hand, which she was looking down at. Behind her was a stack of books of some kind.

Ada tried to enlarge the image of the spines, but these were the kinds of books that were bound in leather, intended to look fancy, but had probably never been read. As far as Ada could tell by looking up the year of her graduating class, she had finished, and Ada could even see the title of her doctoral dissertation: *The Effect of Fiction Reading Aloud on Non-Verbal Autistic Children Aged Seven to Ten: A Long-Term Study.*

The final photo was of 'Director Soledad Sanchez' who was smiling at the camera in a way that made Ada twitch. She had short, gray hair cut in a bob, and she wore glasses that seemed mostly for show. She wore a business-like suit with a pink blouse that had a bit of lace around her throat to make her look more feminine.

She also had a long list of credentials and had apparently

hosted a 'Gala Event' earlier in the year that had raised enough funds to pay for three scholarships for underprivileged students, as well as the rest of the budgeting costs, which, as far as Ada could tell, were entirely reasonable.

There were also a few photos of the school itself, which was housed in an old farmhouse that had been repurposed and had beautiful grassy grounds around it that any child, autistic or not, would have to enjoy. There were plenty of windows to look out on the fields surrounding the house, and few cars to be seen. It wasn't a school that was trying to 'mainstream' autistic students, and there were no neurotypical popular students to bully the others.

She didn't have a name of either the victim or the child who was supposed to have killed her. There was no other information online about the murder that she hadn't seen before.

FOUR

Ada's phone rang as she was trying to lie back down and get her mind to quiet enough to sleep another hour or two. She checked the time reflexively. It was four thirty-two a.m. The caller ID said that it was from 'FBI Headquarters.'

Ada sat up immediately and answered, 'Hello, this is Ada Latia.'

'This is Henry Bloodstone, Adalatia. You used to call me Hen. Do you remember?'

This was not at all what Ada had been expecting, and it took her aback. She hesitated several long moments before getting out a guttural noise that was neither 'yes' nor 'no.'

'We went to high school together. I was in your math class. And your physics class,' he continued.

'That was eight years ago,' Ada said, which she knew was a stupid thing to say. The man surely knew as well as she did how many years ago it had been.

She remembered him as a gawky teenage boy, pimply with glasses. He had annoyed her, but not often. She'd called him 'Hen' as a kind of joke, since he asked her on their first meeting if she ever went by something short as a nickname. And now she did, as it turned out.

He was the last person she'd have thought might turn out to be an agent of the FBI. He'd been intelligent, but not at all the kind of rule-follower she might have assumed would do well in such a bureaucracy.

'Yes, it was. I work for the FBI now, and when I heard of the report you made to the phone system, your name immediately made me pay attention. You've taken off the surname since I knew you, but it's still a very distinctive name.'

Ada had changed her name at marriage and then again after her divorce. She hadn't wanted her ex-husband's last name anymore, but changing it back to her father's last name hadn't seemed like much of a solution. She'd thought about it for a few weeks and eventually decided that the name that suited her best was the name she'd always been known by: Adalatia. She simply separated it into two parts.

'I always went by Adalatia,' she said.

'Yes, I liked that about you. It suited you – that unusual, formal name.'

Ada didn't know what to say to that, so she said nothing. She hated these kinds of conversations. She wanted to get down to business, to the facts. This felt like irrelevant small talk, and while she knew that other humans always liked to establish their relationship to each other, their position on the social hierarchy, and what they could do for each other, she had difficulty paying attention to those kinds of things.

If aliens came to Earth, she sincerely hoped they were aliens who did not have their own ridiculous list of social rules, that they were entirely rational beings that she could talk to easily. Autistic aliens, so to speak.

'Do you still think there's a possibility of this autistic child being murdered and not just accidentally killed?' Henry asked.

Finally, back to the point of his phone call. What a relief. Now she felt she could talk honestly.

'It's not a possibility. It's a certainty. And when did you ever know me to change my mind?' she asked. If he had known her in high school, he should remember that.

'Never,' he said, laughing.

She felt awkward then, as she always did when other people laughed. Laughter was usually directed at her, or it signaled that she was being excluded from something she didn't understand. She hated not understanding things, even the stupid things that other people laughed about.

'That child was murdered,' Ada said. 'I think by a neurotypical adult. Probably one of the school staff members.'

'Well, I read your conclusions based on the one photograph. Unfortunately, we need actual proof and not just suppositions at the FBI.'

'Is there anything you didn't understand?' Ada asked. She knew that most people, but especially men, wouldn't admit if they didn't understand something she'd said. It was another nonsensical thing about normal social interaction. If she didn't understand something, she was happy to say she didn't, and leave space for someone to explain something to her. It was always good to have more information. But other people didn't seem to feel that way. They liked to pretend they understood things they did not.

'Several things, actually.'

'Oh,' Ada said, taken aback. 'Well, tell me which ones and I can explain them more to you.'

'I have a few questions first, actually. Do you mind answering them?'

'Of course not,' she said. 'Go ahead.'

He cleared his throat and said, 'Actually, I was hoping that we could go out for coffee. This morning, if you're available. Then we could talk in person, and it wouldn't feel so disjointed.'

Ada didn't like phone calls, either. But her preference would have been to communicate via text or email, not in person. Then she'd have had time to look through all the words and make sure that they all made sense. Words were a far superior way of communication. Humans and their insistence on continuing to use gesture made no sense. That way of communicating had been fine for Neanderthals and other early human groups who didn't have more sophisticated and specific utterances.

But she also knew that most humans wanted to see faces and pretend to read body language. She didn't think they got much from her, but they seemed to want it. Even Henry Bloodstone, sadly.

'In person seems like a lot of trouble for you. Where are you located?' Ada asked.

'Oh, we have an office in Utah. That's not a problem. I can drive to where you are in thirty minutes. Is there a local coffee shop you prefer?' Henry asked.

Ada was confused by the question. Why would she have a local destination to go to for coffee? If she wanted coffee, she had it delivered to her home, typically in bean form so she could grind it fresh. She didn't want other humans to touch it or interfere with the way she liked it made, and she didn't trust them to make it without changes or contamination. She didn't like leaving her apartment if she could avoid it. She'd made this into the perfect place for her to have calm and peace, so she could concentrate on communicating with aliens.

But this was important, so she would make an exception.

'Why don't you pick a place, and I'll meet you there?' Ada said, and hung up.

In another minute, Henry sent her the address of a local Starbucks, which was fine with her. She put it into her phone and found that she had twenty minutes to shower and dress before she had to leave. Plenty of time.

She took a nap first. She set an alarm to wake herself up five minutes before she had to leave. And weirdly, she fell asleep immediately. All the spiraling thoughts had disappeared because she had a plan for how to deal with the problem now.

When her alarm went off, she felt refreshed and hurried into the shower. She had timed herself many times before. If she was in a real hurry, she could get out in two minutes, twenty-three seconds. This time, she wasn't in such a hurry, so she gave herself three minutes.

After she had dried off, she had fifty-seven seconds to put on the outfit she'd already planned on – the purple paisley elastic-waist skirt with the yellow knit top with an open collar. The sleeves came to just above her wrists, which was ideal for her. She didn't like to have to push up her sleeves if she had to do work with her hands.

With the last twenty seconds, she did a quick toothbrushing and put on deodorant. She didn't bother with combing her hair since she hadn't washed it, just covered it with a shower cap. Every once in a while, she was tempted to shave her hair off entirely, but she hadn't gotten around to it.

At the door of her apartment, she put on a pair of gold sneakers that didn't need to be tied since they were already loose enough to slip on, and she was out the door and into her car. The address was already in her maps app, and she enjoyed the Australian male voice giving her instructions to the Starbucks.

She found a table by the door and sat down. While she waited, she put in her order on the app on her phone, which she'd just downloaded. It was so much easier to type requests into a computer than it was to have to speak aloud to a human, whose face she had to watch for cues, and who would make gestures that they would expect her to understand about whatever special they were trying to get her to buy today.

Henry came in three minutes late. She tried to remember if he was one of those people who strived to be 'fashionably late' in high school, but she realized that she hadn't known him well enough to form those kinds of memories about him. He really hadn't stuck in her consciousness at all. If she'd never met him again, she would have died thinking only vaguely of someone she'd known in high school who hadn't been terrible or wonderful enough to remember clearly.

He had longish brown hair that curled around his ears, and he seemed at least a couple of inches taller than she'd remembered him being. He was dressed in a pair of khakis with a gray button-down shirt and a black belt. It was the most unassuming outfit she'd seen, the kind of thing one wore to appear invisible.

Ada understood that kind of clothing very well. For all of high school, she had worn those kinds of clothes as camouflage. But it hadn't worked to protect her. Not at all. So now she enjoyed outrageous colors like those she was currently wearing.

Henry had already looked around the Starbucks, and now looked around again. This time, she waved a hand to draw attention to herself.

He started visibly, pulled his head back, and then moved toward her tentatively.

'Adalatia?' he asked. 'Is that really you?'

'Yes, it's me. I suppose I look different than in high school. I go by just Ada now.'

'Ada.' He nodded, came closer, and then held up a finger. 'One second. I'm going to go get my order in. Do you want me to get you anything?'

'No,' she said. 'I already got mine.'

'Because you always order the same thing.'

'Yes, I do.' Ada did not understand why he was stating the obvious. She thought that was what the autistic person in a relationship was supposed to do.

Was she in a relationship with Henry Bloodstone? Yes, but not that kind of relationship.

He put in his order, which sounded quite complicated, and came back over to her. 'You look great, by the way,' he said. 'I didn't mean to imply anything else.'

He seemed to think that she cared about how she looked. This was a neurotypical obsession, as far as Ada could tell. Neurotypical people liked to pay in the social currency of compliments, but Ada had never met anyone who had understood why it didn't work on her. It wasn't that she was immune to compliments, but no one seemed to know what kind to give her.

The idea that she cared about her appearance was strange. Her body wasn't her. Her clothing wasn't her. They were things that carried her around. She was inside of what anyone could see.

If people complimented her about things she cared about – her inventions, her theories, her communications with aliens – those things she'd flush about and stammer out a thank you for. But people who told her that they saw her as a sack of flesh and bones – it just made no sense to her.

'I'm surprised you answered my lead so quickly,' Ada said. 'Are you really an agent for the FBI? I wouldn't have guessed that.' She wasn't sure what she would have guessed, but not that.

'Well, I got interested in research and the agency hired me.' He sounded a bit embarrassed.

'Well, I'm glad you're the one who read it. I thought it would just go into some kind of black hole and be ignored. I was really starting to worry that no one would pay attention at all, and I would have to try to go to the school myself,' Ada said.

'Oh, no. That's not a good idea. Not by yourself. You want to be official. Otherwise, they wouldn't talk to you at all,' Henry said. He fussed in his pocket and pulled out a lanyard with his name and photo and a logo from the FBI on it.

'Do you like working for the FBI?' Ada asked.

Someone called out 'Ada' and she went to get her coffee. She opened the top to check and make sure it was what she ordered. It looked like the simple black coffee she preferred. She took a sip and made a face.

Yes, it was definitely black.

'Mr Blood?' one of the servers called out just as she put the lid on again and headed back to the table at the front.

She was surprised to see Henry go get the order for 'Mr Blood.'

'It's my coffee-shop name,' he explained as he took it without opening it or even taking a sip. He seemed to trust total strangers to listen to his order and take his word that it was what he wanted. Ada hadn't had much experience with that in her life.

'It tends to go with the FBI thing,' he said. 'You know, investigating murders.'

'Ah,' Ada said.

She and Henry both sat back down.

Henry took a sip of his coffee finally and sighed. 'God, that is good. I love a coffee in the morning.'

'Maybe what you actually like is the sugar and fat,' Ada said.

'Are you judging my coffee choice?' Henry asked, putting a hand to his heart.

Ada realized after a moment that he wasn't really offended. 'I just think it's a lot of sugar for the morning.' Did she sound like Rex? She did sound like Rex, and she hated that. 'Never mind. Forget I said that.'

There were still times when she said something she had once thought she truly believed in, only to find out that it was just Rex's voice installed in her brain, and she had to work on uninstalling it like any other piece of software. Or malware, as the case might be. She had once thought he was so smart. Not smarter than she was, but as close to as smart as she was as she would ever find.

She'd been delighted that he was interested in her. She had given up any thought of finding romance because she hadn't thought she could find a compatible match. She'd liked that he had his own opinions, which he'd told her boldly. She'd liked that they argued with each other. She had thought she had found someone at last who wasn't intimidated or disgusted by her. And she had listened so many times to what he'd told her with certainty was true about the world.

But now she knew he'd been lying to her from the first. She had to find all those little tags of information that she'd accepted readily and added to her bank of 'facts' and take them out one by one. It was taking a lot more time than she had anticipated when she'd first started on the project. She hoped that, at some point, she'd be able to forget he ever existed. But not now, it seemed.

'Me working for the FBI? I can see why that would surprise you,' Henry said. 'I admit, it's not at all what I thought I would do back in high school. I think I imagined that I'd be some kind of theoretical physicist. Or an astronaut. Or someone who talked to aliens.' He laughed at this.

Ada did not laugh, and his smile quickly faded.

'But I wasn't as good at the theoretical stuff as I thought, once I went to college. And I was good at psychology, and I took a course in crime scene investigation, and somehow ended up at the FBI. It turned out to be a good fit. And I find it satisfying. I feel like it's making the world a better place. That matters to me.'

This simple statement made Ada's heart warm. She'd been debating about whether or not she would be able to trust Henry Bloodstone on a deeper level. Of course, she'd have to go with him to NAVITEK, but she hadn't been sure if she would just be using him to go along with her or if she'd really tell him everything she thought.

'It's quite a coincidence that you found me there. I mean, not that you were looking for me specifically.' He tugged at his collar. 'But I'm glad that I noticed your tip and glad that I can come and talk to you about a real case. I don't know what you've been doing since high school, though.'

He waited and seemed to expect Ada to tell him something. She wasn't going to tell him about Rex. Or about Good Cosmetics. That wouldn't be useful to the case at hand, even though there was the connection to the makeup brand and colors she'd invented.

So she said, 'I work for myself. I like doing independent projects. I often consult on high-level topics that require thinking outside the box.'

How she hated that phrase, though she used it anyway. She was not in the box, whatever box people seemed to think of. It had never been something that she was ever praised for, being outside the box. But in the business world that she'd been briefly part of, people were always saying that they were 'outside the box,' though, as far as Ada could tell, they were barely able to raise their eyes outside the box. They were firmly still inside the box and mostly had no interest in doing any significant movement other than pulling other people into the box with them, and all pretending how much outside the box they supposedly were, if they kept their eyes closed.

Henry nodded. 'I see. Yes, that makes sense. I suppose I can't really see you in a corporate environment, sitting in meetings and worrying about how much money you could make.'

'I have enough money,' Ada said cryptically. At least she did for now.

'Is it all right if I ask you some questions?' Henry asked.

'What kind of questions?' She tensed.

'Can you tell me how you found out about this case? It's not in the news, as far as I can tell, not even the local news.'

'An acquaintance alerted me to it,' Ada said carefully. This was the exact truth, and she always found it easier to say the exact truth, though she had recently become aware that sometimes telling the exact truth gave people the wrong impression. That was not her fault. Just because people didn't ask more questions, or assumed things about her that were not true, was not her fault.

'Is your acquaintance in law enforcement?' Henry asked.

'No, not at all,' Ada said.

'Are they part of the school staff? Or possibly a parent of another child there?'

'No,' Ada said. 'No, it's not like that. They told me about it because they know I'm autistic and they thought I would be interested.' That was most of the truth. As much as Henry needed to know.

'Did they know you'd contact the FBI?' Henry continued.

'No. Hen, *I* didn't know I'd contact the FBI. I was just getting desperate. And I didn't know you worked for the FBI. How would I? We haven't had any contact since high school. You went your way and I went mine.'

He gave a rueful smile. 'Yes, and it's not as if you followed my career with interest. From afar.'

'I didn't think about you at all, Hen.' Was that a rude thing to say? It would have been true of almost anyone from high school. She hadn't thought of the teachers, or the other students. She didn't have any friends, so she hadn't thought of friends.

Her life after high school had been quiet and isolated. She would have said lonely, except that she'd never really had any idea what that word meant. She liked being alone. She'd never had a moment in her life where she wished other people were around her when she was alone. Not even when she'd been married to Rex.

Did that say something about their relationship? She hadn't thought so at the time, and she didn't think so now, either.

'All right. Good. I just needed to make sure that you didn't have any conflict of interest.'

'I don't. I don't know anyone at the school or in law enforcement. Other than you.'

'Good.' He nodded. 'Just a few more questions, all right?' He didn't wait for her to agree this time. 'When looking at that photograph, you seemed to have had an expert response to it. Do you have any training in forensic pathology?'

'No more than any other person who understands the basics of human biology and has access to the internet,' Ada said.

'And you don't write crime novels or something like that? You're not working on a big movie idea to sell to Hollywood?' Henry asked.

Why was he asking this? 'No, that sounds disgusting. People who enjoy thinking about murder? Writing about murders? I can only imagine that they aren't very nice people.' She shuddered a little.

Henry laughed again and reached across the table to take her hand. 'Oh God, Ada, I had no idea how much I missed you until you came back into my life.'

She pulled her hand back immediately. She had never liked being touched. It was one of the things her mother had said about her infancy, that she had been a baby who was entirely self-contained, who didn't speak or make eye contact or even seem to know who her parents were – or care. Her mother had been angry about this – that, at such a young age, Ada hadn't given her the proper attention and respect.

Henry let his hand drop and then he reddened. 'I mean, not that you're in my life again. I just mean that you're funny, and I think I somehow forgot that about you.'

'I am not funny,' Ada said stiffly.

She had a vague sense that she was, once again, the butt of some joke she didn't understand. Whenever people laughed at her, it was always with some element of cruelty or superiority. Her whole life, she'd listened while other people laughed about things she didn't understand. To her, comedy was mean, pointing out other people's weaknesses and letting other people know all about them. That was what social scientists insisted was part of the basic human herd instinct, but Ada didn't think so. In her opinion, that kind of cruelty had developed far later in human development. But then again, so many definitions of 'humanity' excluded autistic people of various kinds. No wonder most people thought of them as some kind of monster.

'I'm sorry. I apologize. I'd also forgotten how much you dislike jokes.'

'I don't like being laughed at,' Ada said.

'I wasn't—' Henry started to say, and then gave up. 'All right, as I said, I remember now you don't like that. I promise I won't call you funny again.'

'Thank you.'

'Now, about the NAVITEK school. I have looked up how far it is from here. Maybe four hours of driving,' Henry said.

Ada had already looked up the address and directions from her apartment. 'If you drive too fast,' she said.

Henry looked like he was going to argue with her about that, and then he said, 'All right, let's say five hours then, driving the speed limit.'

What else did he think was the point of having a speed limit if people were going to just ignore it? Ada didn't understand why society created rules and then most neurotypical people changed the rules in their own heads. Why not just make a different rule?

'I think that we need to go to NAVITEK and interview the staff about what happened to this child. I've already contacted the director,' Henry said.

'Soledad Sanchez,' Ada said.

'Yes, her. She's agreed to allow us to come on campus for three days, starting tomorrow, and she's willing to set up interviews for us to talk to the relevant staff. Apparently, there's a field trip on two of the three days, so the students will be gone for the next two days,' he said.

'Allowing you?' Ada echoed. 'Aren't you the FBI? Why is she telling you that you can come for three days?' Ada thought the FBI would tell the school when they were coming and how long they'd stay for.

'It's not always politic to force things on people. Interviews will go better if there's cooperation. And I said us, not just me.'

Ada hated the word 'politic,' because it was used to tell her that she didn't understand anything about how social interaction worked, but also because it meant that someone was not telling the whole truth.

She stared at Henry Bloodstone. In high school, he'd seemed a decent sort of person. For a neurotypical. She couldn't remember a time he'd lied to her or manipulated her. So she was going to give him the benefit of the doubt. For now.

'All right,' she said. 'So you want me to come with you?'

He waved a hand at her. 'You're the one who started this. I thought you should be there. And also, I admit, I'm no expert on autism and I thought there would be areas that you would be better suited to understand than me.'

Ada shook her head vehemently.

'What? What did I say?' Henry asked.

'I'm not an expert on autism. I'm an autist. There's a difference. I know what it's like to be autistic, from the inside. I can talk about my autism.'

'Isn't that better than any neurotypical person, even if they've studied autism all their lives?'

Ada answered sharply. 'So a thief is an expert on burglary, even if they only do one kind of burglary? An athlete is an expert on nutrition science? If you speak English, then you can explain the grammar and teach any non-native speaker how to learn the rules and sound native?'

'I suppose not,' Henry said. He didn't sound convinced.

'I'm autistic, but certain parts of my experience with autism are unique to me. And there are traits of autism that I don't have at all. It's called a spectrum for a reason. There are multiple definitions given by multiple experts. It's not as if you can give someone a blood test to see if they have autism. It's about asking the right questions about certain topics and then rating the answers to see if there is significant enough variation from the norm,' Ada said.

Henry did something awkward with his hands, directed at her.

'So, no, I'm not an expert in autism.' She might be an expert in alien communication, though so far her experience had been that the more she studied the topic, the less it seemed clear if there were any experts or if any of them agreed on anything. She felt sometimes as though the more she learned, the less she knew.

'Fine. You're not an expert in autism, then. But you can definitely help me navigate the school and the interviews. I want you with me, Adalatia. I think there are things that you can see that no one else can. Details, contradictions maybe. I mean, you've already shown that with the photograph of the girl, Ella.'

'Is that her name?' Ada said.

'Yes, Ella Kimball.'

She took in a deep breath and let it out slowly. 'Ella Kimball,' she repeated. It was important to her to know the girl's name in a way she wasn't sure she could explain. Too often, autistic people were seen as just a stereotype, as a representative of the whole group. And as she'd just explained to Henry, no autistic person was like any other autistic person. Just like no neurotypical person was like another neurotypical person. They were people, too. People first, autistic second. They deserved to be treated that way, and it seemed that Ada was the one who could do that.

'All right,' Ada said.

'You'll come, then?' Henry's face seemed to change. His whole body was tense and alert.

Was that a good thing?

'Come to the school? Yes, if you want me.'

'Good. We'll drive up in the morning and talk to the director. Then I'll get us a hotel to stay overnight for the next three days.'

'So will I be an official consultant of some kind?' Ada asked, surprised that Henry didn't talk about this first. Surely there was an order to this kind of process.

'Unofficial consultant, I suppose,' Henry said. 'But don't worry about that. It won't matter.'

'If you say so,' Ada said. Henry was the expert on the FBI.

'You're available for the rest of the week? No other appointments that you'll need to reschedule or anything? No one who will need you?'

'I don't have any appointments this week,' Ada said. She didn't have any appointments for the rest of the year, not just the rest of the week. That was how she preferred her life.

Her first adult therapist had asked her once if she ever got lonely.

'I don't think so,' Ada had said. 'Why would I be lonely?' It wasn't something she'd ever thought about before.

'You're not in school anymore. You don't have a schedule that has you meet with other people regularly, talk to others, interact with others. You're very isolated, working at home.'

Ada had shrugged. Yes, she was isolated. How was that a problem?

'You don't ever want to go to a coffee shop and just be around other people?' the therapist had asked.

Ada shuddered at that. 'No, definitely not.'

But maybe the therapist had been right, after all. Maybe she understood something about her that Ada hadn't. Because it hadn't been two months later that she'd met Rex and had fallen in love with him for no good reason. Only because, perhaps, she had been lonely and hadn't known it.

And now here she was, at a coffee shop. But thank God she wasn't with Rex. Henry would never be the same problem for her. Henry was just Hen.

'I have your address from your phone number. Reverse search,' Henry said. 'So I can pick you up in the morning. What time?'

'How about seven a.m.?' Ada asked. That would give her plenty of time for her morning routine.

'So early?' Henry said, looking vaguely surprised.

'How about seven fifteen?' Ada said instead.

'All right. Thanks for that extra fifteen minutes,' Henry said with an odd tone. 'I'll see you then. We can go walk around the school, see the scene of the crime. The body has been taken to a mortuary, but that's not our area.'

'Will you be asking for the body to go to a morgue so a medical examiner can do an autopsy?' Ada suggested.

'Hmm. Maybe. Let's see where things go at NAVITEK.'

'But if the body is prepared for burial, won't much of the evidence be destroyed?'

'Ah, good point. So I will make some phone calls on that issue tonight. We need the body not buried even if the medical examiner doesn't do an autopsy immediately.'

Ada didn't know why Henry wouldn't just have an FBI medical examiner look at the body, but he was the expert on the FBI.

'After we speak to the staff, hopefully we can speak to the other children. Witnesses,' Henry said.

'Can I speak to the other autistic child?' Ada asked.

'The boy who is suspected of smothering the victim? I don't know if he's verbal or not. I understand that some autistic children aren't. But if it's possible, we'll ask Director Sanchez to facilitate that.'

'I believe I could communicate with a non-verbal autistic child,' Ada said. Even though she'd just argued with Henry that she wasn't an expert on autism, she thought this would not be difficult for her.

'All right, then. I will see you tomorrow,' Henry said. He finished off his coffee, and Ada took a few sips of hers before throwing it away on her way home. It wasn't the right kind of coffee, her own coffee.

FIVE

When Henry rang the doorbell, it was seven twenty-three. Ada had been waiting for eight minutes by that time. She had been sitting on her couch, wondering if it was possible that Henry had forgotten, if he had been doing some kind of long con on her the day before and didn't work for the FBI at all, or if she should text him and ask him how late he was going to be.

Then the doorbell rang and she stopped worrying. She felt her heart skip a beat (literally) as she stood up and moved toward the door. She always felt a burst of anxiety when someone rang the bell or knocked, or when she got an email from someone unfamiliar, or when she got a text message. Any of these things required her to put on a kind of social mask that was difficult to sustain. She was always afraid that she would act in some wrong kind of way and would then be told a list of all her flaws or, worse still, be rejected entirely and never contacted again.

But Henry was different, Ada told herself. At least, she hoped so.

She opened the door. Henry stood there in a very ordinary black suit and possibly the most ordinary plain red tie she'd ever seen. She'd thought yesterday's outfit was bland, but this one was even more boring.

'Wow, that is—' Henry said, waving at her clothing.

She had on a purple-and-green paisley jumpsuit that covered her from neck to ankles, and down to her wrists. She rather liked clothing that covered her body. It wasn't exactly modesty, because she didn't think there was anything shameful about her body, though she supposed it was possible that she'd learned far too early that just because she thought her body was fine didn't mean other people would agree.

More fabric meant that there was more color, more style, and people tended to focus on that rather than on her. She liked it. It was a kind of disguise, rather different from the neutral tones she wore in high school, but far more effective.

'I don't know why you keep surprising me.'

'Because you thought I would never change?' Ada asked. 'You certainly have.'

'Yes, but I suspect much less obviously,' Henry said.

Ada wasn't sure that was true at all. She had changed her clothing style, but in every other way she was so much like she was in high school that she couldn't imagine anyone who was more so. She was the same height, the same size (though she did technically wear a smaller size because clothing manufacturers had changed their sizing even if her numbers remained the same). She had learned things that she hadn't known in high school, but she sorted information the same way. If she liked different things now, it was only because she hadn't been introduced to them at that time.

She was the least changeable person on the planet, and she knew that was partly because of her autism, but she wasn't ashamed of it.

'I'm ready,' she said, trying to hide her annoyance with Henry's hesitation.

'What? No last-minute rushing around?' Henry said. He sounded genuinely surprised.

'You are eight minutes late,' she said, looking at her watch. 'Nine now. Why would I be rushing around when I am the one who chose the time?'

Henry tilted his head to the side, considering. 'Because it's very early?' he asked. 'And because you're a woman?'

That was so blunt and sexist that she couldn't just walk out the door without addressing it directly. Ada shook her head at him. 'There's no reason that having female genitals would make one late any more than having male genitals makes one early. I swear, I will always be confused and annoyed by the long list of traits that are assigned to one gender or another. What about having a uterus means that I will like the color pink and not the color blue? Or that I will enjoy activities like cooking and cleaning and not running marathons or weightlifting?'

Henry put up his hands. 'You are right. I'm sorry. I certainly didn't mean to start off with a sexist comment. Will you give me another chance?'

But Ada hadn't finished her venting. 'Gender is, in my opinion, entirely a social construct. It's not something you have on the inside. It's something that people press on to you from the outside. Women are this and that. Men are this and that. And be careful because every fifty years or so, it will change completely to the reverse. Like in the eighteen hundreds when little girls were dressed entirely in blue because that was a feminine color, and little boys were dressed in pink because red was a masculine color and pink was a boyish version of that.'

'Interesting,' Henry said.

Ada didn't check to see if he was, in fact, interested. He needed to know this information about her view of gender if he was going to work with her. He needed to know it sooner rather than later, because if he couldn't stand it, then he could just go to the school on his own or not go at all. After so many rejections, Ada found it better for someone to hear all of the bad parts of her personality up front so that the rejection happened when she hadn't become attached to them yet and it wouldn't hurt as much.

'In other countries, little boys are considered far more susceptible to illness than little girls. Little girls are hardy and don't need to see a doctor. Only little boys need extra care and attention. And do you know what happens because of that?' Ada asked.

'No, I don't,' Henry said.

Just as well, since Ada was going to tell him anyway. 'Little girls in those cultures die at much higher rates than little boys because they don't get medical intervention. Because the reality that this idea cloaks is simply that this culture, like ours, considers boys to be more valuable than girls, and so deserving of the expense of better medical care.'

'I see,' Henry said.

He was waiting, Ada decided. 'I'm finished now,' she said.

'OK. Well, if you want to tell me more about gender being a social construct, I'm ready to listen. I went to college and took a gender studies class. I'm not a total idiot.'

Ada took a breath and realized that part of the reason she'd done this was because it served as a kind of threshold conversation as she prepared to step out of her apartment and into Henry's car, into another world that she would not have control over. Other people might have made small talk. She babbled about something that she cared about, but that perhaps wasn't entirely appropriate.

'Does the gender lecture have something to do with Ella Kimball's murder?' Henry asked.

'I don't think so,' Ada said.

Henry glanced behind her. 'Your apartment is . . . not at all like what I thought it would be,' he said briefly.

She supposed that someone else might consider that a request to be invited in. But Ada didn't like other people in her apartment. Since she'd gone through the divorce, no one had been in her apartment, and she liked it that way. The fact that Rex had purchased nothing here, had been able to make no pronouncements about any of her choices, made her feel so safe here, like a cocoon.

'What did you expect?' Ada asked.

'I don't know. I guess something less colorful. And, uh, maybe less crowded?' Henry said, with a lopsided smile.

Ada loved the green-and-orange floral couch and the purple-and-pink tasseled cushions atop, one of the things that Henry was staring at, though his eyes also moved to the huge abstract paintings in black and orange on one side and blue and yellow and mauve on the other. The carpet was a bright gold color that had been on sale for reasons she didn't ask about. It was soft and lovely to walk about barefoot on.

It was true that she had as many bookshelves as she could fit behind her other furniture, as well as numerous blankets for when she got cold – which was often. And there were a number of fidget toys that she used when she needed to think. She had to move them when she needed to pace, which wasn't as often as her needing the fidget toys, but was still at least once a day.

Henry glanced around, seeming to take in everything.

Ada found herself slightly embarrassed, which was ridiculous because it was her apartment and she purchased things solely to please herself now, not someone else. Which was just as well, given how bad she was at guessing what might please another person, and whether or not they were telling her the truth when they thanked her for her gift.

'Do you want coffee or something?' Ada asked, aware again that this was the kind of thing that was generally expected as a token of welcome, even if they were in a hurry. She didn't know Henry well enough to know how early he usually woke or what his morning routine was, nor how this might have changed it.

'No, thanks. I've had about a gallon of coffee in the last six hours,' Henry explained.

'OK, let's go.' She grabbed the backpack by the door.

'I can carry your suitcase,' Henry suggested. He looked around, turning in a full circle.

'I'm not bringing a suitcase,' Ada said.

'But I'm sure you need more than that . . .' Henry waved at the backpack.

'Why are you sure of that? I packed everything I need. And an extra pair of underwear just in case,' Ada said, tapping the backpack.

Henry reddened at this. It took a moment for Ada to realize that he was embarrassed because she'd mentioned underwear.

The rules that neurotypical people had about taboos were always confusing to her. Anyone could talk about food, but sex and underwear were topics that were supposed to be reserved for same-sex conversations. Or for parents and children.

She could think of other taboo topics. Bowel problems. Cancer treatment and the unpleasant effects of it, though the word 'cancer' itself was allowed. The cost of cancer treatment was also not allowed. The cost of many things was not allowed, though deals on fashion items, housing, and concert tickets were often encouraged and apparently increased social capital.

She could go on. In fact, now that she thought about it, it would be an interesting list to make for aliens, when they arrived. Ada assumed no intelligent creatures from another planet would have the same rules, but who knew? Maybe they would have their own lists.

'Anything for the drive?' Henry asked.

'I'm quite capable of packing for a three-day trip, I assure you.' Ada remembered her mother insisting on going through her bags when she was younger, ready to go to a summer camp, and adding things that she would never use to her bags, which she then had to carry around and figure out if she'd rather throw them away or if her mother would expect her to pretend to use them and then bring the remainders home.

'But, I thought—' Henry was stuttering.

Ada walked out to his black SUV, simply waiting for him to open the door so she could climb in. She put the backpack at her feet.

'Wouldn't you rather put that in the trunk?' Henry asked.

She opened her eyes wide at him. 'Maybe now is a good time for you to stop making assumptions about me. I know myself quite well and I know what I need. I am autistic, not helpless. I've had autism all my life, and I know how to work around it and when it is an advantage rather than a disadvantage.' Such as now, when she didn't need or want chit-chat.

There was no known cure for autism, nor any medications that could treat it. It was a brain disorder. Some autists thought of it as a mere difference, not a disability at all, but part of a wide spectrum of neurodiversity that included hypersensitivity, ADHD, and possibly OCD, as well. These autists insisted that it was only because society itself was inherently prejudiced against autists that it was ever a problem.

Other autists, Ada included, considered autism a mixture of ability and disability. Usually, she was at peace with what her autism included – the sensitivities and even the meltdowns, the hyper-focus and the extreme focus on details no one else noticed. But other times, she hated her autism and would gladly ask for a 'cure' for it if one was available. She was also sure that if she went through with it, she'd regret it for the rest of her life and never recognize herself as 'Ada Latia' ever again.

'You may be the most efficient person I've ever met,' Henry said, as he started the car and pulled it into reverse. It was seven thirty-two according to his car's clock. Ada looked at her own phone and saw that it was actually seven thirty-three. She wondered how often that caused Henry to be late to things. But probably most people didn't notice.

'I can buy anything if you've forgotten it.' He held up a credit card. 'FBI card with a budget of several thousand dollars per case. As long as I put in the paperwork.'

'I don't forget things,' Ada said.

'Of course you don't,' Henry said.

SIX

The drive to NAVITEK took a little over the four hours that Henry had estimated. It was in total silence for the first forty minutes. Ada liked silence. She suspected that Henry did not. He kept opening his mouth, started to say something, and then stopped.

Ada liked the time to think without distraction. She was still going through the list of staff members from the website, trying to decide which one was most likely to have murdered a child under her care. Thinking intensely for Ada was a kind of rest. She felt as though the rest of her body hummed around in the background then. It gave her a wonderful feeling of well-being that was quite rare in her life.

'Are you that angry at me?' Henry asked suddenly.

'What?'

'I thought that what had happened between us in high school would be forgiven and forgotten by now. It's been eight years at least. And I did tell you I was sorry at the time,' Henry said.

Ada noticed that his hands were tight on the steering wheel, the knuckles white. 'You told me you were sorry? I really don't remember.'

'You're pretending not to remember, but it's obvious you're angry at me. You've been silent for nearly an hour.'

'Fifty-eight minutes,' Ada said, tapping at the clock on the car, which now read eight thirty-one.

'Exactly. So it's obvious that you have to still be upset about what happened way back then. I was just a teenager, you know. I was an idiot, and I don't think you should make assumptions about who I am now based on who I was then. I'm sure you wouldn't want anyone to think you were the same as you were in your teenage years.'

Ada had had a conversation like this with neurotypical people so many times in her life that she'd lost count. They remembered things that she didn't remember, and she remembered things they didn't remember. It was such a strange reality. She didn't know if her reality was wrong or theirs was, but she hadn't had any luck changing her ability to see the details other people saw rather than the ones she did. And she didn't see much reason to, either, because their details were not objectively relevant.

'I am nearly exactly the same as I was when I was a teenager. I might look different because of my choice of fashion, but I am in most ways identical to the high school version of Ada. I have the same grasp of the intricacies of science, the same pessimistic view of humanity's future, the same quick ability to synthesize, the same lack of understanding of emotions and body language. You must realize that.' She wanted to set the standards, so she didn't disappoint Hen. She really, really disliked disappointing people.

'All true,' Henry said.

'I haven't changed at all in anything but superficialities. You are the one who has changed in far more extensive ways.' He was far more attractive than he had been back then, in a purely objective sense. He paid more attention to personal hygiene, was more of an ideal weight, and he dressed in what she supposed was considered fashionable, however bland it seemed to her – black suit with a white shirt and red tie. His insistence on continuing to rehash forgotten memories was annoying.

Henry smiled faintly and said, with one raised eyebrow, 'Your apartment isn't what I would have expected, knowing you back then. You were so black and white. You wore black most of the time. With occasional bits of gray and white, or some dark green or blue if you felt especially festive.'

'Yes, that is true. I've changed my clothing style, but inside, I am the same. And if you remembered me then, you remember that I never lied. Not for any reason. And I also had a very good memory,' Ada said.

She had no problem acknowledging when she was wrong and other people were right. It was information, something to think about. She was, perhaps, not being fair to Henry, though it had nothing to do with what he seemed to think it did.

'You really don't remember me apologizing to you in high school?' Henry asked. 'Or why I needed to apologize?'

'I do not,' Ada said succinctly.

Henry cleared his throat and, after a long moment, said, 'I asked you out on a date. On the bus ride home from the science fair, senior year. You wouldn't even look at me, you were so upset about it. Or I thought you were.'

Ada thought back to the bus ride home from the science fair. She'd been on that bus five times, from eighth grade to twelfth grade. She remembered the project she had brought to the fair, about pheromones. She did not remember Hen talking to her on that bus ride.

She'd won first prize in the state that year, and she'd been upset about it because she'd hated the project. She'd only done it because the science teacher had insisted on it, had told her that it would make sure she won a prize, and that it would look good on college applications. She'd been so frustrated that he'd been right, because she felt it showed the whole institution of science was rotten to the core. She was ashamed of winning that prize. She'd wanted – and expected – to come home on the bus with no prize at all, but with the satisfaction of being able to tell her teacher he was wrong.

So what did that say about her willingness to be wrong? She asked this of herself and realized that it was another thing that had changed about her. She cared much less now than she had. But she admitted to herself that she did still care about being wrong, especially when it was about things that mattered. To the world, and to herself.

'Like most men, you seem to think that any reaction a woman gives to you is because of you. Has it occurred to you that I might have had another reason for responding with silence to your invitation on a date?' she asked.

'I think that any man knows what it means when a woman is silent in response to him asking her out,' Henry said, taking his eye off the road briefly to look at her. Why neurotypical people seemed to think that eye contact was so important during ordinary, everyday communication, Ada would never understand.

'I think any man is an idiot. I didn't hear you ask me out because I was thinking about something else and I had my earplugs in, as I always did and still do on bus rides – if I have to take them now. They are noisy, and I get over-stimulated, and then it takes me hours to recover afterward. Silence is my preference, then and now. Because I prefer not to have autistic meltdowns, either in public or in private. They hurt.'

Henry took this in. After a long minute, he said, 'You really didn't hear me ask you out? You weren't angry at me all these years for my presumption?'

This time, Ada said nothing. She felt he did not deserve a response, and she was also parsing the reality that she'd been asked out by a young man in high school. No other young man had asked her out until Rex many years later. She hadn't particularly worried about it. Hen hadn't been one of the handful of young men she'd fantasized about asking her out. Still, he hadn't been terrible. If she'd heard him ask her out, she might have said yes.

Or she might not. She didn't know what to do in most social situations, then and now. She tended to make a mess of it. As she was doing now.

'I'm sorry,' she said. She tried to sound genuine. She was sorry that she hadn't known he liked her. She was also sorry because she thought it might have changed . . . other things. If she had known that she wasn't the kind of person who had no real choice in whom she dated. She'd always assumed that Rex was her one chance to have a romantic relationship, and that she'd best accept what was offered.

Beggars can't be choosers and all that.

It was a strange grief to process a part of her past she'd never known existed.

The rest of the drive was blessedly silent, at least as far as Ada was concerned. She wasn't sure if Henry was angry or not, but she'd spent most of her life accepting that people would be angry with her for reasons that she never understood. In this case, at least she understood, after a fashion, why Henry was angry. That was better than she had imagined. She didn't have any interest in Henry romantically, or in anyone else for that matter. She'd been cured of any idea of a romantic attachment for herself rather thoroughly. But she did hope that they could work together in a professional relationship.

SEVEN

NAVITEK was in one of the smallest towns in Idaho that Ada had ever driven through. There was a gas station that had some kind of fast-food place attached, and she was tempted to ask Hen to stop for fries and ice cream. She didn't often allow herself the chance to indulge in unhealthy food. Because it was, well, unhealthy.

But she reminded herself this was a work outing. Food was not important. She had to focus on the town and gather all the information she possibly could so that she could solve a young girl's death.

There were, by her count, sixteen homes on the main street in town. All but two of them had been built in the 1950s or 1960s, faded blue and pink and green, siding that was pulling off in bits and pieces, lawns that were yellow or just plain dirt-brown. Several of the lawns had an old car or two on them, one of the cars upside down. Ada stared perhaps too long at that, trying to decide if this was a kind of political or artistic statement, or if it had been turned upside down in a windstorm. Maybe it was just in the process of being fixed?

She had to drag her attention away from contemplating that problem. Her brain wanted an answer to the questions: Why and who and how and when? She knew where. Here.

But trying to figure out the purposes of other humans was always tricky. She'd never studied the intricate parts of cars, but she could see how one could drown in those facts. She admired other people who had their specialties, who got sucked down deep inside a tiny little world like she did. It was the people who drifted from subject to subject, sipping but never drinking deeply, who made no sense to her. She had an innate suspicion of them. What was the purpose of their being alive?

'Those two are different. Newer. Related to NAVITEK, I think, since the school's only been around the last five years,' Henry said as he drove past the two new homes. They were small, almost condos rather than houses, and right next to each other, closer to the turn-off to the school than anything else. There was faux stone on the outside of each, and a little circular driveway that led to a small garage area. One was yellow, the other a plain gray.

'Probably the teachers and staff of the school,' Henry added.

There was nothing else on the road to the school but NAVITEK itself. There was a fancy logo that matched the one on the website, with a wagon wheel behind and some vines around it, looking nothing like the scene behind the sign, which was a couple of old farmhouses that had been put together with a rather industrial-looking covered hallway in between. Whoever had taken the photos on the website had done a very good job of making it look better than in real life.

She'd stopped studying serial killers the year after her diagnosis. She didn't like the way that so many people talked about autists and serial killers in the same breath, since they both supposedly lacked normal human empathy.

Ada had empathy, even if she didn't show it the way that other people did. And sometimes she didn't understand that other people were upset because they didn't tell her that they were, and they thought she should guess based on their non-verbal tics. She even asked them if they were upset, and they'd say no, and then still expected her to know that they were lying. It was all very confusing.

Serial killers weren't like autists in Ada's experience. Serial killers were neurotypical people, but more exaggerated than others. They pretended to feel things and they showed their pretend feelings with body language and facial expressions. They were experts at that. And other people believed them because they perfected their pretend skills in a way that Ada was both disgusted and fascinated by.

Logically, Ada could understand why, in a system where most people told the truth, lying could work to one person's advantage. It benefited the sociopath who was able to get a whole group of people to accept them, to trust them, to give to them. But just because Ada could see that it would be a useful skill didn't mean she could attain it. She had tried at times to do so, but she wasn't very good at it, and she always stopped before she got better because it felt morally wrong to her. She didn't lie well and she didn't want to learn to lie well.

'Are you ready to go in?' Henry asked. He had his hand on the door, and Ada realized that he'd already turned the SUV engine off. She had drifted away from the present.

'Sorry,' she said. 'I lost track of time there.'

He smiled faintly. 'Yes, I remember you used to do that. I always liked it. I was so sure you were thinking about very important things back then.'

'Yes, well, I thought I was, too,' Ada said.

Rex had disabused her of the idea that anything she did actually mattered. For so many years, she'd wanted to believe that what she was doing would make the world a better place, but she'd given that up. Mostly. Except for her hope to contact aliens.

As she and Henry got out, Ada noticed that there were only five other vehicles in the gravel parking area at NAVITEK. There was a gravel path to a disused barn behind the second building, but it didn't look like it was used much.

She and Henry walked toward what seemed to be the front door, though it wasn't marked in any way, other than the cement path from the parking lot to the black door with a chrome knob on it.

Henry opened the door for her as she reached for it herself and touched his hand before jerking away. The contact made Ada think of Rex. He had done things like that for her. But he had always been lying to her. Kindness now made her sure that someone was lying.

Inside, Henry led her down a short hallway to a door that read 'Director, Soledad Sanchez.'

He knocked on the door, and after a moment, a voice called out, 'Come in, Mr Bloodstone.'

Henry opened the door and waved Ada in. The office was very small and sparsely furnished.

'Oh, hello. And you are?' the woman inside asked. She looked very much like the online photo, possibly even with the same suit. Her makeup was more colorful than it had been in the photo, however. Her lips were a bright orange, her foundation light enough to show the color spectacularly.

Ada reminded herself not to focus on the details. Sometimes

she got lost in the details, and she needed to focus on the woman herself, not the neurotypical camouflage she wore.

'My name is Ada Latia,' Ada said.

'I'm Henry Bloodstone with the FBI.'

'But aren't you both with the FBI?' Sanchez asked.

Before Ada could say she wasn't, Henry interrupted her.

'Yes,' Henry said. 'Ada is consulting with the FBI. She's an expert on autism.'

Ada opened her mouth to explain she wasn't an expert on autism, just autistic herself. But Sanchez was already looking her up and down.

'You are autistic yourself, aren't you?' she asked.

That made things simpler. 'Yes, I am,' she responded.

'Ah, I'm not an expert in diagnosis, of course. But I have been at the school for the last three years, and, of course, my two sons are both diagnosed autistic, as well,' Sanchez said.

'Two sons? They are both here at the school? Is that why you work here?' Ada asked directly.

Sanchez considered this. 'My husband disappeared after Gavin was diagnosed, about seven years ago, at age five. Taylor was diagnosed just months afterward, at age two. Gavin is twelve, and he's quite verbal and high-functioning, which is why it took so long. Taylor has more support needs.'

Ada remembered one of the school counselors trying to convince her mother that she was 'high-functioning' or 'low support needs,' and that her mother should be happy about a bright future for her. Her mother was not happy.

'Some parents think an autistic child is a burden,' Ada said. 'And some think it reflects badly on them.'

Sanchez nodded. 'Exactly what my husband thought. Which is why we're best rid of him, actually. If he doesn't love my sons, I'll do it doubly.'

Ada tried to read the expression on her face. It was intensity of some kind, but beyond that, she couldn't parse it.

Sanchez went on, 'It was hard the first few years while I was going back to school to train in business management and special education, but it has been for the best for the three of us. I can help my boys get the best education possible for both of them now.'

This sounded like the perfect response. Ada couldn't fault it at all. She wished her own mother had been so fierce in her love and devotion.

'You said three years? Was the school here before then?' Ada tried to remember the website, but it hadn't had anything on it from before three years ago.

'Yes, I've been at NAVITEK for three years. I'd been looking for a position like this one for a while, working in a school far from here that wasn't nearly as good. The old director here was ready to retire, and I was ready for some new challenges for me and my sons.'

Ada nodded toward the window that showed the farmland around them. 'You're pretty remote here.'

'I think that was the idea. No one could object to a school for neurodiverse children if it was this far out of the way.'

Ada swallowed hard at the idea of a community that would protest a school for autistic children, but she didn't doubt it was possible. It sounded as if Sanchez had specific experience with the problem.

'We're here to investigate Ella Kimball's death, as you might have guessed. Can you tell me what you observed about her, as the director of this school? What was unique about her and what was typical, as a start?' Henry asked, drawing the conversation back to the case at hand.

'Yes, of course. Ella was a pretty little girl. Ten years old. Small for her age, delicate,' Sanchez said. 'She was doing well here, as she became more comfortable and trusted us more. She was actually hyper-verbal, eager to use words, though not always in a typical way. Sometimes it was just echolalia, repeating things she'd heard. Other times, she was able to use words to communicate in full sentences. She was obviously highly intelligent.'

All the good autists were the intelligent ones. Wasn't that why the Nazis had had a special process to tag them out, with Dr Hans Asperger? Find the ones who were useful to the state, who could be trained in math and science. Keep those from the extermination camps the other disabled children went to. And let all the other autists understand how to make sure they were seen as good enough to live.

'And her parents?' Henry asked.

'They live out of state, in California. They're coming to pick up the body from the mortuary soon. But I understand you've asked the mortuary to wait before releasing her?' Director Sanchez stared at Henry.

'Yes, we don't want any evidence destroyed, so the body shouldn't be released as of now,' Henry explained.

'Well, I don't see why the FBI needs to get involved. This was a clear accident,' Sanchez said.

'Well, that's what we're here to determine. If you don't mind answering a few more questions,' Henry said, and then he didn't wait for Sanchez to agree. 'About the boy who was in the room with Ella when she died – what is his name?'

Sanchez stiffened at this. 'He didn't understand what happened,' she said. 'I can't let you treat him as a suspect. He did nothing he thought was wrong.'

'We need to speak to him to confirm that. Is he verbal?' Henry asked.

Sanchez sat down behind her desk and held her hands in front of her body. 'I will not be a party to a witch hunt. All of the children here are autistic. They are vulnerable and they need protection. Both of the children who were involved in this incident should be seen as victims, and even if the boy didn't die, he is not culpable. I won't let you charge him in some misguided attempt to prove that the case is being treated seriously.'

Sanchez was experiencing some deep emotion, but Ada couldn't tell which one. Anger? A sense of injustice? Fear?

Henry touched Ada's shoulder, and she flinched instantly.

'I'm sorry,' he murmured, and then gestured for her to sit in front of the desk. When she was seated, he sat down next to her.

'I'm here to make sure that this death is properly investigated,' he said. 'Ada is here to make sure that I understand the autistic intricacies of this case. I'd like for you to trust us and to participate in helping us find out the truth.'

Ada hated how she could feel the weight of the emotions in the room, even if she couldn't identify them. They transferred into her in some way that she didn't know how to explain. It sounded like mystical nonsense, but it felt as though she'd just been given a drug that sped up her heart rate and made it more difficult for her to breathe.

She desperately wanted to start rocking back and forth. But that was socially unacceptable, and she wasn't safe enough to do what she needed, not with Henry here, and the director, who was a complete stranger. Instead, she pressed her fingers into the palm of her hands as tightly as she could. It wasn't painful, not exactly, though there would be nasty red marks later, and sometimes it took hours before she could fully feel her fingers again. But it did help her deal with the sensory dysregulation.

She'd learned how to do this when she first started school. Her mother and teachers had tried over and over again to get her to stop. But their reactions had just made her more attached to the behavior as something that she had to hide because it was absolutely necessary. In school, she'd sometimes put her hands under her desk, or under a coat or a backpack. Or she'd gone into the bathroom and sat in a stall, pressing her fingers into her palms until she felt safe again.

'Your son Gavin was the one in the room with Ella, wasn't he?' Henry said gently.

Sanchez hissed as if in pain, and Ada could see her neck muscles twitching.

'You said that he's verbal, Director. We'd like to speak to him. You're welcome to sit in the room with him, as long as you don't interrupt our questioning,' Henry said.

Her son. Ada was still trying to process this. No wonder Sanchez had been so full of potent emotion that it had streamed out into the ether of the room between them.

Ada let go of a long breath and slowly felt her own emotions take control of her body again. It was always so unpleasant when she felt as if her own skin and bones and organs and muscle had been possessed by some other life form. 'Unpleasant' probably wasn't the right word, but she didn't know what else to call it.

Sanchez slowly lifted her head from the desk. She rubbed at her eyes. She gave a brief look at Ada, and it didn't seem to be a kind one. Then she turned back to Henry. 'My son was verbal, yes. Before this happened. He is in a fugue state at the moment. I don't think an interrogation by law enforcement will help,' she said.

'I assure you, we want to help your son,' Henry said. He waved at Ada. 'I've invited her to come precisely because she believes she can communicate with your son, even if he is non-verbal. We need to speak to a witness so we can understand what actually happened here.'

'What actually happened?' Sanchez demanded. 'You mean because you think that if he's verbal and if another child died in his presence, then he's a murderer?' She stood up now, and even Ada could see that she was about to demand that they leave.

Good, Ada thought. That would be a relief. Then she could ask Hen to drop her off at the nearest city so that she could find her own way home. She could not possibly endure so many hours in the car with him so soon after the trip here.

'Director Sanchez, please. We didn't come because we think your son is a murderer. Ms. Latia saw the photo of Ella Kimball's death and she made some very cogent comments about the body being arranged by some outside actor who couldn't possibly have been your young, autistic son. Whoever this other person is, we need your help to discover their identity and their true culpability.' The words seemed to burst out of him.

Ada was always slow to put the emotional content to the intellectual content of conversation. It was annoying when she couldn't respond immediately because of this lag.

Ada could tell that Henry was also upset about the accusation that he had come to arrest an autistic boy. He was red-faced now. He had that kind of pale, freckled skin that turned red easily. She remembered that now, from high school. It had made her like him because it made him more vulnerable, like she was. He was picked on, too, because he showed his feelings too easily. It made him different from the other boys.

'You think that someone else was involved in the death?' Sanchez echoed back.

Ada realized she was doing the same thing, trying to work around her lag in interpreting emotion and body language. She had this tic of echoing things back. Ada's father had done the same thing. It had annoyed her mother, and she'd mocked him for it.

Now is not then, Ada told herself. This was another problem of her autism, that she had a hard time separating past and present. Everything always seemed to be happening at the same time, because her brain was processing things all at once, not in sequential order, as would have been more convenient.

'You are saying you think that this wasn't an accident, but murder, and that it wasn't my son Gavin who was at fault, but someone else at the school? One of the staff? Me?'

'No, not Gavin. No one autistic,' Henry got out.

'I don't think we have to talk to you,' Sanchez said. 'I have a lawyer who is already involved in this, and I will be contacting him as soon as you leave.' She stood and walked to the door, holding it open.

'You can do that, but that could cause much more disruption of the school. Even more members of the FBI would have to come in, and classes would have to be stopped entirely,' Henry said.

Even Ada knew that was a threat, though probably one that Hen could follow through on.

Sanchez considered this, then her whole body sagged. 'Can I give you a tour first? Show you around the facility? We like to think that it's at least as much a home as it is a school. Once you've seen it at its best, then we can talk about Gavin again. I've already set up appointments with the staff for you.'

'A tour would be superb. Thank you for your hospitality, given such short notice,' Henry said.

EIGHT

Sanchez stood up and moved around them, waving them through and then locking the door behind her. She gestured with her hand down the corridor, explaining as she walked.

'These two buildings are the main instruction areas. There are larger rooms on the main floor in this building that we use for a cafeteria and the kitchen next door. There's an exercise room that allows the children to run and play in groups when that time is designated, but it's also used as a room for children who are having meltdowns or who need space to run around and make noise.'

She opened the door to the cafeteria. There were six tables set up with eight chairs each. Ada automatically did the math there. Forty-eight students.

But Henry asked more directly, 'How many children do you have here at the moment?'

'We have forty-two. Or we did before Ella passed. Now we have forty-one,' she said.

'And how many years has NAVITEK been taking students?'

'Well, the original alternative school – first called IDOP for Idaho Open – opened thirty-four years ago. But as you might guess from that name, it was very different then. It wasn't for autistic students specifically. It was originally intended to be a kind of wilderness school. Back then, the barn was meant to be for milking cows so that students had experience with hard physical labor. The fields were still used for growing in. Mostly corn and alfalfa, with a few smaller plots for tomatoes and zucchini and herbs used in the kitchen.'

'Why and when did the school change purpose?' Henry asked.

Something about his tone made Ada suspect that he already knew the answer to this question, but she hadn't seen anything about this on the website, so Henry must have found it elsewhere. Probably something the FBI had access to that she did not.

'Well, IDOP was sued when one of the students was injured falling off a tractor during a school activity. The insurance was canceled, and once that happened, it just wasn't a viable business anymore. The director before me, Eileen Gay, bought all the property for a song and it took her a few years to build it up for autistic students. The first year, I think she only had two, and she taught them both herself. No staff.'

Sanchez stopped and opened the door to a room that was as big as the cafeteria, but filled with shelves of toys and puzzles, boxes that were labeled clearly with both words and images as 'Legos,' 'wooden blocks,' 'Lincoln logs,' 'Tinkertoys,' 'K'nex,' 'stacking cups,' 'clothes,' 'stuffed animals,' 'blankets,' and 'letters and numbers.' The small carpet helped to divide the room into more close-knit spaces, one with Care Bears, one with emojis, one with blocks in different colors, and one in yellow that said simply 'sit here.'

Ada found herself itching to go inside and try things out. She'd never had a space like this to explore when she was a child. Her parents insisted that Legos were dangerous if you stepped on them and that she wasn't responsible enough to take care of them. They didn't like any kind of toy that had different pieces. She'd been allowed one stuffed bear, which she slept with every night and tried once to take to school with her in her backpack, but her mother found it and scolded her.

There were a couple of easy chairs and one child-size couch, but mostly there were bean bags that could be pulled around and placed wherever desired. That made a lot of sense to Ada. There were also dividers set up in several corners where students could go and find quiet. And there was a treadmill that she suspected wasn't used for typical running of miles.

'It's not very big and it's not much like a normal gym class, but I think it has certain advantages,' Sanchez said.

'I'm surprised you don't use the outdoors much.' Henry gestured to the one window on the far wall that was open. There were several others that had been covered in thick blinds or curtains to make the room less bright with light. Mostly, it was interior light that allowed them to see, but the lights were all set up so that any of them could be turned off and leave one part of the room dimmer than the rest.

'Ha, well, that's what I thought when I first started here. Eileen tried to warn me. She said that there was just too much space out there, too many chances for kids to get into trouble. She was one hundred percent right about that. In the beginning, Gavin and a couple of other children went out there one day with one of our early staff members. The three boys bolted off in three different directions, and she couldn't catch them all. So that was the end of that.'

This explained much about what Ada had seen when they first came in, the path that was overgrown and the lack of fencing.

'You could use leashes, couldn't you?' Henry asked.

Ada felt an immediate visceral reaction to this. Leashes were for animals, not for humans. She wouldn't want to have a leash used on her. Would Henry? Would anyone?

But Sanchez answered with no change in tone. 'That can be a practical solution, yes. Though some parents object to their children being treated that way. You see, with parents of autistic children, it's very much a sensitive topic that they feel their children are granted full humanity.'

It was a good answer. Ada appreciated it and found herself calming down.

'Of course,' Henry murmured.

'We also tried putting in a fence out back, so there would be some more safety. But the first fence we put up wasn't sturdy enough and it quickly came down. Autistic children can be surprisingly strong and cooperative if they have the same goal. We tried a far more expensive fence that came with a guarantee.' She made a strange smile at this. 'But it turned out that when our children broke that one, too, the guarantee didn't cover autistic school use. So we came back to this solution. Indoor living.'

'And the treadmill?' Henry asked, waving at it. 'Is that for the staff when they need a break?'

Sanchez laughed at that. 'No, the staff can go outside whenever they want to. They have their own living spaces that you must have passed when you came in. Not fancy by any means, but serviceable. The treadmill is for children who need to walk or run to get out their energy. Some just need to walk, to use their arms and legs in a coordinated motion. So we made sure they had this.'

She waited a moment to see if Ada had any questions, but she didn't. Lucky children who didn't have parents telling them who they were supposed to be and what they had to do at all times.

'Is this the room where Ella died?' Ada asked.

Sanchez stiffened. 'Yes,' she said. 'Though, at the time, only

Ella and Gavin were here. The staff member who was assigned to them stepped out briefly. Normally, students are supervised unless they are in their own bedroom spaces.'

Ada tried to find the spot that she'd seen in the photograph, with the neat vacuum lines.

Sanchez seemed uncomfortable, but did walk toward the corner of the room, where there were a few boxes of toys, though the bean bags hadn't shown in the photo. 'Gavin and Ella moved some of these things around, but it was here.'

Ada imagined that the other children hadn't been told that this was where their schoolmate had been found dead. But it was possible many of them wouldn't understand death, and that Ella not returning to classes was as far as their minds could go.

Ada herself had struggled with understanding death when she was younger. It was another reason she'd been fascinated with serial killers and had studied the graphic photos of the victims that were used in the trials. Her mother had been horrified about it, but it had taken months for Ada to grasp the finality of death, that the bodies had once been living, breathing people. When she had, it had changed everything about that obsession for her.

'Is the staff member who had charge over them still here?' Henry asked.

'Yes. She hasn't been fired, if that's what you're asking.'

'That's what I'm asking. I want to be able to interview her, if possible.'

'All right. I will put her on a list of interviewees, but you should understand that I don't consider her to be at fault at all. And I've told Ella's parents that any fault is to be mine and mine alone. I am the one who set up the schedules. If there was a mistake, it should be laid at my door.'

That sounded very responsible, Ada thought. She was still trying to move around and tilt her head at just the right angle for the photograph.

There. That was it. Yes, now she could see how the body had been arranged. And yes, the bean bags weren't there then. Someone had purposely set things up so that the photograph didn't show how large the room was. It had looked like a much smaller space. Not institutional at all.

Now that Ada was here, she had many other questions, though

some of them hadn't been formed into words yet. The room had to have been cleaned. Who had done that? Where had the body been taken right after it was found? Was it left here, and the children had to play elsewhere – or not play at all? Did Gavin understand what had happened to his friend? How close were the two children? Had they played together often?

'What have Ella's parents had to say?' Ada asked.

'Oh, well, they will be here soon to pick up her things. I suppose they will tell me then just how they feel.' Sanchez didn't show any emotion that Ada could see. She seemed still the professional, if a little stiff.

'Are you concerned about the consequences for the other students? Is there a possibility that other parents will decide to take them out of the school?' Henry asked.

Sanchez waved a hand. 'I'm not concerned about that right now, no. We take very good care of the students here. Their scores are far and away above anything that any similar school has been able to produce. And we provide full-time care, not just during school hours. It's hard to replace this kind of service at any cost, and ours are very affordable because of the donors that I've been successful at recruiting each year.'

Ada thought about being a student at this school. Maybe it would have been better than living at home, though she would have hated the adjustment. It always took her a long time to get used to anything new. But not living with her parents might have been a huge improvement in much of her life.

They moved away from the larger space and down to the last rooms in this converted farmhouse. Sanchez led the way, walking at an easy pace.

'Here is one of our smaller classrooms.' Sanchez opened one of the last doors before the connecting structure between the farmhouses. 'This is often for the youngest or the oldest students because we have fewer of them, and they sometimes need more special attention.'

Ada looked at the simple chairs in a circle, around a brightly colored green-and-yellow rug. She itched to touch the fibers of the rug but restrained herself.

'And here are a couple of the bedrooms for the students who board with us privately.' She opened the first door.

'This was Ella's room,' she explained. 'Her parents haven't come to pick up her things, but we've had staff pack things up to make it easier for them. The other room is for Gillie, but I wouldn't want to intrude on his privacy.'

Curious, Ada stepped into the room. It wasn't larger than a bedroom in any house would be. But the bed itself was an expensive brand with a canopy top in pink and purple ruffles. There was a matching white dresser and a white bed stool with a pad on top. The windows had both blinds and curtains, and there was a large walk-in closet, where Ada saw all of Ella's things, packed in two large suitcases and four boxes.

'That is a lot of stuff for a child of that age,' Henry commented.

'Well, her parents wanted her to feel at home. They don't live close by, so she wasn't able to travel home, not even on weekends,' Sanchez explained.

'Are there only two students who board here?' Henry asked.

'No, there are fourteen,' Sanchez said. 'My two sons among them. Better for many of them here than at home because of the stable routine. Routine is very important for autistic children. It helps them feel safe and secure.'

Ada definitely agreed with that. Her parents had not understood or cared about this. It was a constant of her childhood, the changes that suited her parents and not her. She had to adjust and adjust again and never suggest that she'd prefer the old way rather than whatever new and improved way that was supposed to be so much better. New bathroom. New lighting. New curtains. New wood flooring that hurt her bare feet so that she had to wear shoes even while inside. She hated shoes. They were prison for her feet. But she knew she had to wear them, even so.

'Did Ella keep it this clean?' Ada asked.

Sanchez made a choking sound and then said, 'No, she was quite messy, in fact. It sometimes distressed those around her. But we did our best to help her with our cleaning staff. She wasn't always happy about that, but it was necessary. Of course, at the moment, it has all been packed up to prepare for her parents' final checkout.'

As Ada walked around the room slowly, it was hard to make conclusions about Ella's personality, given that this wasn't how she had left her room. Ada wished she had seen it before it was cleaned and packed up. She wanted to know if Ella was one of those autistic children who needed total order and control in her outer world, or if she was messy and hated it, but wasn't able to do anything about it.

Ada had been messy when she was younger, but her father decided one day, 'If you can't care for your things, you won't be able to have them.'

He packed up everything, not in suitcases like this, or in boxes, but in garbage bags. He'd carried them off as she wailed and asked for another chance.

'You've had a dozen chances,' her father said.

She'd always thought that he had thrown her things away. She'd been furious about it, had felt as if she'd lost part of herself that day. She'd changed entirely, unable to allow herself to play with anything because it might be taken away if she didn't put it back correctly. She ordered things, counted things, looked at things, collected things. But she didn't move them or play with them.

It wasn't until her mother died that she discovered the garbage bags full of her childhood possessions in the attic. She didn't know if that made it better or worse, that he'd kept them there and never returned them, but also hadn't thrown them away.

'We saw a few smaller buildings coming in. Are they for staff?' Henry asked, gesturing generally in the direction of the smaller, newer houses.

Sanchez nodded. 'For the teachers and for myself. The other staff live further away and drive in each morning.'

Henry whistled. 'That must be a long drive. This is a pretty isolated place.'

Sanchez sighed. 'We have to reserve the closer buildings for the teachers. The other staff often have to drive an hour each way, it's true. At some point, we hope to add more buildings, but we'll have to see how this year's budget falls out,' she said.

'Where do the other students board?'

'I'll show you,' Sanchez said. She took them through the walkway to the other building. It was colder here and smelled faintly of mold. Ada could tell that this was the older building and that it hadn't been updated. The rooms were larger, but there were bunk beds in each one, sometimes more than one set. There were also fewer possessions.

'Ella's parents were able to pay for her to have a private room, I assume,' Henry said.

'Yes. I wish that wasn't the way it worked for autistic children, but it is. There's a privilege in having parents who can afford better care.'

So Ella's parents had been wealthy.

'But all the students here are privileged, aren't they?' Henry said. 'Even if not as privileged as Ella.'

'Yes,' Sanchez agreed. She had reached the end of the second building. 'Back in the barn, we have some activity spaces. Would you like to see those?'

'Thank you,' Henry said.

The door opened and led down the crumbling cement path. The grass had grown high beyond the path, and it looked as though it hadn't been mown for a long time.

The barn was painted various shades of red in different spots. Ada couldn't tell if it was because they'd run out of paint or if someone hadn't been able to match it. Clearly, they hadn't wanted to repaint the whole thing. There were a handful of windows, but not on the second floor.

As soon as they walked inside, Ada sneezed. The mustiness was overpowering. She had to stop a moment to wipe at her eyes.

'Are you all right?' Henry asked.

She got out a handkerchief from her pocket, something she never left the house without, and wiped at her face. She nodded briefly.

'It's an old space. We've tried to modernize it, but it's not always the top priority when it comes to allocation of funds,' Sanchez explained.

The rooms were large and oddly shaped. There was one central bathroom that it seemed all the children had to share. Ada could see that there was a schedule posted on it, a half hour each morning for the girls and a half hour for the boys. There were two showers inside and two sinks and toilets, without any separation or privacy.

Ada had refused to use a group shower in junior high school gym class, and she'd faced teasing by the other girls as well as pressure from the gym teacher and the school counselor, but even when she tried to make herself do it, she simply couldn't. She felt too naked and stared at.

'There are a few smaller rooms upstairs for the younger children. Those are a little nicer,' Sanchez said, and gestured at the staircase.

Henry didn't wait for her to lead them up. He went himself, ducking at the top because the lintel was too low for his head.

Ada followed after him, with Sanchez coming last.

There was no window in this upper room. There were six beds, along with a couple of toddler beds against the walls. Ada wrinkled her nose at the smell of urine that was strong here.

'The smaller kids are often still in diapers, day or night, which is why we keep them together. The soiled bedding is taken out daily and cleaned, along with the disposal of the diapers each morning and night. But the smell does remain. We're working on how to deal with the ventilation up here, but free-standing fans could be a potential hazard to the younger children, so we haven't done that.' She stopped, and Ada noticed that her cheeks were flushed. She wasn't sure what emotion that indicated.

'We're not here to judge the facilities,' Henry said.

Well, that wasn't their primary purpose, but Ada thought they could hardly prevent themselves from doing so. She certainly couldn't.

'Facilities for autistic children were very bad just a generation ago. Mostly a problem of shame and lack of funding. We are working on both of those.' Sanchez smiled, but to Ada's untrained eye, it didn't look like a happy expression.

'Now, if we can head back to the office, I can—' Sanchez started.

'Why are there no children here today?' Ada asked.

'Ah. Well, the children are out on a field trip today. That's why they're not here. We thought it would be a good idea for them to spend some time outside of the school this week. In case . . .' Sanchez trailed off and didn't finish the sentence as they moved along the path toward the second converted farmhouse. The door was opening, and a small, well-dressed woman was stepping out, her facial expression and body language clear enough that even Ada could read it: fury.

NINE

'Director Sanchez, there you are. I've been searching for you for twenty minutes. You weren't in your office, and you didn't answer your phone. We expected you to at least be available to help us collect our daughter's personal items,' the woman said, her hands on hips covered in a white linen pantsuit with a gold belt that matched the necklace and bracelet she wore.

A stout, sweating man in a tailored tan suit and pink tie came out of the door behind her. He looked more defeated than angry.

Ada saw immediately the woman's resemblance to Ella, the girl in the photo. They were startlingly alike, down to the small, upturned nose and the delicate jawline, as well as the dark hair color and small hands.

A flash of memory came to Ada as she remembered her own mother being told again and again that her daughter looked like a carbon copy of her, and how her mother hated to hear it. It made her feel as though she had to take the blame for all of Ada's flaws, and she was resentful of that. She had seemed to want to pretend that Ada was unrelated to her genetically, or at least that part of the fault for Ada's problems lay with her husband.

'I'm sorry, Mrs Kimball and Mr Kimball. I was working with these two consultants with the FBI, who have come to look into your daughter's case,' Sanchez said, gesturing at Ada and Henry.

Ada was in front, the closest to Mrs Kimball, and she wasn't prepared for the woman's sudden reaction.

'The FBI? How dare you take my daughter's body for further investigation?' Mrs Kimball slapped Ada across the face so hard that Ada stumbled backward and fell to her knee.

Henry leaped past her, and for a moment, Ada was surprised he hadn't stopped to help her. But then she realized he was trying to protect her from further attack.

'Please step back,' he said sternly to the Kimballs, putting out his hands. He glanced back to check on Ada, who had gotten to her feet.

Her whole face felt like it was on fire and her ears were ringing. She had the beginnings of a nasty headache that she knew would only get worse with time, until she could sleep in a dark and quiet room.

Mrs Kimball shouted and gesticulated wildly with her hands at Ada and Henry. 'It's bad enough that we have to bury our daughter, that she died here in a school where we were assured she would be safe, but now people like you are insisting that we can't take her home with us for the funeral? We have to make a second trip and have the casket dug up so that we can put her body in it properly days or weeks later? People like you are sick. How can you live with yourselves?'

Mrs Kimball had now moved closer to Henry and put her hands on his chest. She'd pushed against him at the end of each sentence, but Henry hadn't moved. He looked like a statue, showing no emotion at all.

Somehow seeing that made Ada feel a little safer. But only a little.

'Don, why are you just standing there?' Mrs Kimball demanded of her husband. 'Doing nothing, as usual. Always nothing.'

Even Ada could hear the note of disdain in that voice.

But her husband didn't respond in anger. He seemed very calm. Or just unemotional.

What kind of a father was unemotional about his daughter's death? Ada felt more connection to Mrs Kimball than to her husband, even if the woman had just hit her. She wished that her own mother had ever cared that much about her.

'Sybil, let's get back inside and get her things to the car,' Don Kimball suggested.

He was mostly bald, with a paunch, and under the sleeves of his suit, Ada could see sweat stains. His face was dripping with it, and though it was warm, Ada wondered if he had some condition, because it was not that hot, even outside.

'You shut up and leave me alone. All of you!' Sybil Kimball swung around, holding her arm out and now whacking her husband in the chest with it. 'I deserve to have my say. My daughter is dead, and there is no explanation for it, none at all. I did my best for her all these years. I sent her to the best school I could find. I had such great expectations for her. She was so smart. She was going to change the world, change how people saw autistic people.'

The woman broke down in tears, her arms wrapped around her head, which had fallen to her chest. Her whole body shook.

Don Kimball tried to pat at his wife, but it only enraged her more, and she swatted at him until he stepped back with a huff.

As far as Ada was concerned, she would have been happy to go back in the direction she'd come, anything to not have to hear this woman's loud noises. She cared about the woman's grief, but the sound of her weeping was also an assault on her senses. It made her worry that it could trigger a meltdown, which wasn't what she wanted to happen right here and now at all. Not in front of all these people, and certainly not in front of Henry.

Noise was always a trigger for sensory overload. The wrong kind of noise, anyway. Ada could listen to her chanting recordings and that was soothing, even if she turned it loud enough that the noise in the apartment next to hers was drowned out. But that was noise with a clear rhythm and pattern. Mrs Kimball's weeping made Ada's head spin, and she felt like her head was going to fly right off her body to get away from all this.

She knew what she was supposed to do when someone was crying. She'd been taught that she should make soothing noises and, if she had a close relationship, pat or hug the person who was grieving. She was supposed to say that everything would be all right or that there was a purpose for all this.

Only of course it wouldn't be all right for Ella's parents that their daughter was dead. And Ada didn't believe there was a purpose for all this, at least not one beyond the murderer's need to prove their power.

Lying to someone who was grieving didn't seem like a kindness to Ada. She never wanted people to lie to her, whether she was sad or not. It seemed as though it would just make everything take longer, all the healing part.

So she just stood there, waiting for Sanchez or Henry to do something.

It was Henry who moved forward first. 'We're doing our best to find answers. I hope that you can trust us. I swear to you that we will find out what happened to your daughter. That's the only reason we need to keep her body. Can you understand that?'

Sybil Kimball sobbed more.

Henry cleared his throat, and Ada thought that he was going to step back, giving up. But she was learning something important about Henry: he was not a man who gave up easily, and perhaps not ever.

It was something that she liked about him very much. She had given up too many times in her life, but, at her best, she could be dogged and fervent in her focus and in her forward momentum. What Henry was showing now was what Ada wished that she could always show.

'If you wouldn't mind, we'd like to talk to you and your husband about your daughter. You could help us get to know her a little better, and that might help us to understand what happened,' Henry tried next.

The woman took in a deep, sharp breath and pulled herself upright.

Ada was sure that she was going to start shouting again.

Henry continued in that same confident, reassuring tone. 'We could all sit down for a few minutes, and you could tell us some stories about your daughter. The good stories, and the bad ones, if you don't mind. We want to listen to all of it, all about her. And then you and your husband can take her things if you want to, just a little later. What do you think about that?'

Ada had watched as Mrs Kimball had swung her arms down and then lifted them again. She wanted to warn Henry to watch out.

But then the woman put her arms around him and gave him a loud, wet kiss on his cheek. 'Thank you,' she said. 'I'd like that very much. Ella was a wonderful girl. She deserved better than all this. Better than me. And him. Better.' The last echo was quiet and sad, and it sounded almost like a poem.

TEN

'I can show you the way to a private room. Down this hallway,' Sanchez said briskly, moving forward now as if she had been in charge from the beginning.

Ada wasn't sure, but it seemed as if Sanchez was making sure that she was keeping far enough ahead of the two parents that neither of them could reach her to touch her. Or strike her.

Henry swung his arms wildly to keep up, and that left Ada at the back. She was at that stage of exhaustion where she didn't feel tired for some reason. She felt like she was at the top of a mountain hike and it would all be downhill from here. Downhill was easy, wasn't it? She could practically roll down.

But she'd been here enough times before to know that it was a warning sign. It didn't mean she was all right. It meant that today was likely to end in a full-blown meltdown. She very much did not want to have a meltdown at the school. Not because Henry was here. Not because she cared particularly what he thought. Nothing to do with that.

It was only because she cared about this case and wanted to make sure that Ella Kimball's murderer was found and properly punished, and that the Kimball parents had the truth about their daughter, since that was the only thing anyone could offer them now that might possibly matter, weighed against the finality of their daughter's death.

Ada let herself walk with even strides, not trying to catch the others. She didn't want to risk a sprain from hurrying. She wasn't as clumsy as she had been in elementary school, always the last child picked for any physical activity, and sometimes shoved to the side so that she could be claimed as 'injured' and not able to participate. Any team did better if she sat out and they were down one player than if she tried to hit a ball or run a relay or any of the activities that had been part of her childhood school games.

She wasn't breathing hard when she reached the door that she had seen the others go into. It wasn't the director's office, just one door down from there. Henry had glanced back at her and given her a thumbs up. She'd nodded to him, and he'd looked at her one more time in question before going into the room.

Taking a moment's pause, Ada tried to prepare for the emotions she'd be facing inside. They would feel heavy and hot, like a sauna that pushed against all her senses, like one of those massages she could not bear because she hated strangers touching her, especially all over her body, no matter how gentle.

Ada knew she had emotions herself. It wasn't that she thought she was emotionless. It was just difficult to understand what they meant. And even harder to understand the emotions of other people and to make sure they didn't overwhelm her. Her own emotions seemed to always be buried deep, hard to uncover unless she dug down for them – which she didn't often do.

Finally, she opened the door and stepped inside.

'I was just explaining the questions you had about Ella's photograph online,' Henry said, looking up at her when she came in.

There was a table, and he and Director Sanchez were seated in the two chairs across from Ella's parents. There was no fifth chair, and after a moment's hesitation, Ada leaned against the wall.

Henry waved to his chair to offer it to her, but she shook her head. She really would prefer to be over here, a little bit apart.

'But that doesn't mean . . . I thought you had real evidence,' Don Kimball said. 'If you're keeping her body. Some kind of poison or weapon.'

Sybil Kimball smacked her hand on the table, and her husband picked it up and rubbed at it, probably to keep her calm, Ada thought.

'That's why we're keeping her body. We're investigating further what might have been passed over as an accident. We want to be sure before we make any accusations,' Henry explained.

'But it was your son who suffocated her!' Ella's mother said, pointing an accusing finger at the director. 'You've brought these people in so you can excuse him for hurting her, and make yourself look innocent when you should have taken better care of her. Admit it!'

Henry stood in front of the director. 'She had nothing to do with calling in the FBI to investigate, I assure you. It was entirely on our side.'

Henry wasn't saying that it was because of Ada, and she appreciated that, given Sybil Kimball's response to her already.

'So you have nothing – is that what you're saying? Why are we here, then, and not gathering our daughter's things?' Don Kimball asked.

Had he forgotten what Henry already said? Ada always found it strange how easily neurotypical people seemed to forget what had happened, in the distant past and the near past. She supposed that there were times when she wished she could forget things easily. Instead, she had almost perfect recall, even of the worst parts of her life.

'As I said, we were hoping you could tell us about Ella. It could help us understand what happened,' Henry said. He looked toward Ada, but she was content to observe from the side for now. She was standing near the door she'd come in. Just in case she needed to exit quickly from whatever emotional outburst might be likely from Sybil Kimball next. Her face still stung, though she was doing her best to ignore the physical pain. It wasn't that bad. She'd definitely experienced worse.

'What do you want to know? About her birth? How much she weighed? When she took her first steps? What her first word was?' This from Sybil, rather sarcastically.

'I'd like to know when you first suspected she was autistic. And yes, I'm curious about her first word,' Henry said evenly.

'I could get her file,' Director Sanchez offered, putting a hand out as if to leave the room.

'I'd like to hear it from her parents directly,' Henry insisted without even looking at Sanchez.

'She was . . . such a perfect baby,' her mother said after a moment, that tone in her voice that Ada recognized as fond memory.

'So beautiful, so easy to take care of. I had no idea anything was wrong until she didn't start speaking. And even then I thought it was nothing to worry about. I talked to the doctor when she was two, and he became concerned. That's when he did the tests. Eye contact and watching her play. She didn't cooperate with other children. She couldn't hold a crayon and draw. But she understood what we said. I knew she did. She was very smart.'

The last part was defensive. Smart autistic children were, of course, the only good kind, as Ada well knew.

'Her first word was at age four. She said "umbrella." I don't know why, but she liked that word. Three syllables. She liked big words. She liked unusual words. She would find one and then repeat it over and over again,' Sybil said.

'Do you remember when she started saying "indefensible"?' Don asked. He smiled and let out a little laugh, patting his wife's hand, but she didn't laugh with him.

He looked toward Ada and explained, 'A girl that small saying that word, precisely, correctly. She'd put it in a full sentence. People thought we'd coached her to do it, but we hadn't. It was all on her own.'

That was the kind of trick that was amusing the first time, and quickly became less amusing, Ada had observed in her own life. Most parents, and adults in general, thought autistic children should be seen and not heard. Especially if they used words that made the adults around them feel less confident about themselves and their own superiority.

'It was part of a whole series of words,' Sybil said. 'Indefatigable. Indefinitely. Indefeasible. Indecency. Indecorum. Indecisive. Undeniable. Undesirable. Underappreciated. Underserved.'

'Undescended,' her husband added with a laugh and a faint blush.

'She began to read through the dictionary. With her finger like this.' Sybil held out her finger and moved it up and down, squinting slightly. 'She read faster than anyone I've ever known. People used to say that it was a joke, a trick of some kind, that she couldn't possibly have any comprehension. But I said, go ahead, test her.' She waved a hand. 'And they did.'

Her brief smile faded.

'She was amazing in so many ways,' Don said.

'But at school, she was trouble. Even in kindergarten, the teacher didn't like to be corrected. And Ella didn't like it when the schedule changed, even a little. She wouldn't go out to recess, either. She didn't like it outside.'

Ada had never met Ella, but now she wondered if they'd have liked each other. Neurotypical people always thought it strange if people of different ages were friends, but there was no reason that made sense to Ada why they shouldn't be. But Ella was dead now, and Ada would never get to meet her. The randomness of the universe was often painful. It could have been her at Ella's age, Ada knew. But it wasn't.

'You'd already had her tested by then, right?' Sanchez said more than asked.

Sybil nodded. 'Yes, so we knew there could be problems. We kept thinking she'd adjust. So we let her stay home the rest of the year, thinking first grade would be more academic and less social.'

'But it wasn't,' her husband said.

'So that's when we started looking for other options. There was a charter school nearby, and we tried that for first grade. But it had most of the same problems. It wasn't specifically for autistic children.'

'And we were worried that she wasn't getting any academic stimulation there,' Don added. 'We didn't want just babysitting. We could have paid for a babysitter at home if that was all we wanted for her.'

They wanted their daughter to perform 'smart autist' for them, Ada thought. For other people. So that she would still bring them status.

Ada knew her own parents had wanted that. On a certain level, as an adult, this made sense to her. Why have children if it was a zero-sum game? There had to be some kind of return on investment for all of the money and time spent raising a child. But it was considered rude to say such a thing so bluntly out loud.

And Ada also wished that somehow her parents had seen her as enough. As autistic and enough.

'We wanted her to go to college. To become a brilliant scientist. Or something brilliant. An actor. A musician. There are so many possibilities if autistic children get the right education and don't end up traumatized,' Sybil said. She looked at Ada, trying to explain it to her. 'They can really be anything. The prejudices are so strong, and we didn't want that for her. We wanted her to be able to become whatever she wanted.'

'And what did she want to become?' Ada interrupted.

'I–I don't know.' Sybil's face crumpled, and tears fell down her cheeks again. 'She used to say she wanted to be a ballerina. But I don't think she really had the body type for that. She liked music and she liked moving, but I think she wasn't really interested in that.'

The idea that an autistic child should be a ballerina seemed ridiculous on one level, but on another – why not? Autists often had intense focus on their special interests, and they could be very good with music. With creativity of all kinds, not just math and science, as were the stereotypes that Ada had been so often pressed into.

'We did have a dance tutor come in for a few weeks,' Sanchez interjected.

'Yes, Ella told us about that. She enjoyed it. But she didn't spend time practicing,' Sybil said.

'She told me a few weeks ago, when I talked to her on the phone, that she wanted to be a biologist. Something about frogs,' Don said.

Sybil wiped at her face. 'Really? Frogs? I don't remember that. But I suppose it might have been. We'll never know now.'

Ada thought about her parents. If someone had asked them what her interests were, would they have known? They had seemed to dismiss her talking about serial killers so often, she couldn't tell if they would have remembered. She couldn't ask them now because they were both gone, her mother dead and her father disappeared since the funeral. But she didn't think they had ever known her in any case. That was the saddest part of her memories of them.

'She was a good reader. And writer,' said Sanchez. 'She might have grown up to be a poet. Or a playwright. She was really special. We will all miss her so much.'

There was a long silence that was interrupted only by the sound of Don patting his wife's back as Sybil tried to get herself together.

'How often did you see Ella since she came to this school?' Henry asked finally.

'Oh, we visited every parents' night they had. And, of course, she came home for two weeks every summer,' Don insisted.

Henry turned to Sanchez. 'How many parents' nights do you have?'

She said, 'Two each year, in the fall and in the spring. It's a wonderful chance for the children to show their parents how far they've come. And, of course, they get to meet the parents of the other students, and that's a good way for them to learn more social skills. Not just with the staff.'

'I see.'

Two days a year? Ada had spent more time with her parents than it seemed the feted Ella had with hers. Did they really love her as much as they seemed to, or was it just an imaginary daughter they loved? Maybe her being dead was the reason they could continue to spin out their imagination of what their daughter might have been. She could have turned out perfectly. Even autistic children did that, though they went to very expensive schools.

'Did Ella tell you about any of the other children she was close to?' Henry asked.

'Oh, well, there was Gavin, of course.' Sybil hesitated, unable to come up with another name. 'I don't remember if there were others. When we came to visit, we wanted to spend time with her, not with other autistic children.'

Ada suspected these parents would not have felt the same if Ella had friends who were neurotypical, but she could not know that for certain.

'Do you remember if there was a particular class that Ella liked? Or a teacher that she wanted to make sure you met?' Henry asked.

'Yes, there was. She loved the communication teacher.' Her mother looked at Sanchez.

'Madeleine Lynch,' Sanchez put in.

'Yes. Lovely woman. She was so warm around the children.'

'I've set up an appointment for you to talk to her, as I said,' Sanchez put in. 'If that is all, perhaps we can let the Kimballs go for now?' She looked back and forth between Henry and Ada, but only Henry could give permission.

'Yes, of course. Thank you, Mr Kimball. Mrs Kimball,' Henry said. 'We appreciate your time during this difficult day. You've been very helpful.'

Now was the part of the conversation that went back to small talk. Nonsense superlatives and adjectives and adverbs that were only used to make people feel good about themselves. That seemed to be the main point of much of the conversation pieces that Ada was so bad at. Information giving, on the other hand, she was very good at. Though many people would judge her as 'cold' or 'formal' or simply 'arrogant' for all that.

'Any other questions?' Sanchez asked, looking directly at Ada.

She glanced at Henry. Was he all right with her asking a question?

He nodded to her.

In that case, Ada pulled herself away from the door and asked bluntly, 'Can you tell me why you didn't have any other children after Ella?'

Sybil Kimball drew back in shock. This was not the kind of question, apparently, that one asked aloud. Ada was always being told that. And yet these were the kinds of questions that needed to be answered. To understand the puzzle, to put all the pieces together, Ada didn't want to simply guess at the answer.

'We had enough to do with Ella,' the mother said with a clipped tone. 'And it was expensive to care for her.'

'It wasn't because you were afraid you would have another autistic child, and you hated that idea?' Ada asked.

Now Don Kimball stood up. 'Excuse us. We do not wish to answer such personal questions about our life. We'd like to go back to Ella's room and take her things now.' He didn't leave room for anyone to say no.

Sanchez didn't try to stop them.

Henry looked at Ada with a quizzical, raised eyebrow that meant something she didn't understand. Maybe he would tell her later. Maybe not.

ELEVEN

'Would you like to go to your hotel this afternoon? I've set up appointments for tomorrow morning, running for the following two days,' Sanchez said.

Ada's face was still stinging from the slap by Sybil Kimball, and she was close to sensory overwhelm, but she wasn't sure that going to a hotel would help with that. It would depend on the hotel, the scents used there, the lights, and other factors. She checked her watch. It was only three p.m. After all that driving and the conversation with Ella's parents and the tour? So strange.

'We appreciate you making the appointments, but we'd like to talk to Gavin this afternoon while the other students are still gone on the field trip,' Henry said. 'If your son was there when Ella Kimball died, he must have seen what happened. He's the only witness we have to whatever happened, murder or not.'

Sanchez's face tightened. 'I don't even know if he remembers her death. Or if he understands the permanency of death. And he can't communicate what he saw in any case. I've already tried, as have the experts here. I can't see how either of you will be better than we are.'

Her protectiveness of her son seemed to take the form of diminishing his capacities, but Ada had no way of knowing if Gavin was as disabled as his mother claimed without seeing him herself. She hoped she could communicate with him, but she wasn't an expert in non-verbal communication with autists. She just hoped that being autistic herself would help her see things in a different way from others.

'I think it's worth a chance.' Henry waved at Ada. 'She is very capable at this sort of thing.'

His overconfidence bothered Ada. She wanted to try to communicate with Gavin, yes. But the way Henry kept using her to insist on things, to manipulate others, bothered her. Was this part of FBI training? Or was it just his own personal interaction style?

'Well, I suppose that I can't stop the FBI. And as his mother,

I can only hope that you discover that Gavin isn't the one at fault for Ella's death. Isn't that what you're here to do? That it wasn't a tragic accident between one autistic child and another?' Sanchez looked directly at Ada in an uncomfortably intense way.

'I–I don't know. It's what I thought when I first saw the photos, yes,' Ada stammered. She felt as uncomfortable with Sanchez's hope as she did with Hen's manipulation. Why couldn't these people just let her say what she could and couldn't do, and then let her do it?

'If Gavin isn't to be blamed for this the rest of his life, we have to be allowed to speak to him and find out what really happened,' Henry said smoothly.

Manipulation again. Hold a terrible threat over the head of a mother and see if she caves.

Sanchez did. 'All right. He's not verbal right now, and he's with his therapist, but I can go with you and see if she thinks he might be able to accept a stranger for a few minutes. He's not at his best, and strangers are always difficult for autistic children.'

She nodded briskly. 'I will be observing from outside the room, and Tamsin, his therapist, will be inside. If, at any time, either of us feels that he needs to stop, or that the interview needs to end, you'll have to trust us that we're doing it for his own protection, and not because we think that he's guilty of something. Is that clear?' She turned from Ada to Henry.

'We agree to those terms,' Henry said, without consulting Ada on the matter, just in case she had any misconception about who was in charge here. He added more gently, 'And we won't be recording the conversation, so there will be no way for us to use it against Gavin in any circumstance. We're here to gather information to help guide the rest of the investigation. It's informal. Is that all acceptable to you?'

Sanchez picked up her phone and dialed a number. 'Tamsin? Two people from the FBI are in my office and they'd like to talk to Gavin. Yes, I know he's not using words yet, but they think they can communicate with him through other means. Yes, I'm going to give them permission to come visit him informally. No recording. I'd like you to stay with him in the room while I observe from the outside. Yes, now. Or in the next few minutes. All right, I understand that you have reservations. I'll note that.'

A Special Interest in Murder

She hung up the phone and looked up at them. 'It's set up. I just need to tell my assistant that I'll be unavailable for the next couple of hours.' She typed a message on her phone. There was a buzz, and she looked down at the response. 'I have an appointment I can't change in one hour, so it will have to be less than that. All right?'

Henry nodded, and Ada managed to get her body to stand. After everything that had happened today, but especially the physical attack by Sybil Kimball, it felt as if she had to force it to move each step. There was no automatic motion now. This was what happened when she was so overwhelmed that a part of her brain shut down. It was like she was two different people, the one with a body that had to be moved this way and that, and the one that was a brain, thinking and considering and assessing and analyzing.

She hated this feeling, this empty hollowness, but it was better than a full-blown meltdown when she stopped having control of the body part of herself altogether. She just hoped that she could have the full meltdown in the hotel room tonight. It was coming. She could feel that now. It was just a matter of delaying it as long as she could. She'd gotten better at that since she was a child.

They moved through a hallway and passed some unidentified rooms. They went outside, and later she thought they'd gone to the other farmhouse, but she wasn't entirely sure. The truth was that when she was distressed, one of the first things that disappeared was her ability to make sense of the pieces of even a simple puzzle like the spatiotemporal location of her own body.

Henry stopped a moment and waited for her to reach him. He put a hand on her shoulder, which made her jump again.

'I have to remember to stop doing that,' he muttered to himself.

Then he tried to catch her gaze, but she couldn't stand to meet his eyes. Looking directly into the eyes of another human was difficult at any time, but it wasn't something she could do right now. She looked just past him.

'Are you all right?' Henry asked.

She managed to get her vocal cords to make a sound that was like 'Mmm-hmm.'

Henry wasn't convinced. He wasn't stupid, and he had known

her before, when she wasn't as good at forcing her body to do things that it had to do to get her the things she wanted to have. And sometimes things she needed to have.

Henry had to move now because Sanchez was looking back at him impatiently.

They finally stopped next to a door that had a little window inset into it, presumably so that Sanchez could watch them. Sanchez was looking inside right now.

'She's just telling him that you're going to come in and talk to him. He's upset about it, but I don't think he's going to have a meltdown. We'll see. If he starts spiraling, I'll have to pull you out before the hour is up.' She looked toward Ada this time.

'I understand meltdowns,' Ada said stiffly.

'Good. I'll let you in now.' Sanchez pressed a number code into the pad next to the door, and then it flashed green and she opened it. 'Tamsin, this is Henry. And Ada. They want to talk to Gavin about what happened with Ella Kimball.'

Sanchez walked into the room and knelt before her son. She didn't touch him, just made sure her face was closer to his. 'Gavin, these people are friends. They want to help you. I'll be waiting just outside if you need anything. All right?'

Gavin didn't respond to her. Ada noticed how small he was. He was still just barely taller than she was when she knelt down. His hair was thick and curly and fell to his shoulders, longer than his mother's. He wore a floral shirt in pink and orange that Ada loved and itched to find a copy of in an adult size. He also had on a short pink skort that his hands were wrapped up in the hem of.

There was something that was in between masculine and feminine that was so familiar to her, from her childhood but into her adulthood, as well. In her childhood, she'd been forced to conform to her 'female' gender by both her parents. They insisted it was an important part of fitting in and not being bullied. They hadn't been entirely wrong about that, either. She conformed largely now, at least when she had to be in public. It made many things easier. It made other things more difficult, but those weren't things that other people cared about.

'Hi, Gavin. I'm Ada,' she got out.

She found herself feeling surprisingly relaxed with Gavin. She hadn't expected him to remind her so much of her own twelve-year-old self.

She'd sometimes worn feminine clothing happily. At other times, she'd wanted to cut her hair short like a boy's and wear athletic clothing and use a different name. Gender still felt like something from the outside pressed on to her inside, and she just wanted to be herself. It seemed Gavin was like that, too.

'I'll leave you with him,' Sanchez said, and moved to the door.

'I'm Henry,' Henry said, but he didn't put a hand forward or try to touch Gavin. He hadn't said he was going to come in, but he wasn't leaving, and Sanchez didn't say anything about it.

It was nice having the authority of the FBI, Ada thought, though she wasn't sure she'd always want the weight of that authority, either.

'It's nice to meet you, Henry and Ada,' said Tamsin, clearly pronouncing each name.

She was modeling socially appropriate behavior. But she wasn't forcing it on to Gavin.

Ada also noticed that there were no treats in the room, nothing to bribe Gavin with in order to force compliant behavior on him. Good.

'We know that what happened with Ella must have been very disturbing, Gavin. We're here to talk to you about that. Do you think you could do that?' Ada asked.

Gavin didn't look at Ada or Henry. He looked at the floor, or his hands, or the wall behind his therapist.

Henry gave her a gesture to encourage her to move forward, but Ada wanted to keep her distance. That would make Gavin feel more comfortable, she was sure, even if Henry didn't understand that.

Ada thought of when she'd gone non-verbal herself in the weeks right after her mother's death. She'd forced herself to attend the funeral and speak at it, forced herself to say the formula of nice things you were supposed to say in a eulogy, and then had stood with her father and greeted the few people who had come to mourn her mother. After all that, she'd collapsed and gone non-verbal for weeks. She wasn't sure how long, but it had been midway through the next month when she felt as if she came back to herself.

Ella's death must have been at least as traumatic to Gavin, and he was just a kid. No wonder he had gone non-verbal.

Tamsin had several small toys on her desk – a bouncy ball, a fidget cube, and a couple of vaguely human-like figures made in a soft, dark wood that had been smoothed even more by so many hands touching them.

Ada picked up the bouncy ball and started tossing it from hand to hand.

Tamsin stared at her.

Henry looked at her with an annoyed expression.

Gavin still didn't look at her. Or speak.

Ada stopped playing with the ball and left it on the desk closer to Gavin. Then she picked up the fidget toy and began to make clicking noises with it. She clicked along with the fidget toy.

'What—?' Henry began.

Ada put a finger to her lips and made no sound.

Henry seemed to finally get the idea. He moved away from Gavin and then watched while leaning against the wall.

Gavin picked up the bouncy ball and began tossing it between his hands.

Tamsin looked astonished.

Then Gavin tossed the ball to Ada.

Ada caught it without hesitation. She was still holding the fidget toy in her hand and still making clicking noises.

After a moment, she put the fidget toy on the desk.

She tossed the bouncy ball back to Gavin.

He wasn't looking at her or showing any sign of attention, but he snatched the ball out of the air and began tossing it back and forth between his hands, until suddenly he tossed the ball back to Ada, who caught it.

Tamsin let out a sharp gasp of surprised delight.

Gavin turned slightly toward Ada, and they began to toss the ball back and forth, back and forth. Gavin didn't make it easy for Ada. He threw it far outside of her easy-catch zone, but she always anticipated where he was going to go, even before Henry or Tamsin seemed to guess enough to move out of the way. The ball was small and wouldn't have hurt them, but Ada made sure they never had contact with it.

Tamsin smiled at Ada as the game continued.

At some point, Henry looked at his watch, but Ada had lost all sense of time. She was completely focused on this game with Gavin. It was as much a conversation as if it had been in words.

I'm scared, Gavin said – without words.

I know you are, Ada said. *That's why I'm here. To make you feel safe again.*

You can't make me feel safe. You're a stranger. Strangers are dangerous. Not in words, but in motions.

I am safe. I am a stranger, but I'm also a friend. A new friend.

I don't have friends. He looked away.

You do have friends. I am a friend.

The ball went back and forth, back and forth.

Henry cleared his throat loudly.

What was wrong with the man? Why couldn't he see the progress being made?

The next time Ada tossed the ball to Gavin, he didn't catch it. It landed by Henry's feet, and Henry had to get down on his hands and knees to chase after it as it bounced from corner to corner.

Henry came back to offer it to Gavin.

But Gavin wouldn't take it.

Henry gave it to Ada instead.

Ada put it in her lap and watched Gavin.

After several minutes, Gavin picked up the two plastic toy figures on Tamsin's desk. He offered the smaller one to Ada, and she took it.

Then he took the larger one and had it dance in his hands, almost like it was bouncing back and forth like the ball between them.

Ada took the small figure and put it on the floor between her feet.

Gavin knelt down and brought the larger figure closer. The larger figure danced near the smaller figure but didn't touch it. Then the larger figure stopped. Gavin's whole body seemed to grow taut. The larger figure fell down briefly. But only for a moment.

Then Gavin picked up the larger figure and ran off with it, shrieking loudly, soundless cries of distress.

Tamsin moved to soothe Gavin, putting his head close to her

chest. He batted at her with his arms, but it wasn't with any real strength. He quieted after a little while, and then Tamsin got him to sit next to her, as she put a hand on his back in support.

'I don't—' Henry started to say.

Ada put a finger to her lips again and made a shushing sound at him.

He rolled his eyes and stepped back once more, leaning against the wall and watching.

'Thank you, Gavin,' Ada said. 'I understand what you showed me. You didn't touch Ella, did you?'

Gavin made a very small sound, a grunt, not enough to make it clear if it was affirmative or negative.

'You didn't hurt her because, of course, you wouldn't. She was your friend, and you couldn't believe that when you found her, she was dead.'

This time, Gavin's response was a higher-toned utterance, but still not a word.

'Ada—' Henry started.

Ada shushed him rather loudly. She was just getting to the interesting part here. She turned back to Gavin. 'You stayed with her for a long time after, because you thought she might wake up, that maybe she was just pretending. And then you realized she wasn't pretending, that something was very wrong with her. That's when you started making a fuss, and people came and found her, and you with her.'

Gavin started jumping just a little, his hands clapping together. It still wasn't verbal affirmation, but surely no one could say that he wasn't making it clear that he liked what Ada was saying.

'I don't know what you just did, but that was amazing. Are you an autism therapist of some kind?' Tamsin asked, as she played bouncy ball with Gavin, who was now much calmer and started to make sounds like 'Oh,' and 'Yeah,' and 'Woah,' and other things that were word-like if not quite words.

'No, but I know something of what Gavin is going through. When my mother died, I went non-verbal. I'm also autistic,' Ada said.

'But you . . . just—' Tamsin was gesturing at Gavin and then Ada, but she had to catch the bouncy ball and got distracted.

'Thank you. This has been very helpful,' Ada said.

Tamsin and Gavin seemed content with each other. Ada motioned Henry to go out with her, where Sanchez was.

'I had no idea you could do that. That was amazing!' Sanchez said. 'And now we know that he didn't kill Ella. But who did? Is it possible she died of natural causes?'

'No,' Ada said with certainty.

Henry shook his head. He wasn't at all happy. Whatever emotion he was feeling, it wasn't a good one. He wasn't congratulating her the way she thought she deserved. Surely this was even better than her winning the state science fair.

'What's wrong?' Ada asked quietly.

'There's no way we can use any of that as evidence.' He motioned back toward the room with the window on the door where Gavin had been. 'It's useless.'

'But you said that it wasn't supposed to be evidence. Just trying to find information,' Ada said.

'Yes, but I don't see how anything he might have communicated could help. He didn't say anything about whom he might have seen or who might have had a motive to kill Ella,' Henry insisted.

'True, but he didn't kill her. That's something, isn't it?' Ada asked.

'Not enough. It could have meant anything, and if we ever end up in court, all of that will just be laughed at,' Henry said.

That hurt. Being mocked had always hurt her, even if she hadn't understood that she was being mocked when she was much younger. She hadn't figured that out until after her diagnosis. Before that, it had been about her being 'weird.' After, the mockers had a label to stick on her. And it always stung, every single time.

'We have a mountain still to climb,' Henry went on with a sigh. He rubbed at his temples.

Ada felt all the pain from the encounter with Mrs Kimball return to her, and then some, as if blocking it out for the hour with Gavin now brought it back twofold. She began to shake and was afraid she might fall down.

'What's wrong?' he asked.

She just moved toward Henry, leaning on him heavily. She hoped she could make it back out to the car. Then she was looking forward to a long nap. It would probably take several days of little else but sleeping before she came fully back to herself.

'Should we leave for the hotel now?' asked Henry. 'There are things still to do here, if you can manage it.'

He wasn't wrong. So Ada tried to think of something that would help keep her going. Caffeine? It might give her another hour or two. Maybe that would be enough.

'Can I have some coffee?' she asked.

Henry looked at his watch again. 'In the afternoon? All right, but don't complain to me if you can't sleep tonight.'

'I can get some coffee,' Sanchez said, and led them back to her own office, outside, and down more corridors.

Ada could feel the pain in her face, but almost nothing else. She kept her body moving. For now, she still had control over it. It wasn't her, her body, but she was attached to it. She was resentful of that now more than ever before.

TWELVE

After the coffee, Ada felt a little better, the pain in her face pushed back. She knew that she might crash soon, but she was hoping to push it until later in the evening, when hopefully she would be in a hotel room. Alone.

'I'm sorry,' Henry offered.

She tilted her head at him, confused. 'Sorry for what?'

'For pointing out the problems with your conversation with Gavin. You did a good job. Extraordinary, really. When we first walked in, I wasn't sure that there was any hope he'd be able to communicate.'

'He's dealing with trauma. But he's still inside there. I think he's a very intelligent boy,' Ada said.

'He liked you,' Henry went on. 'He really, really liked you.' He gave her a big, broad smile.

It made Ada uncomfortable. She'd done what she had intended to do – no more, no less. It was always difficult to understand how to respond to compliments from people who weren't autistic. They tended to compliment her on exactly the wrong things. Either they were being sarcastic and didn't mean it as a compliment at all, or they complimented her on something she'd done accidentally.

Compliments were one of several prominent social currencies. People offered them to you as if they were a gift, but there was always a tax that was required, usually in another currency. And no one ever specified how the tax was expected to be paid. If you asked them, they would insist that of course they didn't mean that at all, how ridiculous of you to assume that they expected recompense. The compliment was freely offered.

But it never was.

Ada stared at Henry, trying to figure out what he expected in return for the compliment.

'The students will be returning from the field trip soon,' Sanchez said. The director had been walking them back to her office, and then she sat at her desk, typing quickly on her computer, as she glanced at them. 'I've got appointments for tomorrow and the next day, if you'd like to head out now. I'm sure you have things to take care of. Phone calls to family and such.'

Ada did not have family to make phone calls to, but she let Henry reply. He hadn't said anything about a romantic partner or even a wife or children. She didn't know anything about his current life, except that he worked for the FBI.

'If you don't mind, maybe we can interview anyone else here who isn't on the field trip? If there is anyone?' Henry asked.

Ada realized immediately she should have told Henry she needed to go to the hotel now. She was too close to meltdown, and she didn't want Henry to see it full blown. But at least the others would be more used to seeing an autistic person in such a state, and it might be less embarrassing.

'I suppose there's Tina Abrams. She's the friendship facilitator, and she didn't go on the field trip. She's at her staff housing, but she could probably come here quickly enough,' Sanchez offered.

No, no, no, no, no, thought Ada. But she couldn't bring herself to say 'no.' Maybe her time with the non-verbal Gavin had affected her in ways she hadn't anticipated.

'What is a friendship facilitator?' Henry asked.

'Exactly what it sounds like,' Sanchez said, slightly impatient. 'She helps put the children together in friendship pairs that might work well for them. She tries to keep them together for more than a year, so that they feel stable with each other. It's been shown to be very helpful for autistic children, who can be slow to form bonds with others because they need more time to process social cues.'

'So she sets people up on friendship dates?' Henry asked.

If it was meant to be a joke, no one laughed.

Sanchez slowed down, as if Henry weren't smart enough to understand her the first time. 'She pairs children. She paired Gavin and Ella up because they had some similarities she thought were important. She makes sure that they have scheduled friendship time together, and that they have several classes together.'

'Weren't they different ages? Wouldn't they be in different grades?' Henry asked.

Sanchez sighed. 'Yes, but there are only forty-two children here. So we can't divide them into twelve different grades or there wouldn't be enough students for any classes. We keep them in wide age ranges. And in any case, neurodivergent children often don't think of age or grades in the same way that neurotypical students do. Some argue that they're more open. Others say that they're simply delayed in their social development, so they don't notice the mistakes older or younger students make. But the result is the same here. Friendship facilitation.'

'I see,' Henry said. 'Yes, we'd like to talk to her. Wouldn't we, Ada?'

Here was a chance to say no again, that she needed to take a break, to have private time in a dark, silent space. But the shame that came from talking about her autism and her special needs came rushing back. And it was hard to get words out.

'Nnnn,' she said to Henry, but he didn't understand.

'Great,' Henry said, then turned to Sanchez. 'Let's do it.'

The director typed on her phone. 'I'm checking to see if she's available today instead of tomorrow and the next day, when I have you scheduled to meet with every single member of the staff.'

'Thank you,' Henry said.

'Is there anything else you need, while we wait?' she said, staring back and forth at her phone and at Henry.

'Yes. I was wondering: if it was an hour until Gavin thought to ask for help, who did he go to? Who found Ella's body?'

'Ah. Well, that would be me,' Sanchez said. 'He's my son, so he would come to me in an emergency, even if he didn't fully understand what was wrong with Ella. I came in and I was also upset, though my main focus was calming Gavin down until I could call an ambulance.'

Ada looked at her, trying to decide what it was about what the woman had just said that felt wrong. She was often bad at telling what intonations were off or why, but she also had a sense of things not fitting together that other people didn't.

'And it was this Ms Abrams who decided that Gavin and Ella should be together at that time? Was she the staff member who was supposed to be watching over them and wasn't?' Henry asked.

Sanchez pursed her lips before responding. 'She was called out to deal with a different social problem. Children in the cafeteria were throwing food.'

'Ah.' Henry smiled softly at this. 'That seems a normal enough thing.'

'It may be normal at other schools, but not at this one. It is unacceptable here, and Ms Abrams knew I would take it seriously. I texted her to deal with it immediately, and she had been waiting for our math tutor to take over with Ella and Gavin, since they were at similar levels. But she had to leave them when Ms Glock didn't come. She'd sent a message explaining she had to leave early that day, but Ms Abrams didn't see it until . . . well, until after all of this had already happened. And ultimately, as the director here, I'm the one who is at fault for the results of my decisions, including sending Ms Abrams to the cafeteria. But I didn't think . . .' She trailed off. 'I should have gone to take her place with Gavin and Ella. Or at least checked in with them sooner. I'll never forgive myself for that.'

Ada remembered Sanchez saying something similar to Ella's parents, the Kimballs, that she was taking responsibility for what had happened because she was the director of the school. But it felt like those were just words.

'Had she left Gavin and Ella alone before?' Henry asked.

'Yes, a couple of times, but for no more than ten minutes. As I said, I thought she would be able to manage the cafeteria situation more quickly.'

Now Ada realized what was wrong. Sanchez was acting as if Gavin had gone out of the room to find her, but as far as Ada could tell from his version of events, that hadn't happened. So why was the director implying something different from what had actually happened? Unless Gavin was wrong, of course. Or Ada had misunderstood him.

The conversation between Henry and Sanchez was going too quickly for her to interject. She could bring up the question tomorrow, she told herself. When she'd had a chance to rest.

'And the photograph of Ella that was taken at her death?' Henry asked.

Sanchez looked confused. 'What photograph?'

Henry got out his phone and showed the photo, first to Ada

and then to Sanchez. 'This is the photo that was released on social media when the story first came out. You didn't take it?'

'Of course not.' Her vehemence was loud. 'No one on my staff would have had permission to take a photograph like that. It would be a violation of . . . of . . . too many things to count. I didn't know that it had even gone out. How terrible.' She put a hand to her mouth.

'But someone must have,' Henry said.

Sanchez's phone buzzed, and she glanced at it, eyes tearing up. 'Oh, that's Tina Abrams. She should be ready to see you now. She's walking down and will meet us in the room I've set up for interviews.' A wave of her hand as she stood up.

'Did you approve of Gavin and Ella's friendship?' Henry asked as they moved once more toward the door.

'Me? If you're asking if I got to choose whomever I wanted to be my son's friend, then no. That was entirely in Ms Abram's domain. I would never have interfered in her choices.' A pause, and then she added, 'But I did approve of it. I thought that they were a good match.'

'Why is that?' Henry asked.

Ada kept moving forward, feeling heavier with each step. Sometimes she wished she could be like Spock's brain in the original *Star Trek* series, no longer burdened with the weight of a body, and all the operations that had to go on inside of it, all at the same time. So much energy wasted on her sack of flesh and bones.

She had enjoyed the fictional characters Spock and Data as a child, though her parents hadn't liked *Star Trek* and had sometimes made fun of her. Nonetheless, they'd used permission to watch one of the shows as an effective bribe when they wanted her to do something. It was one of Ada's few chances to see on television people she thought were autistic like she was.

Spock was an alien, and he was one of her earliest obsessions with space and the idea of alien species that might come to Earth. Data was, of course, a robot, and in some ways, she thought that was even better than being an alien, because he didn't have any flesh and bones. He was entirely circuits and information. What could be better than that?

'What did Ella and Gavin have in common?' Henry asked as

Ada tried to convince her sack of flesh and bones to keep moving normally.

'They were both interested in frogs. It sounds like a superficial similarity, but Gavin would talk on and on about frogs if anyone would let him. And Ella let him. I think she might have been almost over her interest, but not Gavin,' Sanchez said as she led them down the hall again.

Ada remembered Ella's mother mentioning frogs, but not her remembering Ella really liking them. Had she or hadn't she? Another question to think about for tomorrow.

The director put up a finger as her phone buzzed again. 'Just give me a moment, and I'll be back,' she said, and stepped into one of the rooms.

THIRTEEN

Ada couldn't hear if Director Sanchez was speaking on the phone, but she was also not fully herself. Her brain didn't work at one hundred percent when a meltdown was coming.

'You do three times as much as most people in half the time,' one of her therapists had told her once. 'Having an occasional meltdown seems like it just evens things out a bit for the rest of us.'

It had felt kind, but in some ways, Ada thought it was also true. Even with her meltdowns, she still accomplished more than most people did in a day. It was just that it never felt enough. She was always haunted by her parents' standards for her, and by their impatience with her meltdowns.

'No time for wasting time,' her father had said so many times.

Ada closed her eyes briefly while Sanchez was gone.

After a moment, she could feel Henry next to her. He didn't touch her, but he was standing very close. She opened her eyes and met his eyes, which were very intense.

'What is wrong?' he asked.

She didn't understand what he was asking.

'Wrong? A girl was murdered,' Ada said simply. 'We're investigating it.' There were a lot of things wrong here at NAVITEK, as far as she could tell. Which specific one could Henry mean?

He made a tsking sound. 'No, what is wrong with you? Right now – what is it? You're practically vibrating. I feel like you turned into Mary Poppins and might start floating out of the room or something. Are you going to start singing?' He didn't smile, so this wasn't a joke.

'No, I'm not going to start singing,' Ada said.

'Then let's get this interview done. That will make the other two days a little less crowded. We can possibly head home after that and make it before midnight. All right?'

'Yes, of course,' Ada mumbled. She was starting to feel numb.

Her lips and jaw were working, but she couldn't feel them. Her body was going on autopilot. Soon, she wouldn't be much use for anything. She'd seem like she was fine, except that she wouldn't be able to talk or move, and she wouldn't remember what happened except in patches.

She hated this part of herself. It made her feel so weak and ashamed. She knew that she shouldn't feel that way. It was just that she'd gotten over-stimulated, and this was her body's way of resetting everything so that her brain would work again as soon as it could. But neither of her parents had ever had a meltdown as far as she knew. They'd always been in control of their environments, at least as adults, and they certainly hadn't admitted to childhood meltdowns. Because they weren't autistic, according to them. They had no defects. Only Ada had those.

The door opened and Sanchez poked her head outside. 'Thank you for your patience,' she said, and gestured to the next room down the hallway. 'It should just be a moment if you'll wait there for Ms Abrams.'

Ada and Henry went into the room, which had a table and four chairs around it. Her face still stung, but the pain seemed less intense now. She hoped that wasn't just because she was in too many other kinds of pain to notice it. That had certainly happened in her life before.

'I'll be back in an hour, if that sounds all right?' Sanchez said.

'Fine,' Henry said, and waved her out.

'You sure there's nothing wrong?' Henry asked again.

Before Ada could answer, the door opened, and a very tall, thin woman with extremely strong perfume came inside. Most everything else about her was overwhelmed in Ada's mind by the scent of that perfume. Something that smelled like rotten flowers. How anyone could think that was a good scent, Ada didn't know. She'd mostly overcome her sensitivity to various common scents like cleaners and basic hygiene gels. But this was something she'd never smelled before, and it was awful. Her eyes were watering.

'Ada?' Henry was asking.

'Yes,' Ada made herself say.

'I'm Tina Abrams. Director Sanchez asked me to come speak with you. Something about Ella and Gavin's friendship pairing?'

Ada had to bite hard on her bottom lip to bring herself back to the moment. She'd zoned out. She hoped she hadn't made any noises. She glanced at Henry, but he didn't seem to be edging away from her.

'I'm Henry Bloodstone,' Henry said, offering a hand. 'I'm with the FBI.'

Abrams shook it.

'This is Ada Latia. She's working with me on the death of Ella.'

He hadn't referred to her as an expert, Ada thought. That was good.

'How very tragic,' Abrams said. 'So sad what happened to her. But I can assure you that whatever happened, Ella's death was purely an accident. Gavin doesn't have a mean bone in his body. He and Ella were quite close.'

Ada felt as if she were seeing everything from a distance, through a foggy glass. She always had trouble parsing body language and facial expression, but her usual keen grasp of details was gone. The woman was wearing something – red and white, with black accents. A scarf around her neck. Or was that a necklace?

'You left them together to deal with a problem in the cafeteria?' Henry asked.

'Yes, I got a message about some uproar there, and I thought that Gavin and Ella would be fine together. They were good friends. I'd observed them together on many occasions,' Abrams said.

'Had you ever left them alone before?'

Abrams hesitated before answering this. 'I tried not to.'

'And why is that? Did you think there could be danger for Ella?'

'No, of course not,' she insisted. Then took a breath. 'I don't think autistic children are bound to be violent, if that's what you're asking. And I didn't see anything between Gavin and Ella that would have concerned me. I put them together because they seemed good for each other. They *were* good for each other, until—'

'Until Ella ended up dead,' Henry said.

'Yes, well, no one could have predicted that. They were

supposed to have math tutoring at that time, and I'd already finished my planned material with them.'

'What was your planned material?' Ada asked, interrupting Henry. She felt a strange rush of sound around her but tried to ignore it.

'My planned material?' A waved hand. 'Just set questions for them to ask each other about their interests. I think it was frogs. They both liked frogs.'

That was an important piece of information about the two, it seemed. Ada was going to try to remember it.

'In any case, I told them to play quietly until I got back. But then I forgot after the incident at the cafeteria. I thought someone else would go get them. And I suppose someone eventually . . .' She trailed off.

'What do you think could have happened that triggered Gavin attacking Ella?' Henry asked.

Ada didn't understand why Henry was saying this. Hadn't they already agreed that Gavin hadn't attacked Ella, that someone else had killed her, not the autistic boy? Why would Henry ask something like this? It made no sense to her.

Abrams shook her head. 'I really couldn't make a guess like that.'

'But Ella is dead, and you knew the two children very well. You put them together because you thought they would be compatible, isn't that right?' Henry asked.

Her hands were waving about, making Ada more confused. 'Well, yes, I suppose. This is one of the best schools for autistic children in the country. If it could be duplicated, we could help thousands of families. But, of course, no one can be reasonably expected to foresee the future.'

We.

Words, words, words.

Ada's face throbbed once, like a glitchy strobe light, and then felt numb again. She preferred the numb.

'What made you put these two together? It was some months ago, wasn't it? They've been friends for more than a year, isn't that right?' Henry asked.

Abrams pursed her lips. 'You must understand, it wasn't specifically about them when I first put them together. I had a whole group I was trying to pair up. I just made the best overall pairings I could, given all the other children.'

'Now it sounds like you're saying that they weren't well matched. Are you good at your job, Ms Abrams?'

Ada didn't like how combative Henry sounded. She would have bristled if he were asking her questions like that. It almost sounded like her mother.

Abrams straightened. 'Of course I'm good at my job. I graduated first in my class at Harvard. And at Yale. Who are you to question me?'

Ada twitched at the reminder of the kinds of credentials that her parents had had, that they had wanted her to have. They had been so embarrassed when she had refused even to apply to any of the top universities. She hadn't wanted any of that. She hadn't needed it, either.

Henry looked at her, and she realized he wanted her to ask a question. She eventually got out, 'Did you like Gavin? Or was it Ella you didn't like?' She only realized when she spoke that she had guessed Abrams disliked one of them based on some cue she couldn't define immediately.

'What? Of course I liked Gavin. And Ella. I care about all the children under my care. Maybe I didn't understand their interest in frogs, but autistic children often have unusual special interests, at least for a time. It can be a good way to get them to bond, even if it's not as emotionally significant as something neurotypical people would bond over,' Abrams insisted.

'Emotionally significant?' Ada echoed.

'Yes, like a shared experience. Having a loved one die. Or having to move often in childhood. Or being made fun of for reading books.' Abrams smiled, as if this was a small thing. 'Autistic children don't have the same social acumen, so they don't process their experiences in the same way. That's why it may seem as if we're pairing them based on more superficial factors.'

Superficial. Yes, of course, this woman thought autistic people were superficial in their special interests.

'You don't think that their bonding was because they had empathy for each other?' Ada asked. 'Because they both understood what it was like to be autistic in a world that doesn't love autistic children?'

'What? I don't—' Abrams began to say. Then she stopped. 'I don't think that either of those children had the capacity for empathy that you're suggesting. That's one of the main diagnostic criteria for autistic children. They struggle to understand that other people are actually real, that other people have different experiences from their own.' She sounded like she was going to lecture them about this, as if Ada and Henry must be very stupid, and she was going to have to start at the very beginning, however tedious she herself found it.

Ada knew she was not at her best, and that she should probably have let Henry take back control of the conversation, but she couldn't help but respond. 'Have you considered that you're the one who lacks empathy because you can't see the world the way that autistic children do?' She didn't try to hide the anger in her tone.

'What?' Abrams sputtered. 'I don't think you are in a position to explain to me how autistic children see the world. I've spent my entire life—'

And that was the last thing that Ada heard before the meltdown started.

FOURTEEN

This meltdown was like all the other times, from her childhood to the last meltdown she'd had, which, not coincidentally, was when Rex had sent her the divorce papers. She hadn't pushed herself this hard since then. She'd been very cautious with her time and energy, and she didn't think she'd left the house for more than an hour in the last year save for this case.

It was as Ada imagined touching a live electric wire would be. For several moments, it felt like the world was on fire, like everything was loud and hot and all over, inside and out. She could feel her body start to jerk. She tried to make her mouth move so that she could ask Henry to carry her away from here, into the car, away from where anyone else could see her. It seemed a stupid thing that she, an autistic woman, was embarrassed by other people seeing what was a classic symptom of autism, but she knew that the worst part of a meltdown was never the meltdown itself.

It was what happened afterward. How she would try to piece together all the things that she missed, and how she'd have to try to explain it so that it didn't seem like she wasn't fully human.

But after the heat and the noise and the shaking, there was a blessed silence.

This was the good part of a meltdown, the only good part, frankly.

Her brain shut out the too-much-ness that she had been forcing herself into, and it made it not too much anymore.

It was quiet and dark, and time seemed to stretch out to infinity.

This was what death was probably like. And if she wasn't so scared of waking up from being dead, she might think about suicide more often.

Death couldn't be so bad if it was just nothing. Emptiness. Not being conscious of all the too-much-ness of the world around her, and the not-enough-ness of herself. So many things that she was supposed to know and process and put together, puzzles she didn't see and couldn't solve.

The pain in her face came back, pulsing with the beat of her heart.

Ouch.

She didn't want that.

But she couldn't push it away anymore.

That was the first sense she had that she was coming back into herself.

She noticed that she was breathing, which is to say that she could feel her body again. Not that her body was somehow separate from her mind. She knew that wasn't true. But the weight of it had gone away, the borders of it, and now it was coming back.

When she could feel she was breathing again, that meant she was aware of her chest, her lungs, her skin, her heart, her head against – something – and her fingers cold and cramped and her legs splayed out like that?

She jerked and could feel her eyes open, and her dry, cracked mouth try to say something.

'Ada, are you there?'

She could hear the muffled words from a familiar voice. Who was that? Wasn't he gone? She couldn't trust him.

No, this was Henry. Hen. Hen was safe.

Probably safe.

Was he still safe now?

'Ada, I'm here. I've got you.'

She turned her head to try to see, but the room was dim.

'I can turn on the lights, if you want,' Henry suggested. 'But I thought you would rather I stay next to you.'

She could feel now that her fingers were entwined with his fingers. She thought she was on the floor when she woke up, but no, that was too soft to be a floor. She had to be on a couch of some kind. There hadn't been a couch in the room she'd had the meltdown in. So where was she? How did she get there?

'How long?' she finally got her mouth and vocal cords to work together to say.

Henry hesitated, and then seemed to be looking down at his watch, which glowed in the dark. She could see the time on it as well as he could, but she appreciated him translating it into words.

'It's six past four. I think you've been out a little over an hour.'

'God,' she said.

'I'm so sorry. I shouldn't have pushed you like that. You tried to warn me. When I asked if you wanted to stay, you made that sound, and I should have known that meant you were struggling.'

What was his tone? Irritated? She couldn't tell.

'Where is she? Abrams?' Ada got out again.

'Probably went back to her car and went home. Why does it matter? She's not the one who collapsed,' Henry said.

Ada found herself flushing. She hated when that happened. It made her emotions so clear to other people. Usually, she was blank-faced, so no one could tell how she was feeling any more than she could guess what they were feeling. It was more fair. This was very imbalanced.

She pulled her fingers away from his, clenching her fists, at least partly to get circulation and warmth back into her extremities. She sat up.

'Whoa! Are you sure you're ready for that?' Henry asked.

She held herself rigidly still to make it clear she was fine now. She wasn't fine now. She had a headache and still felt very muzzy. But she didn't need medical attention or anything.

Henry put up his hands. 'All right. I'll leave you alone. I was just trying to help.'

'You did help.' She bit her lower lip. Took a deep breath. 'Thank you for taking me here. It's nice and quiet. And private.'

'I figured you wouldn't want other people to see you like that,' Henry said, looking away.

Was he embarrassed by her? She couldn't tell. 'What did you think of Abrams?' she asked, trying to focus on the investigation again. If she was useful to him, then he'd be less embarrassed, surely.

She was always trying to make sure that other people got enough in return for their relationship with her, and Henry seemed to have already paid a lot, both in the past and present. She didn't understand social capital and was sure that people who knew her didn't think of her as higher in the social hierarchy than she was. She couldn't offer Henry any status for being close to her, but she could at least offer him her knowledge and expertise. It had seemed before, at least, that had mattered enough for him to stay with her.

'Abrams? I don't understand why anyone would hire her to pick friends for autistic children. I had to wonder if that woman had ever had a real friend herself. She has no idea what real kindness is,' Henry said.

Ada had very few friends. She hadn't made any in high school and she hadn't gone to college. The friends she'd made in the business world had drifted away from her when she'd stepped back. They'd been Rex's friends, not hers, as it turned out.

'What she said about Ella not having any empathy . . .' She didn't finish, but Henry was already nodding.

'Yes, I agree that she might be wrong on that. But not many people have your level of empathy, autistic or not.'

Ada blinked at him. The words penetrated slowly. She flushed again, this time with pleasure rather than embarrassment. 'Thank you,' she said. She meant it. It was the nicest compliment anyone had given her in a long time, and she was fairly certain it was meant sincerely.

Henry continued, 'But I don't know that I believe Abrams killed Ella. I don't really see a motive. Do you?'

Ada thought about it, but she didn't have a simple answer, at least not off the top of her head. Her head, or rather her brain, was not working at its peak at the moment. 'I don't know,' she said honestly.

'We can go now. We don't have any more appointments tonight. What do you think about tomorrow?' Henry asked.

It was a sensible question, but she was so exhausted.

'I think we should come back in the morning. I'd like to take a break overnight,' she said quietly. 'There's a hotel somewhere nearby?'

'Yes, I already have one booked.' He looked at his watch.

Ada had pushed too hard and now she could barely speak, let alone think. She hated being so useless. The only good part of her was her brain, the way that it could see so many things and make sense of them. But times like now, it just turned off, and then what was the point of her being alive?

'We can go now if you'd like. I should go tell Director Sanchez that we're on our way out and that we'd like to come back tomorrow. If necessary, I can come back alone and interview a few staff members on my own, maybe ones who might not be as useful.'

FIFTEEN

Ada let out a groan as she tried to rise.

Henry stepped back and then looked her up and down. 'Are you really OK? You don't need to see a doctor or anything? Go to a hospital? Your face looks terrible, worse now than before.'

She waved a hand. 'Of course not. I'm perfectly fine.' Rex had always said she was fine after meltdowns. They didn't matter, of course. Insignificant. Just ignore them and look the other way.

Hen stared at her.

Did he want an explanation?

'What happened?' he asked.

'I was stupid,' Ada muttered. She tried to move toward the door and found herself stumbling.

Henry caught her.

The warmth of his arm felt nice. And then it felt like a cage. She pulled away from him. 'Let's just go, please.'

'In a moment,' he said. 'I just want one thing.' He put his face next to hers, demanding she make eye contact with him. 'You're not dying, are you? Cancer treatment? Chemo? Or an untreatable brain tumor?'

She couldn't answer while she was using up so much energy looking at him.

Finally, he looked away and she could breathe. 'I'm not ill, no. I'm not dying. Just autistic.'

'So Abrams was right about it being a meltdown?'

Ada said, 'Yes,' very precisely. Her precision in language was coming back. Good. That felt normal. It felt right. It was who she was. She needed to be herself again.

'Do those happen often?' he asked. Not forcing her to answer, not making her look him in the eyes.

'Not if I can help it.'

'It seemed awful. I'm sorry. I didn't know that was coming.'

'I did,' she said.

'And you kept going?'

She shrugged. 'Nothing else I could really do.'

'Well, let me know if it's going to happen again. I'd prefer to be prepared. And if there's anything I can do to help stave it off, I'm happy to do that, too.'

'Thank you,' she said, and sighed.

He touched her arm briefly, and she turned her face to him, not quite meeting his eyes. 'My wife died of a brain tumor. Four months ago now. What happened to you looked from the outside a lot like her first convulsion attack. It was terrifying. I thought you were going to die. I'm glad you didn't.'

'I didn't know that.' She hadn't thought of him as getting married in the years she hadn't known him. Rex would have said that was her autism, that she didn't think about other people's existence when she wasn't around them.

Henry said, 'Of course you couldn't. She was pregnant at the time. We had to make a decision to have her do chemo and have an abortion. It was a terrible choice. And then she died anyway.' His face looked terrible. He had to be very upset, and she had brought it back for him, all unintentionally.

'I'm sorry,' she said. It didn't seem like enough. It never was.

'I didn't mean to make this all about me. You were the one suffering, not me,' Henry said.

Ada shook her head. This was the kind of thing she didn't understand about neurotypical people. They made things into contests that weren't contests. She stepped toward the door, swaying again, but this time when Henry touched her, she shook him off. 'I'm fine now. I just need to get my bearings.'

So Henry stayed a few steps behind as she found her way down the hallway and then saw the familiar front door that she and Henry had come in some hours ago. She pushed against it, unable to make it open, until Henry came up behind her.

'Let me,' he said.

She cursed under her breath. She hated it when she couldn't do things for herself.

He only had to push slightly differently and the door opened. He waved her out, moving behind her again.

It was embarrassing to have him following her like this, as if she were a toddler who couldn't be trusted on her first walk out in the real world.

He insisted on opening the car door for her, then closing it once he had buckled her into her seat.

The next thing Ada knew, the car was moving down the road and she was disoriented, so she put out her hands as if bracing herself.

'I'm not that bad a driver,' Henry said, turning to give her a brief smile, then focusing on the road again.

'My parents thought I could control the meltdowns. They kept insisting that I wasn't trying hard enough,' Ada said.

'The fuck,' Henry said. His expression was dark.

'If I'm careful about not leaving my apartment too often and making sure I go only to places that I know won't overstimulate me, I can keep them from happening very often,' Ada said.

'That's not what I meant.'

'I think I was always a disappointment to them. You'd think I'd get used to that, disappointing other people. But if you'd prefer, I can get a ride back to Utah from the hotel and you can finish the investigation entirely by yourself.'

Henry pulled to the side of the road and smacked the steering wheel with his hands.

'I can get out here if you want.' Ada put a hand on the door.

'No. Don't do that,' Henry barked. Then he sighed. 'Ada, please stop assuming that I'm angry at you. I'm angry that your parents made you feel like a disappointment, even as a child. I could see that in you, in high school. You would flinch as if someone had hit you over and over again.'

'Oh, they never hit me. They had too much self-control,' Ada said.

'Well, forgive me if I don't have much respect for parents who made you feel like shit when you were just yourself.'

'I embarrassed them,' Ada said, the words automatic. Her parents weren't the problem; she was.

'No, they were embarrassed because of their own limitations. I think you're amazing and I want your help for the rest of the investigation. But, Ada, if you don't want to go back tomorrow, please tell me. If I've pushed you too far already, I apologize sincerely. I don't want to make you have another meltdown like that. It was obviously very unpleasant. For you, I mean, not for me.'

A car drove by then, the driver in the front seat staring out at them and then honking as if he decided that they didn't have a good enough reason to be stopped on the side of the road.

Henry didn't seem bothered by it at all. He didn't move his hands to the steering wheel. He was perfectly confident of the space he took up in the world. That was something that Ada didn't think she would ever truly understand.

'I want to go back. I want to finish the investigation. I really do. But after a meltdown, it's difficult,' Ada said. 'It takes some time for me to feel myself again.'

Henry nodded. 'All right. Tell me what would help. Food? Quiet? Music? A television show? A massage? You name it, and I will do my best to make it happen.'

She considered the offer. No one had ever asked her what would help after a meltdown. She'd always focused on trying to keep them from knowing how difficult it was, because it would make her feel like a burden, and they would see her as less than human.

'Quiet, yes,' she said.

'Who was he?' Henry asked after a moment, his tone sharp.

'What? Who was who?' Ada asked.

He gestured toward her, waving up and down. 'Whoever it was that made you afraid of yourself. I know your parents were bad, but you seem to be worse than you were in high school. You're flinching at me, and I haven't done anything to make you afraid of me, I don't think.'

'No, of course you didn't. It's not your fault.' Ada hated it when she felt as though she had no words left, but she was so tired.

'All right, I won't pester you about it. Let's get you to a quiet place. I've got a reservation for two rooms, one on each side of the hotel. You can decide which of the two you'd prefer, and I'll take the other one.'

How had he guessed that she'd want two different choices? 'You don't care, truly?'

He winked at her before pulling the car back on the road again. 'I can sleep outside in a thunderstorm, in an airport in the middle of the day, or during a fireworks show. I have a gift for it.'

He kept driving, and she found herself falling asleep again. She trusted him somehow, even in her sleep. That must be from years ago. She always preferred familiar things because they were safer. Familiar people were rare, because people didn't stay around her long. She always did something to make them leave. Some annoying thing they couldn't handle. That was why she never asked for much.

It was dark when she woke up and found Henry was still driving. 'Almost there,' he said, noticing her.

'Rex,' Ada said, saying the word before she thought too carefully about whether or not it was a good idea. Though she was the least impulsive person she'd ever heard of, this once, for Henry, she was impulsive. Maybe you could be impulsive if you trusted the person you were with enough.

'What?'

'You asked who it was. It was Rex.'

'Ah. Rex.' He said the word as if he were tasting it for the first time and found it bitter.

Or maybe he didn't say it like that at all. What did she know? 'He's my ex-husband.'

'Ah.'

He didn't think anyone would want to marry her. He wasn't wrong. That was why it had been Rex. 'Anyway, he didn't like it when my autism got in the way. He thought that I should be better than that.'

'Fuck him,' Henry said.

Ada pulled herself upright and tugged at the seat belt. She always wore a seat belt because the science was clear on them being safer, but she hated the feel of the belt at her neck, that tug as if a hand was at her throat.

'I don't fuck him anymore, actually,' Ada said.

Henry stuttered. 'I didn't mean—'

She leaned over and put a brief hand on his leg. 'It was a joke,' she said. 'I can make jokes, actually. People think autists have no sense of humor, but we do. It's just different.'

'Ah. Well, I'm glad you're not fucking him anymore. Doesn't sound like he did it very well.'

'Ha. I won't argue with that assessment,' Ada said. 'Though he always said it was my fault, that I wasn't expressive enough.'

'Because you didn't howl with pleasure like his porn videos,' Henry said bluntly.

Ada laughed at that. 'Oh, I didn't know that laughing would help with the headache. I don't think I've ever laughed after a meltdown before.'

Henry pulled into the parking lot of what looked like a nice hotel, not a motel at all. 'Ada, you deserve better than that asshat. I hope you know that. And if you have meltdowns now and again, you should understand that I think it is absolutely worth it, considering what you give in return. I could not have gotten this far in this investigation without you.' He turned to her, not forcing her to meet his gaze this time, just allowing it. 'Do you believe me?' he asked.

'I believe you,' she said to her surprise. And she did.

SIXTEEN

That night, Ada picked the southern hotel room, which was further from the freeway.

Henry helped her out of the car and walked her to her door, though she tried to insist that she was fine and didn't need anything.

'Just a moment,' he said, and held up the second keycard. 'I'll be right back.'

She didn't like the idea that he had a key to her room. She needed more privacy than most people did. 'Need' seemed inadequate to explain it.

Henry knocked when he came back, holding an ice bucket that was full of ice.

'What?' Ada asked, confused. 'Are we drinking to something?' That was all she could imagine as the use for the ice, but Henry didn't have a bottle of alcohol. Not that she would have drunk any. One thing she had learned about her body was that alcohol did not mix well with the after-effects of a meltdown. Talk about a hangover . . .

'It's for your face,' Henry said, gesturing to it.

That was when she felt the stinging pain return. She'd thought it was gone, but it was not. It had just been waiting for her to pay attention, it seemed.

She grabbed a piece of ice and put it to her face. 'Ooh,' she said, jerking at the sudden pain.

'Does that make it worse? I'm sorry, I thought it would help,' Henry said.

'No, it does. Just took a moment to get used to it.' She sighed and let herself relax into the cold, numbing her face again.

'There's a plastic bag, as well, if you want that,' Hen said.

'Thank you,' she said, and let him pack up the ice in the bag and hand it to her. The pain wasn't as bad now, and she could take the bag of ice off and on, so she didn't freeze her skin.

'I'll leave you, then. Unless you need anything else? If you want to order room service, it will go on my card. For the FBI. Or I can bring you something from a fast-food place, if you prefer. Or you can order from Door-Dash.'

It sounded like he was rambling.

'I'm fine. I'm not hungry,' she said.

'And tomorrow?' he asked.

'I don't know yet.'

'Well, if you're not awake when I'm ready to leave, I'll assume you need to take the day off. But you can text me at any time and I'll come back and get you.'

That was a long drive, but Ada nodded, appreciating the kindness behind it.

There was something in Hen's eyes she recognized in some way, but couldn't think of the name for. It came to her after he'd left and the door closed behind him.

Hurt.

He was hurt somehow, and she didn't understand it.

She was the one putting ice on her face.

If aliens ever came to Earth, she hoped they'd be able to explain humans to her, because she wasn't going to be able to explain a lot of things to them.

In the morning, she slept until six past six, when her body clock woke her up with a jolt because she usually woke up at six precisely and anything that disrupted her routine was a potential threat. She tried to calm herself down and go back to sleep, but after another thirteen minutes, she gave it up.

She got out of bed, had a shower, and went down to get some coffee. Her face felt a little sore, but no more throbbing or stinging. The ice must have helped. Good. Her head ached generally from the meltdown, but mostly she felt . . . tired. She felt as though somehow her body had gotten heavier than it used to be, that she had to drag it around. Her body reacted sluggishly, and she kept forgetting how to make it move. Right leg, then left leg, opposite arms. Lift coffee cup, tip liquid into mouth, then swallow. Repeat.

Coming? Henry texted her at seven twenty-five.

She didn't respond.

She went back to her room and climbed back into her bed, pulling the blanket over her head to make it a little darker.

Leaving now. See you tomorrow, Henry texted at seven forty-five.

Now she was alone. Good. That was what she wanted, wasn't it?

She knew she needed quiet to recover, but also she hated that she had to rest. She hated the boredom of resetting her brain, of turning everything off and starting over.

The routine of this was now ingrained in her, and she still balked.

She put on her face mask and her ear plugs, pulled the covers over her head again. Sensory deprivation. She sometimes wished she had one of those expensive tanks. She was sure that it would work better, but it probably wouldn't be faster.

The last time she'd been in one, the technicians got freaked out because she stopped moving and they thought she'd had a stroke or a heart attack or something – she didn't notice the timer beeping and she'd been in for sixteen hours. The technician had accidentally left her in overnight and gone home. It was only in the morning that the same technician realized she was still in there.

She hadn't noticed the passage of time at all. It had felt delicious. It had felt like the first time in her life when she hadn't hated her body and all of the signals that it gave her, constantly giving input and overloading her brain. It had been more restful than sleep.

It also cost several hundred dollars, and the technician had told her that she wasn't allowed to make another appointment.

'I had to put a note on your account, and the management doesn't want you to come back. They think you're too high risk.'

Maybe it was just as well; otherwise, she might have spent the rest of her life focused only on earning enough money so that she could go back and spend more and more time there. She'd never understood addiction until then. She'd always thought addiction was about people wanting to feel more, but afterward she realized it was about them wanting to feel less.

Her phone buzzed an hour later.

Henry texted: **I'm already back at the school. I'm doing a couple of interviews without you here. I'll summarize them tonight when I get back, or in the morning if you'd rather. Then we can** both come back, and if you want to re-interview anyone, that will be fine.

After that, she put the phone on silent and went back to the routine. Face mask, ear plugs.

Ada had tried to explain to Rex about meltdowns, about how she was learning to predict them coming further and further in advance. In her childhood, it had been almost impossible for her to see what was happening, and so she'd had meltdowns often at school. Some teachers and one administrator had accused her of faking it. The others just seemed to see her as less than human. Certainly, that was how her peers acted, if she couldn't manage to get to a bathroom stall first.

'I can take care of you,' Rex had said.

She'd wanted so much to believe it. But when she'd had her first meltdown after she and Rex got together, she'd found out that he'd filmed her. He'd insisted that he wasn't going to post it online.

'I just wanted to show it to you, so you could see what it looks like from the outside. I thought it would be useful for troubleshooting and to make sure you know what to do if it happens outside the home.'

She'd believed him. God knows why she'd believed anything he'd ever told her. But she had. His face had always seemed to have such easily read expressions. She'd felt so safe because of that. She thought it meant their intimacy was allowing her to understand him better.

Now she knew that was because he was faking it, overdoing everything. No one else would have been fooled by him. No one neurotypical. But she'd been so vulnerable, so stupid.

He had posted that first meltdown, and other meltdowns of hers. Making her look incompetent, ridiculous, not human. No wonder so many of her business contacts had gone with him when they had split. That had been the plan all along, or so she assumed now.

Why had she been so vulnerable? Yes, because she was autistic. But it was more than that.

She was autistic so she'd never had a romantic relationship before. In high school, she'd watched all the girls around her going on dates and having boyfriends. They talked to each other about breaking up and getting back together. She hadn't been part of those conversations, except in passing, but she'd heard enough to know that she wasn't interested in that kind of drama. She wanted someone who loved her, who wanted to be a permanent part of her life. She thought she could skip the other stuff.

Only she hadn't. She was just delayed. That was what her second therapist told her, that she would figure out most of the social things, just a little bit later than neurotypical kids did. She should be patient with herself and not rush anything.

Which was why when Ada told her about the man who so quickly insisted he loved her and wormed his way into all the parts of her life, and that therapist had asked, 'Are you at all concerned that he might have ulterior motives?' Ada had stood up and left the room and never gone back.

'You don't need a therapist. You have me,' Rex had said.

And she believed him. Because she was acting like a fourteen-year-old girl who was in love with her first stupid, immature boyfriend. Only she had a lot more money than that girl did, and she had no parents to protect her anymore – or girlfriends, either. She'd never had any girlfriends, and that had made her extra vulnerable.

In the hotel, with the facemask and earplugs on, she drifted off to sleep and had a vivid dream about Rex murdering her and leaving her just the way Ella had been left, posing her dead body and putting makeup on her.

'There. Just right,' he said as he snapped a photo of her and then walked out of the room.

She was dead, but somehow she knew she was dead. She couldn't move or breathe, but it wasn't the kind of restful dead she'd always hoped for.

When she woke up, it took several minutes for her to realize that the dream had been just that: a dream. There was a transition period between dream and waking that she hated. The Ada that had dreamed about Rex was still in love with him, and she couldn't scream that she needed help because she was dead. The Ada that was waking struggled to make sense of where she was now and how she'd gotten there, and what had happened to Rex, and that she was actually still alive.

She could feel wet, cold tears on her face, and she waited until she was sure she was back in her own body before she wiped them off and took off her face mask and ear plugs. The headache was pounding now. It always got worse before it got better. She got a glass of water and drank it all down, then refilled the cup and took a sip, nursing the second glass for another couple of hours until she had to get up to pee.

At times like this, she found herself wanting to call Rex. Not because she thought he would be nice to her, but because she wanted what was familiar again, even if it didn't feel good. It would make her feel more inside of her own body, and right now her brain felt like it was still floating, detached from the rest of her. That was where the headache came from, the fact that her brain kept moving in and out of her skull.

Of course she knew it wasn't really happening, but telling herself that didn't stop it from feeling like it was real.

Rex was gone. Rex didn't love her anymore. Rex had never loved her, not really.

Logic wasn't always helpful in this transitional stage. It was like her brain was some infantile version of herself, clinging to what used to be.

She had always hated transitions. Even as a child, it had taken her an hour to get up and get moving. She'd struggled to eat breakfast because it was the first meal of the day. She'd hated leaving her crib, and then she hated getting out of her bed. She hated opening her blinds to look at the new daylight outside. She hated opening the door and going downstairs.

But she'd hated just as much going to bed the night before, getting her brain to slow down enough to sleep. She hated coming home from a day at school, or at work when she'd left the house to work. She'd hated it when Rex left the house, and also when he came back.

It was better if she had a schedule that she could rely on, but her parents and teachers were always ruining the schedule, not understanding how important it was to stick to it, minute by minute. And then they'd complain that she was the one who wasn't following the instructions, even though they were the ones who changed things first and expected her to catch up.

She'd learned to tell herself what had to be done, whether she liked it or not.

You have to wake up and start the day.

You have to go to sleep now or at least lie down and close your eyes and try to get your brain to turn off.

You have to remember that Rex isn't here, that whatever he says to you doesn't matter anymore.

You have to move and breathe and stay alive.

Not that.

This.

Not this.

That.

Dreams are just images from the past that your night brain makes into stories that make no sense.

Dreams don't mean anything, no matter what Freud or Jung say.

Dreams are random nonsense, and the best thing for you is to forget whatever they told you is real.

Not real.

Not real.

Not real.

She counted long breaths. One, two, three, four, five.

She was hungry. That was good. Hungry meant her body was starting to be her own again.

She ordered room service from the hotel for lunch. That way, she wouldn't have to leave her room and try to figure out how to speak and walk as if she weren't autistic.

Masking, they called it. But right now it would have made her feel naked, as though everyone could see inside the deepest part of her, where she usually tried to hide who she really was and what she really struggled with, all those things that everyone else thought were so easy and automatic.

SEVENTEEN

A knock at Ada's door jolted her.

She opened it, expecting room service, only remembering later that she'd already eaten the hamburger that was left on the tray outside her room because she'd asked for privacy and no knocking.

She was wearing the comfortable pajamas she'd brought with her, and realized they were likely to drag on the ground because the legs were so long and she had never bothered to have them hemmed. She also had on her slippers.

It was Hen. Henry. He looked tired, his eyes red and puffy. 'Oh, good. You're awake.'

'Yes,' she said stupidly.

'Can I—?' He gestured at the room behind her.

She hesitated. She didn't want him to come into her hotel room.

'I'm sorry. I thought you'd like to talk after being alone all day. But if you need another night to rest, that's fine.' He turned to go.

'Wait,' she called him back. 'Can we go to your room instead?'

He froze, and then slowly turned back. 'When a woman asks to go to your hotel room, it's not usually to go over interview notes,' he said, smiling with his eyebrows exaggeratedly waggling.

It took Ada a moment to catch that he was making a joke, even though she didn't really understand why it was supposed to be funny.

'Haha,' she said, in that way she'd learned to make it sound as if she got the joke but wanted to move on.

'I'm on the other side of the hotel. You OK walking over there?'

'Of course.' It wasn't that her muscles were sore. It was just that it took all her conscious effort to get her legs to keep moving. Every time Henry stopped, to get in an elevator, to turn a corner, or to get out his key, she had to tell her body the new instructions. There was always a lag, and she bumped into him twice.

The dragging of her pajamas wasn't even a top concern. She'd replace them later, if necessary. She had money for expenses on that scale.

'Do you want to talk about the interviews today? I talked to the cook and the cleaner and the nurse. Staff, not teachers. I decided to ask for all the others to be postponed until tomorrow.'

'Not yet. Tomorrow,' she said. She didn't feel settled in her body again, but she thought she would soon.

'Do you want me to order something for you to eat? I got something on the drive back, so I'm fine.'

'No, thank you,' she said.

'Maybe a drink?' he said. Then, after a moment, he shook himself. 'Stupid question. Of course you don't want a drink. I bet you never drink. Too much self-control.'

It didn't sound like a compliment. So she answered with curiosity rather than annoyance. 'Is that how you think of me? As having self-control?' She thought it was strange, given the meltdown yesterday.

'Yes, of course. Even yesterday, when you were about to collapse on the ground, you just kept going, asking questions. Who could do that if they didn't have self-control? If I'd known that was about to happen, I'd have freaked out and tried to escape, get away from other people,' he said.

His hair was dancing around his head in strange points and cloudy shapes. She liked his hair. It had just a bit of curl in it. It made his face softer.

'I couldn't stop it. I delayed it. I'm proud of that part. They used to happen a lot, but now they happen less. I'm proud of that, too.' She didn't think she'd ever be able to control meltdowns completely, but maybe she did love self-control too much. It made her feel as if she'd won a contest of some sort. Against herself. And her parents.

He made a face, like he was scrunching all his skin together in the center around his nose. 'When my wife was sick, she had seizures. They looked a lot like what happened to you. The sicker she got, the more often they happened,' he said. 'Let me assure you that I didn't get better at dealing with them just because they happened multiple times a day. If anything, I got worse because my sense of being utterly powerless increased. I could see her slipping away, and I couldn't do anything about it. I had no idea, when she went away like that, if she'd ever come back again. The last time . . .' He trailed off.

'I'm not dying,' Ada said. 'Is that what you thought when it happened?'

'I didn't think anything. I was just trying to react to it. But Abrams knew what it was, and she told me that I didn't need to call an ambulance. She actually said that you'd be grateful if I didn't do that because it would be unnecessary and draw attention to you. She said you wouldn't like people staring at you and asking you questions, especially not while you were in that state.'

Ada was surprised that Abrams knew enough about autistic people to see that. That made her like the woman a bit more than she had. It also made her think she was less likely to be the murderer of an autistic girl who covered it up and blamed another autistic child.

'Are you sure you want me to go back with you tomorrow?' Ada asked. 'I mean, after what happened yesterday?'

Henry leaned in and reached for her hand, but he stopped himself before he touched her. 'Definitely. You make it so much easier. I feel like I'm stumbling in the dark alone there. I don't know the rules. About autism. That's why I didn't interview anyone except staff without you. I feel like you have to be my translator with all of their jargon.'

'The staff could be guilty,' Ada said, reacting to the immediate information rather than any emotional tone his words offered. 'You know, it's prejudiced for you to think otherwise. Rich people and poor people, educated and uneducated people are equally capable of murder.'

He raised his eyebrows and laughed. 'Just when I think that I get you, you surprise me again.'

'Because I have a liberal political perspective?'

'Because you are funny at such surprising times.'

Ada felt herself closing down. Her head dropped and she pulled her arms in close to her chest. 'I wasn't being funny.' How stupid she was to think that she could have a relationship with a neurotypical person, even just a friendship. They could never have anything in common, not really. A neurotypical person could never really understand her.

'I don't understand. What happened? What did I do?' Henry asked.

She couldn't find the right words for several long, uncomfortable minutes. Finally, she got out, 'I don't like it when people laugh at me.'

'But . . . I wasn't laughing at you. Ada, you have to believe me. You said something funny. You have to see that it was funny about the equality of rich, educated people and poor, uneducated people when it comes to murder. Like they're all just human, all capable of killing in the right circumstances. Or wrong circumstances, as the case may be.' He let out a harsh laugh at that.

'How is that funny? It's just true,' Ada said. The room smelled like him. It was his room. She didn't belong here.

'Yes, that's what makes it so funny. Because it's true. Don't you see?'

His face was doing stuff she couldn't understand. She didn't want to look at it directly. It was like staring at the sun. It could hurt her.

'I say true things all the time. Why are some funny and some not funny?' she asked.

'I don't know. I guess I just responded in the moment. I didn't mean to hurt your feelings. I just thought you were making a joke.'

She let out a long breath. 'Jokes are tricky for me. I'm never sure if I understand when other people are joking or if they understand when I am. And that in itself makes me feel like I can never be accepted as normal, that I will always be on the outside. It is a frightening place to be – the outside. Humans are meant to live in herds. We need others for protection. But not me. No one needed me.'

He didn't say anything, just listened and watched with those deep, dark eyes.

'When I was a kid, the other kids laughing meant they were laughing at me. It meant there was about to be an attack. So I learned to tense up when I heard laughter. It meant that I might need to flee for safety. Even if the threat wasn't physical. I learned to laugh along with other people, even if I didn't understand the joke, because that helped me fit in.'

'God,' Henry said softly, 'your childhood sounds awful. I thought everyone had the same kind of bad childhood and teen years, but I think yours is another level of bad. I'm sorry.'

'You don't have to say you're sorry. It wasn't you who did it. Even in high school, you were one of the decent ones.' As far as neurotypical people went, anyway.

'Yeah, but you hardly spoke to me. I always thought that you imagined you were above me. I mean, intellectually, you were. But it never occurred to me that you were afraid of me.'

'Of course I was afraid of you. I was afraid of everyone.' What else could he possibly imagine?

'I can see that now.' His head tilted to the side and his eyes looked just past her, as if he was seeing something important.

She turned, but she couldn't see anything but a wall with a very standard piece of hotel art on it and a mirror above the vanity.

'I told my wife about you, you know. When she was dying. Delia couldn't bear to listen to anything but the sound of my voice at the end, and she begged me to keep talking to her. She made me promise that I'd keep talking even if she didn't say anything back. Her greatest fear was that she'd be still inside her head and that everyone around her would act like she'd already died. She wanted me to stay with her until the very end, until she wasn't breathing anymore, and they were ready to take her body away.'

Delia sounded like a very sensible woman to Ada.

'I told her about you and my little crush on you. Of course, I was over you by then. I loved her far more than I could ever have loved you at that immature age. But I told her about everything I said to you and everything you said to me. Not that it was very much. I told her all the awards you won. That you got a perfect score on the SAT, all the parts. I told her that you got six full-ride scholarships, and you turned them all down because you thought it wasn't useful to go to college when you learned better at home, reading books and seeing lectures in your own space.'

Ada remembered saying that to him once. When she looked back at it now, she could hear how arrogant it must have sounded. Her refusal to go to college had had nothing to do with arrogance and everything to do with her own terror of having a meltdown far away from home and being locked in a hospital psych ward while her parents let her 'learn about consequences' to see if she'd finally figure out better self-control.

'Crush,' Ada echoed, as it just dawned on her that Henry had used a word that she'd never heard anyone use in reference to her before.

'Oh, yes. I was completely in love with you, and I was keenly aware of the fact that you took so little notice of me that you didn't even know. After you ignored me when I asked you out on the bus, I figured that was it. No means no, but that doesn't mean I stopped having a crush,' Henry said. His cheeks were slightly red, as if he'd been out in the cold, but not as if he'd been slapped.

'You told your wife that you loved me? While she was dying?' Ada often wondered why it was that autistic people were so often told that they didn't understand social rules and that they constantly hurt other people's feelings by not thinking through their words carefully enough. But the way Henry was talking, it seemed like he had broken lots of rules, and with his wife.

'I was pouring out my soul to her. Delia knew that it didn't mean I didn't love her. She was my mature love. You were . . . a high school puppy love. Not real. Just imagined.'

'I see. Thanks for that.' Now he'd hurt her feelings, which she knew was stupid because, just a few days ago, she hadn't known that he'd had a crush on her, and it hadn't hurt then. How had anything changed between them? It hadn't. So whatever he said about the past shouldn't matter.

'No, I didn't mean it like that. I just meant that I didn't hurt her feelings. She said she wished that she'd been able to meet you. I followed your career. That company with your ex-husband. Good Cosmetics. All that success. It was impressive. I felt a little bit of reflected glory, thinking that I knew you once upon a time. I loved you before other people even knew who you were.'

Ada felt cold now. She was trying not to shake, but she wished she could pile some of the blankets on his bed on top of her.

'You don't have that company anymore, though, do you? After Delia got sick, I got lost for a while. When I came back out of it, I couldn't find you. Until you sent in that note to the FBI. I thought you'd gone underground or something. Maybe that you'd gotten sick.'

When she spoke, Ada said the words with precision, each sentence complete: 'My company went to Rex in the divorce. He was the one who built it up to be what it was. Or that's what he claimed. It would be nothing without him. So it's his now and I do . . . other projects. Ones that aren't as likely to attract attention like that.' At least, so far her interest in communicating with aliens had gotten very little attention indeed, certainly none from Rex.

'You didn't fight him, Ada?' Henry asked. 'That company was yours. It was so much yours. I saw it. Surely other people could have seen it, too.'

She didn't care anymore. 'He wanted it so badly, I let him have it.' She half shrugged half shuddered. She hadn't wanted it anymore, not after she understood that he had never loved her. He had only ever loved the company.

She shook and then moved to the door. 'I'll be ready in the morning. Six thirty if you want. I can meet you in the breakfast room and we can get coffee there to go.'

'Hotel coffee?' He made a face, and it took her a moment to parse that he was saying he thought that was disgusting.

'Or, if you prefer, we can stop for whatever kind of coffee you prefer on the way.'

'You don't care about good coffee.'

'I care about what coffee does, not how it tastes. It's the caffeine that matters.'

'So you wouldn't care if they just had caffeine pills in the breakfast room, along with some water?'

Was he laughing at her again? Or was he just asking for information?

'I keep caffeine pills on hand for just that purpose,' she said logically. 'But coffee is hot, and it has a slower uptake than a full caffeine pill.'

'But it's just the result that matters, not how it feels going down?' There was something in his tone that felt like laughter.

'Of course,' she said, bracing herself for new mockery.

It didn't come. 'In fact, the school doesn't open until eight a.m., so we don't need to leave until seven to get there.'

'All right. We leave at seven. But I will be in the breakfast room at six thirty,' she said.

EIGHTEEN

'Your face!' Henry said when she first walked into the breakfast area.

She put a hand to it and could feel a bruise rising along the broken skin. It felt much better than it had yesterday, but it looked worse. She supposed that any other woman would have examined it carefully in the mirror this morning and then tried to put on some makeup to cover it up. She didn't have any. She'd used it occasionally when she had the company, but not anymore. She didn't have a single item from Good Cosmetics in her apartment now.

'I'm fine,' she assured him, and bent to get her coffee.

'You look awful,' Henry said.

'Well, maybe that will frighten them into saying the truth,' Ada suggested. She lifted up her coffee cup.

'Black?' Henry asked, as he put cream and sugar in his own.

'Yes,' she said. She'd tried coffee with sugar and cream in it. It tasted the same to her, no matter what. It was always bitter.

Henry looked back at her and winced again, seeing her face. 'I didn't realize she hit you so hard. Is that why you had the . . . problem?'

'It was an autistic meltdown, and no, I don't think it was from the slap to the face. Although it could have begun the cascade of problems. Meltdowns are usually a result of a series of sensory over-stimulations. The noise, the lights, the trouble reading faces. All of it put together.' She could talk about it calmly and logically now.

'I see,' Henry said.

Ada didn't think he did, but she doubted anyone neurotypical could really comprehend it. What she didn't understand was why all of those things didn't bother other people. How could they think it was normal to be assaulted by noise and light all the time?

'I'll try to make sure no one hits you today,' he said.

She caught the hint of a smile and realized he was trying to make a joke. Again. Neurotypical people seemed incapable of going a single day or even a single hour without them. 'Thanks,' she said, even though she wasn't at all sure that he could prevent the same thing from happening again.

'You ready?' he asked.

'Yes, of course.'

The drive back to the school was quiet, which Ada appreciated. She sipped at the coffee and Henry did the same.

She felt safe with him, despite what had happened two days ago. They had a shared purpose. They were business colleagues. That was all. Not old friends from high school. Not a former crush and an arrogant autistic alien researcher. Just two people working on an investigation for the FBI.

Ada was wearing her second outfit, just as colorful as her first one, and her gold sneakers. Henry wore the same suit as before (as far as she could tell) with a slightly different tie. A little more colorful, though Ada doubted she could take credit for that, considering he must have packed before he'd seen her apartment or her outfit.

Director Sanchez greeted them in her room, wearing what might have been the same suit she'd had on two days before and that she'd worn in the photo on the website. Maybe she had a dozen suits that all looked the same. She had on a bright red lipstick that Ada liked, but she told herself again that it wasn't important. She didn't work in the cosmetics industry anymore, after all.

'Here you are,' Sanchez said. 'How are you?'

Henry glanced at Ada.

'Fine,' she said.

'Thank you,' Henry said.

'All right. Here's a list of appointments for today. This should be everyone,' Sanchez said.

Henry glanced at the list, then handed it to Ada. She looked quickly down the names. From what she'd seen on the website, this included all the instructors. The staff she had missed the day before, but Henry would be able to fill her in, and, if necessary, she could ask to re-interview anyone she thought important.

Sanchez continued, 'I've left an hour for lunch for you to have a break. Would you like to leave campus for that? Should I build in more time? Or would you prefer to eat in our cafeteria here?'

'That would be useful, I think,' Henry said.

'Then I'll schedule that in,' Sanchez said, turning to the door.

'Excuse me,' Ada said, calling her back.

Sanchez raised an eyebrow. 'Yes?'

'How is Gavin?' she asked. 'Is he doing any better than he was two days ago?'

'Actually, he is better. I appreciate your work with him. I don't think you've had formal training with autistic children, but you seem to have a gift.' Sanchez's face was doing a thing that didn't make sense to Ada, but made her nervous.

The 'gift' phrase triggered Ada's 'compliment' warning alerts. She didn't trust compliments, especially effusive ones. She didn't say 'thank you' because she wasn't grateful for the burden that the compliment placed on her, to find the right way to respond when it seemed like it was an attempt to manipulate her in some way she didn't understand.

The social world was always like this, pretending it was offering her a gift but really insisting later that she hadn't returned payment on something she had never received. There was an economy of social hierarchy that she had never participated in. It was difficult to get others to understand that she hadn't received a bonus in social status from their compliments. It didn't help her at all.

'As a mother, I thank you,' Sanchez continued.

Ada just felt stiff. She knew that she was supposed to say 'you're welcome' or maybe even 'it's nothing' in return. Her mother had told her and told her, had drilled her on the proper response to compliments. But the words meant nothing. They were nonsense phrases and Ada hated them.

'Will Gavin and the other children who knew Ella be able to go to a funeral to say goodbye to her?' she asked into the awkward silence, her mind bouncing to another topic she'd considered on the quiet drive from the hotel.

'If and when the body is released, we'll think about that. But if too much time has passed, that may not be the best thing to do at that stage,' Sanchez said, her face turning back into a more stoic expression that Ada found preferable to the other.

'If a medical examiner is assigned by the FBI, we can't press a timetable,' Henry said. 'The FBI is always backlogged.'

Ada ignored all that. It had nothing to do with her. 'But that doesn't impact the need Gavin and the other students have to experience a kind of closure. I don't know if the funeral ritual itself will matter to them, but they'll likely want to see her body and that she is dead in order to make the event real to them. Otherwise, they may always wonder.'

Ada's parents had refused for years to let her have a pet of any kind. Finally, she'd found a stray cat and had brought it home. She'd been so attached to that black cat with the white patch over its right eye. She'd called the cat 'Cat' the first day, and then decided in a bit of whimsy to call him 'Pirate' instead.

A week later, Pirate had disappeared, and her parents had told her that he'd been run over by a car and that they'd disposed of his body because she was at school.

'That cat was filthy and shouldn't have been in our house in any case. It would be unclean for you to touch it again. It was best for it to be sent to the incinerator immediately,' her mother had said.

And Ada still didn't know if her mother had been lying or not. She didn't know if Pirate had been a nuisance that her parents had decided to get rid of without explaining it to her or if Pirate really had been run over.

It was entirely possible that Pirate had been run over and that her mother really had sent the remains to an incinerator out of an over-concern for cleanliness. But Ada still couldn't know. There weren't records for pet remains the way that there were for human remains. She didn't want the children at this school to face the uncertainty that she had. It would have been better for her to know for certain if her mother had sent Pirate to the shelter for another family to adopt than for her to spend so many years wondering about it. It had to be the same about Ella.

She'd never gotten another pet because she couldn't trust herself to take care of one, and she couldn't bear the inevitable reality that a pet would always die before a human would.

'Ella's parents want to have a funeral in their own state, in California. They have good reason not to trust us anymore,' Sanchez said bluntly.

'But if you explain to them that the other children need to have closure so that they can move forward with their lives, they would have to understand.' Even as she said it, Ada was aware of the reality that not all people agreed with the same logic. She'd had more than one experience in her life of trying in vain to explain something to another person and realizing that they didn't care about the same things that she did at all, and therefore would do what they thought was right, whether or not she thought it was logical.

For example, any time she'd ever tried to talk to one of her friends who had religious beliefs about an afterlife, a heaven, or about sin and forgiveness. These were all nonsensical ideas to Ada, but that wasn't a sentiment that other people appreciated her expressing.

'I think, at this point, Ella's parents feel strongly that it is only their own needs that matter,' Sanchez said, looking to Henry as if for confirmation.

'Sometimes a funeral isn't possible,' Henry said.

Ada didn't know what to say to that, so she said nothing.

'Are you ready?' Director Sanchez asked.

Ada nodded and Henry stood up. They walked down the hall and into a small room that had a table and four chairs.

'This is where we bring parents in to talk to them about enrollment or to discuss alternative plans when there's a problem,' Director Sanchez said. She hadn't come in but was standing in the doorway.

'What kinds of problems are typical with students here, if you don't mind my asking?' Henry said.

'Oh, all kinds of problems. From students not working up to their potential, to physical violence or biting, even jealousy between students or issues to do with burgeoning sexuality,' she said. 'In some ways, it's not so different from any other school with students of all ages.

'The one problem we tend not to have is financial concerns. Most of the parents who come to us have access to plenty of funds to help their children. It is sometimes hard to accept the reality that our school will never be for autistic children of every class. It's simply not the way that capitalism works.'

Ada wondered if Sanchez had practiced saying this until it sounded reasonable. To Ada, it sounded monstrous.

'Did Ella have those kinds of problems? With sexuality?' Henry asked. 'Did Gavin?'

Sanchez reddened. 'Not as far as I know. They were friends, but platonically. Both of them were a little young to deal with puberty, though it's not unheard of at that age.'

'But did either of them express any romantic or sexual interest with their teachers or with the other staff?' Henry asked.

Ada was confused about Sanchez's embarrassment over the issue of sexuality. It was simply a reality that growing children would also have a growing sense of their own bodies and sexuality, and autistic children in particular might not have peers to ask questions about it in the way that neurotypical children did.

Sanchez said, with a wave of her hand, 'Again, not as far as I knew. We normally hear about problems as they come up, but it can take time before a problem becomes acute enough to be addressed by the team.'

'You seem to be very reluctant suddenly to answer questions directly,' Henry pointed out.

'No, I'm not. I just—' She took a breath. 'I just don't want to say anything about a student who has passed away in difficult circumstances.'

'So there was a problem with Ella?'

'No, no problems. Not at all. She was a perfectly normal girl.'

Henry stared at her until she looked at the hallway behind her, then she came in and closed the door.

Sanchez sighed, then admitted, 'One of her teachers had noted that Ella sometimes masturbated with her hands in her pants during class. It was on the list of things we wanted to address with her parents. Autistic children often need direct cues about what is appropriate in group settings and what is not. They don't think of things as private and public on their own.'

'I see. And why didn't you bring this up before?' Henry asked.

'Because it wasn't relevant to her death. Unless you think her masturbating had something to do with her being suffocated?' Her tone was tart. Even Ada could hear her annoyance.

'No, I can't see that. But it could be important information about who Ella was,' Henry said.

'And that is why I didn't bring it up. She was a young girl who deserves to be seen as fully human, as all of our students here do. That kind of information could make the public interest in this case all too prurient. Not to mention how it might affect the reputation of the school, however stupid it might be.'

Ah, now Ada thought she understood why Sanchez had lied. To protect Ella's privacy and her humanity, and also for the sake of the school. It made sense to her, as long as there was a moral reason behind it. She nodded at Henry. She was satisfied now.

'If I can get on with my day?' Sanchez asked, though she didn't wait for an answer before she opened the door and walked out.

The first appointment was in ten minutes. The name on the list was 'Madeleine Lynch,' and her title was 'communication specialist.'

Henry and Ada didn't talk in the interim, which was a relief. Ada could hear the sounds outside the room, students and staff moving up and down.

She tried to ignore the memories of her days in school. Of course, it hadn't been a school like this. She'd always thought that she was glad that she'd gotten a 'mainstream education' because her parents insisted that she wasn't disabled. They hated the stigma of 'autism' and had insisted that the only way to prove that she deserved their love was by working hard to not show her autism. She thought that she'd feel proud of herself for having managed to do something so difficult. But mostly she felt jealous that the students here didn't have the trauma she'd had.

'Do you mind if we talk a bit about these interviews first? What we hope to get out of them?' Henry asked after a few minutes.

'If you think that would be useful,' Ada said, a little disappointed she wouldn't have a few extra quiet minutes to think through her list of traits for the murderer. She still thought it was accurate, though she hadn't found anyone she thought fit her amateur profile yet.

'I think we need to ask questions more subtly, about Ella and Gavin's relationship, about their capabilities and understanding. I don't think we can ask directly if there's a motive for murder in each of these staff members,' Henry said.

He was speaking carefully, and Ada immediately found herself feeling annoyed. He didn't trust her. He thought that she was going to blurt things out. And that it would ruin his plan to lie to people and get them to reveal the truth inadvertently.

'I'm not great at subtle,' Ada said.

'Yes, I'm aware. Maybe I should take the lead in the questions?'

'If you take the lead, what is the point of me being here? I might as well go back to the hotel. Or just head home,' Ada said. She was tempted, too.

'I don't mean that. I want you here. I want you to ask questions. But maybe just not the beginning questions. What do you think about that? I can get people to feel comfortable, and then you can ask some specifics you think are relevant,' Henry suggested.

She looked away from his face, which was confusing to her. 'OK, you can ask the first two questions.'

Henry waited a long moment, as if expecting her to argue more.

She knew how to follow rules, though. The FBI had rules. Two questions first. Simple enough.

'All right. Thank you, Ada,' Henry said.

And then there were a few more minutes of silence before the first interview started. Ada was grateful for them.

NINETEEN

Madeleine Lynch was tall and thin, with dark, curly hair. She wore what looked like a comfortable jacket made of some knit material that Ada wished she could buy. It looked professional but also as though she could move without taking it off or feeling like she couldn't breathe. Here was another woman who cared about comfort more than looks. Ada liked that.

Madeleine's eyes were dark and large, framed by only her own lashes. Her lips were slightly chewed on, and that made Ada like her more than if she'd looked more perfect.

'Oh my. What happened there?' Madeleine asked, gesturing at Ada's face.

'She fell,' Henry put in, as Ada had been trying to figure out how to explain that she'd been hit by Ella's mother.

Ada didn't like the lie. It felt wrong to her. But she decided not to correct it.

'I understand you're from the FBI? Here about Ella's death? It's so terrible,' she began, holding out her hand to Ada first, not Henry.

This was another reason that Ada liked her immediately. Most people, men and women, tended to assume that given two people who might be in charge, it was more likely to be the man. And Henry was, in fact, in charge here. But Henry didn't bring it up, and Madeleine nodded to him as if he were the subordinate, rather than giving him a handshake.

'We're from the FBI, yes. I'm Henry Bloodstone, and this is Ada Latia,' Henry said. 'We've been called in to determine if it was an accidental death.'

'What else could it be?' Madeleine asked, staring at Ada rather than Henry.

But Ada didn't respond. She'd promised Henry two questions, and she hadn't heard even one yet.

'A non-accidental death,' Henry said. 'If you don't mind sitting down, please.' He waved a hand and then sat down himself.

'Can you tell us about this school? How long you've worked here and what you think about it,' Henry said.

Ada was trying to figure out if that was one question or two.

'Oh, yes, of course. NAVITEK is the best school for autistic children in the state, possibly in the nation. With the funds that Director Sanchez has been able to get for us, we have the top staff working here, and the newest treatments available. It truly is amazing. Such a contrast from anything in the previous generation.' She was smiling widely and still staring at Ada.

Ada tried to look away, slightly uncomfortable.

'And what drew you to this kind of work, if I might ask? It seems unusual and quite difficult,' Henry went on.

Surely this counted as the second question, but Ada let the answer come before she stepped in.

'I thought I wanted to be a journalist, so I was majoring in communication. But we had to take a class in different modes of communication, and I was just so fascinated by neurodiverse brains. The more I studied, the more interested I was. So I guess you could say I fell into it,' Lynch said, with a laugh.

'But you don't have a degree in—' Henry began.

Ada cut him off, uninterested in his third question. Or possibly fourth.

'Were Ella and Gavin interested in frogs?' Ada asked abruptly.

'What?' Madeleine's eyes went wide, and then her head tilted to one side.

'I heard that it was a common interest of theirs.'

'Oh, well, I don't recall that interest. But as I said, Ella often talked about whatever she was interested in. She changed her special interests regularly. I suppose it might have been frogs most recently.' She tilted her head slightly to the side.

Ada tried to figure out if that was a tell for lying. She wasn't very good at seeing tells, mostly because they tended to be gestures that she ignored or found confusing.

Henry cleared his throat. 'I have a few more questions,' he said clearly and loudly.

Fine. Ada let him ask his questions if he thought they were so important.

'Did you work with Ella and Gavin individually? It says your specialty is communications.' Henry nodded at the list.

'Yes, I worked with both of them. We have a group session once a week where students get a chance to practice their communication skills together. Students are often grouped with other students who are at a similar level, but there are mixed groups, as well. It can help both ends to have experience with the others.'

'Gavin and Ella were at a high level of communication for students at this school?' Henry asked, waving at Madeleine behind the table.

Ada thought Henry's questions were boring and irrelevant. What was so wrong with asking things directly?

Madeleine responded, 'Verbal communication, yes. Gavin is almost at grade level and Ella was not far behind. Ella could chatter on about anything she was interested in. The difficulty with her was getting her to stop and listen to someone else. Gavin wasn't as eager to get attention. He'd respond to direct questions, but he wouldn't necessarily offer anything that he didn't have to.'

'What can you tell us about Ella and Gavin's relationship? Did you see any tension between them?' Henry again.

'Between Gavin and Ella? Not tension, no. Ella was like a little sister to him,' Madeleine explained.

Ada had no siblings and had a hard time imagining what that might have been like. She thought about this instead of asking another question.

Henry said, 'I have a little sister and she's annoying as hell. She was even worse when she was that age.'

Ada knew that Henry didn't have a little sister. He had an older brother, William, but no sister. He was lying again, and it made Ada uncomfortable.

Madeleine nodded. 'Well, yes. Ella was younger than Gavin, and he was sometimes annoyed with her. But also she paid attention to him. Hero-worshipped him, even. She would copy him sometimes. I think it was consciously done, but maybe not always. She thought he was a good pattern of a human being to make herself into. I . . . well, at the time, I thought it was a good idea, too.'

Ada could tell that Madeleine was emotional about this. Not for the first time, she thought about her mother's funeral and how she hadn't cried and her father had congratulated her.

'You're being very stoic, I appreciate that. None of that maudlin weeping and mucus dripping.' He nodded and patted her arm in a way that she would have loved when she was a child, but now made her uncomfortable.

She hadn't wept for her mother because she hadn't been sad she was gone. Because her mother wasn't really gone. She had been installed in Ada's head and lived there still, most of the time. She felt guilty sometimes for wishing that her mother was truly dead. But so far, she'd had no more success with that than with wishing her father was truly dead.

'What did Ella copy from Gavin?' Henry asked.

'Ah. Well, let me think.' Madeleine tapped her forehead in a way that seemed rather overdone. 'I remember that Gavin had a phrase that he repeated. "Like a camera" and he'd made a clicking sound. She did the same thing.' Madeleine held out the two fingers of each hand and made a frame.

Surely Henry would let Ada ask her questions now. 'Where did you go to school in communications?'

'Oh, just a state college. University of Oklahoma. I got a full-ride scholarship so that's where I went. I never regretted it. No student debt.' She shrugged.

'What do you think the ultimate goal of a school like this one is?' Ada asked.

'To help autistic students, of course,' Madeleine said.

'To help them what?' Ada pressed. She was watching Madeleine's face and body language closely, but she really wasn't sure if she'd be able to interpret what she saw – if there was anything to be seen.

'To help them become functioning members of society. As much as possible, of course. Some students will be able to function more than others, but that's the goal. To be functional.' Madeleine's face was impassive, and her body language seemed normal. Did that mean she was not the murderer?

No, because the murderer would be an expert at deceit and manipulation, especially with autistic people. 'You want to make autistic children into functional adults? In a neurotypical world?' Ada asked.

'Ah,' Madeleine said. 'There's the rub, isn't it? I've been wondering about it since you sat down. It should have been obvious, but I didn't want to make assumptions.'

'What should have been obvious?' Ada asked.

Henry waved a hand again and said, 'I don't think that we need to get into personal details. Let's go back to the question of Ella and Gavin's relationship. And whether you ever saw any anger between them, any fights. Any hint of potential violence.'

Madeleine didn't respond to Henry. She didn't even seem to hear him. 'You're autistic yourself, Ada, aren't you? And you don't like the idea of autistic children being trained out of their autism. That's the current political message from groups filled with people like yourself. Autistic adults who want the world to change so they don't have to.'

Ada felt hot. She wanted nothing more than to escape from this room and go back to the hotel and turn off all the lights. But she couldn't do that. Not right now.

'Ada, you don't need to answer—' Henry started.

But Ada ignored him. This was between her and Madeleine.

'I am autistic, yes,' Ada said, looking at the woman directly now, giving all of the eye contact that she could manage in an entire day all at once. 'And I worry about the message that you're sending the children here, that they aren't valued unless they comply with rules that make no sense to them. What about sensory overwhelm and meltdowns? What about when they become non-verbal or can't comply with other neurotypical expectations?'

Madeleine leaned forward. 'We all know about meltdowns here. About what causes them and how to prevent them from happening. And what to do to shorten their duration and intensity.' Madeleine's eyes seemed very large. Her face was uncomfortably close to Ada's.

'And you also know how to make sure that no one dies in the middle of a meltdown?' Ada asked.

Madeleine sucked in a loud breath at this. 'How dare you suggest that we are at fault for her death! We did everything we could for Ella. And for every child here. All of the staff here would die before we let anything happen to a child. We believe in what we're doing and in this school, but this isn't a specialty that is well paid. If we wanted money, we'd go to Wall Street. If we wanted fame, we'd go to Hollywood. But we don't. We're here. In the middle of Idaho.' She waved to indicate the rural location of the school.

She sounded resentful, but Ada didn't quite trust herself to interpret tone and body language like that. She opened her mouth and closed it again as Madeleine continued.

'Ella was a special child. She had a gift for poetry. She wrote some of the most exquisite poems I've ever seen from a child her age, autistic or not.' Madeleine's eyes began to drip tears.

It could be a manipulated display. Ada couldn't tell. She so rarely cried herself. She hated it, for one thing. It never did anything to help whatever problem was at hand, and it only ended with her feeling dehydrated and headachy. Rather like too much alcohol ending with a hangover, to be frank. She avoided alcohol, too.

'I was devastated when I heard what happened to her. I can't believe she's gone. I keep looking at her poems, rereading them. The world has lost one of its brightest stars and no one even knows. No one but those of us who were here and knew her. Even her parents don't know.

'None of us are allowed to be at the funeral, and we won't be allowed to speak because we're seen as culpable somehow. But whatever happened—' She broke off and bowed her head into her hands, unable to say more.

Or pretending to be unable to say more.

'Can I see one of them?' Ada asked.

'What?' Madeleine's head came up, and her face was splotchy with red marks, and there were tears staining her shirt and dripping off her chin. It was quite a performance, if it was a performance.

'One of the poems. I'd like to get to know Ella better. To understand what happened to her. A poem could help.' Ada had no idea if a poem would help, but she was curious. Poetry was not something that she'd ever really understood. She'd been forced to read poetry in high school, of course. She'd tried to write an essay on a poem once, after it was assigned by her teacher. But it was the lowest grade she'd ever received.

'It doesn't sound like you're even trying to understand the emotion depicted here,' the teacher had written at the bottom of the paper, where the circled grade C– was written in red ink.

Ada had been able to understand things like rhythm and rhyme, and she'd even be able to explain things like metaphors and synecdoches, but beyond that, she'd been lost. Poetry just seemed like nonsense words put together to sound pretty together. She couldn't understand how any autistic person could like or be good at that kind of communication. It was all on a different level that she'd operated on, on a non-direct level.

'All right. I'll see what I can find. Just a moment.' Madeleine got out her phone and started scrolling through it. A couple of times, she had to wipe the screen because of her tears, but she was persistent. Finally, she said, 'Here. This one.' She handed her phone to Ada.

Red
Is the color of
Bleeding sunset.
It hurts when you bleed.
It hurts when things end.
It hurts
When yellow and green and black
Turn red.

Ada copied the screen and pasted it into a message she sent to her own phone. 'Thank you,' she said. She had no idea what the poem meant. She wasn't sure that it meant anything at all. She suspected that Madeleine thought or wanted to think that the poem meant more than it did. But she was going to think about it for a bit and maybe ask Henry his opinion.

'Is it normal for the students here to be left alone together, like Ella and Gavin were?' Henry asked with a sigh.

Madeleine straightened and seemed able to focus again. 'It's not common, but they were good friends. If students are still interested in something after a class is over, teachers might leave them there for a while and come to check back later. Ella and Gavin weren't students we would have worried over. They had never had a problem before.' She looked to Ada, but Ada was still thinking of the poem, which she had memorized immediately and was now repeating in her head.

'Do you think that one of the staff might have killed Ella and used Gavin's presence in the room later to disguise a murder?'

Henry asked, as if throwing a bomb and waiting for it to blow up.

Ada straightened, because this was the kind of bluntness that she appreciated – and hadn't thought Henry capable of.

Madeleine, however, simply shook her head. 'That is impossible. The staff here are professionals. We love these children. They love us. We would never hurt them.'

TWENTY

The next appointment came in immediately after Madeleine left, so there was no time for Ada to ask Henry why he'd waited until the end to ask the real question, and why he'd seemed to want to stop her from asking hers. She knew that people thought she was too blunt. She used to be ashamed about how she was socially and tried to mask and act more neurotypical. She didn't do that anymore.

She didn't think that Madeleine was the murderer, but she'd make a decision when she had all the information, not step by step based on 'intuition' or 'gut feeling' the way neurotypical people said they did. All nonsense.

Madeleine might be lying about her affection for Ella, but that poem she'd read was very telling. Ella must have felt safe with her to write like that for her.

Tina Abrams didn't seem likely, either. She'd been away in the cafeteria at the time of the murder. Besides, she hadn't shown the kind of interest in the case that Ada expected in the murderer. She was arrogant and Ada didn't like her, but that didn't mean she was guilty. Negligent, possibly, but she wasn't the only one who had been negligent in this instance.

'Ms Glock,' Henry said when the next woman came into the room.

'Nora, please,' said the awkward woman with the longest hair that Ada had ever seen. It went nearly to her knees and was free-flowing, though she had several hair elastics tied around her left wrist, presumably for situations in which she was with autistic children who might be tempted to pull that long hair.

'Nora, thank you for being willing to speak to us. Do you know why we're here?' Henry asked.

'I heard it was something about Ella's death. You're clearing the school to move forward with instruction with the other children?' she asked. Her teeth were bucked, but she smiled around them in such a way that it took attention from the teeth. An interesting trick.

Her skin was freckled, pale as it was underneath the colored spots. She wore a pair of pants that were high-waisted, but Ada thought looked very uncomfortable, tight and unbending as the fabric was. To Ada's surprise, she wore no ornamentation, not even a watch.

'We're here because we believe that Ella was murdered,' Henry said in that same direct way that Ada loved so much.

Nora winced. 'Murdered? Surely not.' She put a hand to her heart in the most theatrical response that Ada had yet seen.

'You are the math tutor, I understand.' Henry glanced at the list.

'Yes, I am. I teach math to the younger students in groups, but the older students are generally so disparate in their abilities that it's not as useful to have group sessions, so we tend to do individual lessons instead. They are often pulled out of their play groups to meet with me.'

'You were supposed to be tutoring both Ella and Gavin at the time of her death, is that right? And instead the two children were left alone?' Henry went on. 'What happened that drew you away from your normal schedule?'

Ada noticed how he didn't point out that if she had followed her schedule, Ella might still be alive and Gavin still verbal. The whole school would not be under the stigma of a child dying mysteriously, and Ella's parents wouldn't be threatening a lawsuit for their daughter's death, while they waited for their child's body to be released so that they could bury her. Henry wasn't lying; he was being polite. But to Ada, the distinction didn't matter much.

'I sent a message to Ms Abrams stating that I had to leave early to get to a doctor's appointment. It was an emergency. Or I thought it was at the time,' Nora said. She had her chin up and there was something about her posture that made her look taller and bigger than she was.

'What kind of emergency?' Henry asked with the kind of directness that Ada herself might have used.

'I had a positive cancer screening. My doctor needed to go over my options with me. As it turned out, a second screening was negative. But at the time . . .' She trailed off.

Henry tensed at the word 'cancer.' Memories of his wife must have come up, Ada realized. But he continued.

'So you left in a hurry and didn't check to see if Ms Abrams responded that she'd gotten the message? Did you tell anyone else that you were going to be gone during your regular schedule?' Henry asked.

'No, I–I thought it was sufficient.' She took a deep breath. 'I've been a math tutor at this school for two years. I've missed two scheduled tutoring sessions during that time. No one can adhere to a schedule perfectly, and Ella should have been safe.'

'But she wasn't,' Henry pointed out.

'No child can be watched one hundred percent of the time,' Nora said. There were two spots of color on her cheeks.

'Can you think of any reason that someone here at the school might have wanted Ella dead?' Henry asked.

'No, of course not. Ella was a student here and we all cared for her deeply.'

'She was well liked?'

Nora looked down at her hands, hesitating. When she spoke, her words were halting. 'She was autistic, as all the children here are. There are no popularity contests here. In some ways, that's a good thing. No cliques of kids who are always seen and heard, and other kids who are ignored and silenced. If anything, Ella got more attention than most, but that doesn't mean she was well liked.'

'It sounds like you didn't like Ella,' Henry said.

Ada hadn't made this leap. She thought again that maybe this was a manipulation. Henry was trying to get a response. So he was pushing a button. Metaphorically, of course. He didn't know if this woman liked Ella or not. He was making a leap in the hope of getting a response. That was what people like him did. Neurotypical people who worked for the FBI.

'I had nothing against Ella,' Nora insisted, holding her hands out in a defensive gesture.

'You haven't said that you liked her,' Henry pointed out.

Unlike Madeleine Lynch, who had seemed very fond of Ella indeed.

'I liked her as well as I liked any other student here,' Nora said, her eyes not able to hold Henry's for long enough to finish the sentence.

Henry pointed at her. 'You're lying to me. You didn't like Ella, and I want to know why. She was a child under your care, but you disliked her especially. Tell me why.'

Nora shifted in her seat. She let out a long breath. 'All right, fine. I will tell you that I didn't like her, but that doesn't mean I had anything to do with her death. I admit, I didn't find her particularly rewarding to work with. But I did have a positive cancer screening. I can show you the results on my phone.'

Before Henry could demand to see proof, she'd held out her phone with a message on it, and let both Henry and Ada see it.

Positive cancer screening. Please call office immediately for next steps. It listed a doctor's name and phone number.

'I can have the office send you more, if you don't believe me.'

'I may ask for that,' Henry said. 'But for now, let me understand why it is you didn't like Ella, if you don't mind? Is it because she was bad at math?'

Nora sounded impatient as she spoke, 'Yes, well, she was. She was still working at the level of a neurotypical four-year-old. She didn't understand numbers beyond ten, and she couldn't add or subtract at a basic level. She didn't care, either. Her mind would wander off, and she laughed at me when I tried to get her attention again. Math didn't matter to her. The last tutoring session we had, I tried to tell her that if she wanted to graduate and get a real job, she needed math. She laughed at that, too.'

'And you were angry at an autistic girl laughing at you?' Henry asked.

Nora slapped a hand on the table. 'I wasn't angry. It was just annoying. I would still have gone to tutor her. And Gavin, who also struggled with math, even if he didn't laugh at me when I tried to tell him it was important. But I truly did have an emergency come up.'

Henry leaned back in his chair and crossed his hands over his chest. 'It might have made a difference if you'd been there. She might be still alive,' he said.

Nora blinked rapidly, then rubbed at her eyes. But neither effort stopped the tears from dripping down her face. 'I didn't do anything to her. My personal feelings had nothing to do with what happened to her.'

Ada looked back and forth between the two of them. It turned out Henry's instinct had been correct about Nora, after all. It felt like magic when she saw neurotypical people do things like this. And it made her angry because she could never learn that kind of magic. It would forever be beyond her grasp.

'Why do you work with autistic children if you don't like them?' Henry asked softly.

Another manipulation, Ada decided, though she wasn't sure exactly what it was.

Nora fidgeted with her hands. Then she admitted, 'My younger sister is autistic. She's brilliant with mathematics. I was always behind her, and my parents were always trying to get her more instruction and better teachers. They poured money into her education. She was always growing out of one tutor and then they'd have to find another one.'

'You were jealous of her, then?' Henry said.

'Jealous?' Nora let out a sound that Ada eventually figured out was a harsh laugh. It sounded more like a goose honk than a sound that would come out of a human, and it echoed strangely in the room.

'Yes, I was jealous. I went to the regular school. My parents never had time to take me to any extracurricular activities because they were always busy driving Lola to whatever new teacher she needed to go to. Or to advanced certification. Or to pre-college classes. And math camps. And sessions to help her with the SATs and how to write her college essays.

'And when she was in college and was getting good grades, do you know what happened then?' Her voice had changed. It sounded younger somehow. 'Did they have time for me then? Of course not. They were too busy attending her award ceremonies and presentations and conferences and interviews and on and on and on.

'Do you know how many times they attended one of my award ceremonies? Or one of my swim meets? Or were there when I went to the prom with my first boyfriend? Do you know how many times they told me they were proud of me or asked me what scholarship I was going to apply for or what university I wanted to attend?'

Ada was guessing that it was a small number, but Nora didn't wait for either of her audience members to make a guess.

She held up her right hand in a 'zero' gesture. 'That's how

many times. My mother told me that they expected hard work from me, and that it was a given that I would achieve. She said this as if I would understand why they didn't celebrate me. Because I had everything going for me. I didn't have autism. I didn't have any problems standing in my way.'

Ada thought that Nora's parents had been right to do what they'd done for their autistic daughter. They'd done an amazing thing, to make sure she had the best life possible. And yes, Nora hadn't needed as much. Why couldn't she see logically that this was the right choice? Her emotions seemed to be coloring her ability to see things objectively. But that was what neurotypical people were always like, unable to see logic because of their emotions, unable to see any perspective outside of their own very personal one.

'But if that is true, why would you become an autism specialist?' Henry asked. 'I would think that would be the last thing you'd want to do with your life.'

Nora stared at him and spoke very precisely. 'Autism specialist is a job that has security and decent benefits. It is something I understand at a level most people don't. And I don't have the prejudice that so many people do when it comes to autism. I, of all people, know how amazing autists can be, how they can become functioning, impressive adults who live in the real world and contribute to humanity at levels never seen before.'

'Well, that's not what I would have chosen. You could have done anything with your life,' Henry said.

'Could I? I think not,' Nora said. Then she turned to Ada. 'You're autistic. And everything about you circles around that reality. Nothing you do is unrelated to your autism. Right?'

'I . . . don't know if that's true,' Ada said. She didn't like the question. No one had asked her that before. But she felt obliged to answer it, because she wasn't a liar, and she didn't sidestep questions because they weren't convenient to her.

'What about you isn't about autism, then?' Nora asked.

Ada considered. 'I like heavy metal music,' she said. 'I dance to it, sometimes in a group because it is best that way, when it is very loud and with others.' She paused, trying to think of something else.

Nora let out a snort. 'You listen to loud music? That's what's not autistic about you? Do you bang your head against the wall when you listen at home? Do you make sure when you're dancing that you never touch anyone else?'

Ada nodded briefly at this, despite how stung she felt by the mocking response. She had to answer every question that was asked her. That was the rule of social communication. Her parents had taught her this long ago. There was never an exception to this rule.

But Ada added one other thought. 'I watch science fiction movies about aliens. I'm working on communicating with them in some way. Because humanity needs to have hope for the future. And I don't know if other people would be able to figure out how to talk to people who are very different from us. I know what it's like to be different and to see how inexplicable humans are. I want to make sure that if we contact aliens, they don't exterminate us immediately just because they see the bad parts first.'

There were so many bad parts of humans, as far as Ada could see. When she was a teenager, that was all that she could see about humans. But now she could make sure that aliens saw the bigger picture. It was her main purpose in life. Her only purpose, really. Everything that she did was to make sure that she was still alive when they came, and that she had enough money to make other people listen to her. So she could save humanity from the coming invasion from space. It had to be coming – of course it did.

'Aliens and science fiction movies. Well, that's definitely not autistic,' Nora said flatly.

It took Ada a moment to realize that it was sarcasm. She flinched a little late and then looked away.

'I think it's very admirable,' Henry said. He reached out a hand but then dropped it.

Ada was glad he hadn't touched her. She felt as though her skin had gotten thinner somehow, and her blood was closer to the surface. She could hear the sound of her heart beating, her blood moving around in every muscle in her body. She hated it when her body did this, made itself known to her, but she couldn't stop it.

Henry said goodbye to Nora while Ada tried to gather herself.

'Do you need to go back to the hotel?' he asked when he came back to the table.

She shook her head.

'You're not in danger of another meltdown?'

'No. She agreed with me. I like it when people agree with me,' Ada said, and her body stopped throbbing by the time the next appointment came in.

TWENTY-ONE

Jennifer Langham peeked in, not quite coming fully in the door. 'Hi, I'm wondering if you'd mind coming with me and chatting while I work?' she asked.

She looked very fit, with her muscular shoulders showing under the sleeveless lace shirt she wore. Her hair was colored a bright blue that Ada couldn't look away from. She liked that color. It was the same color as the comforter she'd bought right after the divorce, the one that was too expensive but made her feel very calm whenever she looked at it. The right color could do that.

Henry stood up and motioned for Ada to do the same.

'I understand that you need lunch, is that right?' she asked as they stepped outside and joined her in the hallway.

'Yes,' Henry said. 'Director Sanchez said the school would provide it?'

Langham looked at her watch and said, 'It's second lunch right now. If you don't mind eating in the cafeteria with the students, you can come with me.'

'All right,' Henry said.

'I can't promise the food is great, but it's better than your standard school fare. We have actual cooks who prepare and cook it in the kitchen. I help the kids with some scripts in the lunchroom. To prepare them for what is expected typically at meals.'

'You're the manners specialist?' Henry asked.

'Well, I suppose that's what it says on my résumé. I like to think of myself as an interactive version of Ms Manners. I think it would be a great app on a phone, don't you? Just hold up the camera to any situation and get advice on the fly that will make sure you don't make any faux pas?' She smiled at Henry and Ada.

'You have an app?' Ada asked, because it did seem to her like a very good idea. If there were such an app, she'd definitely try it out for a month or so to see if it helped.

'No, of course not.' Langham laughed and winked at Henry. 'I'm just saying it would be great if it worked. But artificial intelligence is not yet at the level where it could give useful feedback for social situations. There are too many contradictions and changes in culture from situation to situation and room to room. Different rules for every situation, or so it seems to autistic people.'

So it did seem to Ada. So it was.

'What happened?' Langham asked, waving at Ada's face.

'I fell down,' Ada said. She hated lying and she thought it must be obvious that it was a lie, but Langham didn't seem interested and didn't ask any more questions about it.

'Well, we'll try to keep you from hurting yourself again, all right?'

Ada had a strange sense that Langham knew more than she had told her. Someone had told her about the fight with Mrs Kimball, and maybe about more than that – that she was herself autistic. Who would have told her? Director Sanchez? Or one of the other staff members who had been interviewed?

'I bet you two remember the high school cafeteria from your own school days, right?' Langham went on.

They were walking in the section between the two halves of the school that Henry and Ada had been through two days ago with Director Sanchez. But the timing was different now. Ada had to put up a hand because the sunlight coming through the windows was blinding. She stumbled and Henry had to keep her from falling.

'Nice to have someone like you around,' Langham said to Henry, winking at him again.

Ada felt distinctly that she was being laughed at. She'd been put in a room and the door was locked behind her. Henry and Langham were on the outside, staring at her, watching her every move so as to make fun of whatever mistake she made.

'In your typical high school cafeterias, there are often groups or cliques of students who sit at the same table every day. Then there are a few students on the peripheries, students who might move in and out of groups at different times, or students who have never had any group. Sound familiar?' Langham asked.

'Very familiar,' Henry said.

Ada nodded affirmation, though she felt that Langham was the last person who understood what it was like to be on the outside.

Langham waited at the door to the cafeteria that Director Sanchez had only gestured at in passing in their tour before.

Ada stopped abruptly – without stumbling or bumping into anyone this time.

'Well, with our students, it's often the reverse problem. Left to their own devices, they would all sit by themselves and eat in total silence. Then go back to their classrooms without any social interaction at all,' Langham explained.

Ada did not see why this was not an excellent strategy. Lunch was supposed to be a break from studies. Silence and not having to make eye contact or inane conversation seemed to be the best way to ensure she was ready for the next class.

'So we have an assigned seating chart for each day. Students look at it when they come in.' Langham tapped the door and moved just slightly to the side so that Ada could see the chart posted there – printed, not handwritten. Automated by someone, she suspected. At least that part made sense.

'And each table has a conversation topic assigned. The students are required to offer at least one sentence on that topic before they are excused from eating.' Again, Langham tapped the chart.

Ada looked at the assigned topics for different tables today. Sports. Movies. Music. Politics. Food. Art.

There was also a circle around a name in the center of each table, which Ada assumed was the name of an adult who was monitoring the conversations.

'The students get a bonus point that they can use toward an end-of-month auction if they ask another student a question about the topic,' Langham went on.

Ada was aware that Langham was pretending to give them an answer to their questions, but she was now, in fact, in charge of everything that they were talking about. She was the woman behind the curtain, directing their attention in the way she wanted. The questions that Ada had wanted to ask her about Ella's death had been put to the side. It told her a lot about Langham, but that didn't mean Ada was going to forget her other questions.

'We know that all of these autistic students have their own

special interests, but the topics assigned are always something that is unlikely to be an interest. We want them to work on their social skills and to be able to speak to people with whom they have nothing in common,' Langham said, and opened the door.

'You mean you want to make them pretend to be neurotypical,' Ada said.

'I want them to learn good manners,' Langham insisted. 'Something that everyone, autistic or neurotypical, could use more of.' She glanced at Henry, and there was a faint smile there, but Ada couldn't tell what she was trying to communicate with him.

Ada hated the sense she had that she wasn't really here anymore, that Langham was only interested in her when she could make fun of her to Henry. And Henry seemed to be playing along.

'Shall we go in?' Henry asked.

'Of course.' Langham opened the door, and they stepped inside.

Ada noticed first that it was quiet, not at all like her own memories of the school cafeteria. Students were talking, but not loudly or energetically. As Langham had promised, there were no tables that were clearly more important and more boisterous than others. There were no silent, corner tables where only the ostracized kids seemed to go, and where they didn't speak to each other.

The smell was also different. It smelled, well, of food. Real cooked food. Ada hadn't looked at the menu for the day, but it was obvious from the overwhelming smell of cooked beef and tomatoes and melted cheese that it was Italian.

Her mouth started watering. She hadn't had good Italian food for some weeks. She'd grown up with her mother ordering Italian from a local restaurant at least once a week, and it had always been the best food of the week. Her mother had been capable of making healthy food that didn't take long to prepare, but nothing like that restaurant.

It had gone out of business just after Ada's mother had died. She remembered actually going to the restaurant and eating inside, at one of the dark booths that they showed her to. Heavy, tall, blue-tinged glasses of water and large, green cloth napkins. The smell of wine and this smell, the melted cheese and beef and tomatoes, all blended together.

The waiter had explained to her when he brought the check that they were closing the next week.

'The owners are retiring, and their kids don't want to take over. Too much work. Kids these days.' He shrugged.

'How sad,' she said. She wanted to tell the owners what their food had meant to her, but it felt inappropriate. She hadn't known them personally, after all. It had always been delivered. Her parents had never eaten inside the restaurant. Not with Ada, in any case.

Later that night, Ada had woken up crying. She'd dreamed that she and her parents went to the restaurant together, but it was closed. They just kept knocking at the door and trying to call in, but it was dark inside, all the windows covered, no scent of the good food anywhere, just the smell of mold and trash.

Dreams didn't mean anything to Ada. She didn't believe in the nonsense that Freud and then Jung had spouted about dreams having to do with a subconscious mind's wishes. Maybe neurotypical people had subconscious minds that communicated indirectly with symbols, but Ada's mind did not. Ada's mind communicated to her in ways that made a lot more sense, and she didn't need any help interpreting them.

'Come this way,' Langham said. 'You can go ahead and get lunch for yourselves.' She waved at the counters. There was no one else in line.

Henry hustled through the line and came back with a tray of lasagna and some salad and a breadstick. He'd paid for it easily, without any hesitation. It seemed so simple for him, but this wasn't familiar to Ada.

Henry gestured at her to hurry along, and he sat down with Langham. Ada got a tray and held it out next to the big container of lasagna.

A Hispanic woman with a large nose and pock marks, petite but round in torso, hesitated briefly and then scooped up the lasagna and put it on to her plate. The woman had a name tag on that read 'Sylvia.'

'Thank you, Sylvia,' Ada said.

Sylvia nodded without speaking, and Ada wondered if she didn't speak English.

Ada moved along to the tray of breadsticks fresh with real

garlic on them. There were fewer of these. They were obviously popular with the autistic students. They'd been homemade here, Ada was sure, not just reheated.

Trying to get a glimpse of the kitchen in the back, Ada nearly missed the dessert section. There were four different desserts: a piece of chocolate cake, a lemon trifle, a layered gelatin dessert with berries and peaches, and a tiramisu.

Ada wanted to try all four of them, but that would seem greedy and didn't appear to be allowed. She continued to look at the kitchen behind. It was huge, and even if some of the equipment wasn't brand new, it looked like a nice space to move around in. It was larger than her apartment kitchen by far. In fact, it was almost as big as her entire apartment.

'Miss?'

Ada came back to the moment to find the Hispanic woman speaking to her. She didn't have an accent at all. Ada flushed because of her assumptions.

'Which one? Or none?' Sylvia asked.

'The trifle,' Ada said finally. She moved to the cash register and paid for her meal with a card, a system that had been set up so that the staff here could eat, as well.

'The food smells delicious,' Ada said to Sylvia as she waited for her receipt.

'Thank you,' Sylvia said, not meeting her gaze.

Ada noticed that on this side of the cash register, there were also alternate meals on ice for whoever didn't want the homemade food. It didn't look to Ada as if many of the children had taken these choices, but it was kind to offer them. Little boxes of cheese and crackers with fruit drinks, more familiar turkey sandwiches and chips, and cold macaroni and cheese that looked as if it had come from a box. Familiar food that most people would think wasn't very nice. Ada wondered if Sylvia hated making it.

'You're that woman,' Sylvia said when she handed her the receipt. She nodded at Henry, who had to look different from anyone else here. He clearly wasn't one of the regular teaching staff. Nor was she.

'The one with the FBI man. Come here to find out what happened to that girl. Ella,' Sylvia continued.

'Yes, I'm here with the FBI,' Ada said. Again, she felt as if someone she was meeting knew more about her than she should have. It felt uncomfortable.

After a moment, Ada realized that Sylvia must be one of the staff members that she'd missed when she stayed in the hotel because of the after-effects of the meltdown. It felt as if her not coming had been taken as some kind of disrespect. She hadn't meant it that way at all. But how to explain about the meltdown?

'Who do you think you are? Coming here to tell us what happened, as if we know nothing?' Sylvia asked bitterly.

'You're right,' Ada admitted. 'I should have asked you what you know. About Ella. And about what happened to her.' Was there any chance Sylvia would tell her now? She wasn't sure what Sylvia had told Henry.

'She died,' Sylvia said bluntly. 'She wasn't cared for properly. Even here at this expensive school that her parents pay for. She was killed by one of the other children.'

'By Gavin,' Ada said, watching Sylvia carefully. Did she know more?

'Yes. Him. The director's son. They were friends, but what does that matter when they are autistic? They don't know what they are doing,' Sylvia said.

'You don't like the children here,' Ada guessed. 'Why do you work here, then? You could work at another school.'

'I could work at ten different schools. I pass ten schools on my way here. I live more than one hour away from here. I drive here every day. I drive home every day. Does that sound like someone who doesn't like the children here?' Sylvia complained.

Ada was aware that Henry was looking at her with concern on his face. He was gesturing for her to come to the table where he was sitting with the children, participating in their set conversation for the lunch.

But he had already talked to Sylvia, and Ada had not. She'd had no chance to form an opinion about this woman. Why was she putting herself forward here? Because she was angry and arrogant, or was there something else going on here?

'Then why do you come? Why work here? Does it pay well?' Ada asked.

Sylvia snorted in response to the question about pay. Then she said, 'My brother is autistic. He is younger than me, and I helped him for so many years. My parents both worked, and I was the only one who was left. I had no friends, no social life. I never went on a date because my brother needed me. I helped him eat. I helped him go to the bathroom. I helped him do whatever foolish busywork they gave him because they didn't believe that he mattered.'

She was the second person here who said that she worked at NAVITEK because of a sibling with autism. Schools for autistic children had been very different the generation before this one. The autistic children who were labeled as such were often the ones who had the highest needs, and who were least able to mask their traits and look like they were neurotypical.

'I'm sorry that was so difficult for you,' Ada said.

Sylvia's face tightened, and her voice dropped a register. 'Don't tell me you are sorry. I love my brother. Then and now, though he is in an institution now, and I don't get to see him more than once a week. My brother is the reason that I chose to work here. I love autistic children, most of them,' she insisted. 'They deserve better than they usually get. But here, most of them get what they need. What all autistic children should get.'

'Most of them,' Ada echoed. 'So, some of the children here don't deserve better?' This could be important.

'Not all autistic children are good. Just like not all normal children are good,' Sylvia said, her face tight and without expression.

'What kind of bad autistic children are you talking about?' Ada asked. She felt a wave of cold spread over her, just like when she'd first seen that photograph of Ella.

Sylvia waved at the entire cafeteria. 'The rich ones. Some of them. Selfish, greedy, bad-tempered. My brother was never like that. He was never coddled like they are.'

'If you think so many of them are bad, then why are you still here?'

Sylvia put her face very close to Ada's. It was hard for Ada not to pull away from her, but she held her body very still and did her best to continue to look into Sylvia's eyes. 'There are the good ones,' Sylvia said.

But who were the good ones? Ada was afraid that she wasn't going to get any further with Sylvia, so she moved away from the woman and took her tray to the table where Henry was sitting with Langham. She glanced back and saw Sylvia smiling and waving at a couple of the younger autistic children as they came in. She seemed eager to serve them their food.

Ada had no idea what to make of the conversation with Sylvia, except that it had taught her that she had made too many assumptions about the staff and the children here. Maybe about autism, as well.

Autism had made Ada able to see things other people couldn't. It had made her capable of using her brain in ways that most people were not capable of doing. But she also had flaws that came with autism, the inability to understand other people unless they explained themselves to her – and not even then, not always. She could spend days on end in her own little world, not aware that other people even existed.

She had been cruel to Henry in high school. She didn't like that she had done that to him. Did that mean that if aliens did find Earth someday, they would realize that she wasn't worth talking to? That she wasn't a good human?

TWENTY-TWO

Ada sat down at the table across from Henry and took a bite of the lasagna. It was hot and delicious, even better than the smell had led her to believe. She let out a sound of delight.

'It's good, isn't it?' Henry said. He'd already finished his.

Langham said, 'Sylvia is an excellent cook. You should taste her tamales. Or her tres leches cupcakes.' Her mouth looked a little like a smile, but also like a grimace. 'It's unfortunate that her food is also very fattening, so I rarely let myself have a chance to eat it. The children don't worry about that, even if they should. There's not much chance for exercise here.'

Ada looked at the children seated at the table. One of the girls might conceivably be called overweight, but she was also at that awkward stage just barely into her teens, and Ada remembered how it felt for people to make comments about her body then. They thought that because she was labeled autistic, she was too stupid for their rude laughter and pointing. She had not been, and this girl also was not unaware of what was being hinted at.

The girl put her face in her hands and pushed her food away.

'Lunchtime is for social interaction, Lois. You can't just turn it off because you don't like it,' Langham chided.

Ada hadn't liked Langham before, but now she thoroughly disliked her. What kind of a woman makes herself feel good by belittling a child? Maybe the same kind of person who frames a child for the murder of another child?

It felt as if instead of her narrowing the possibilities for who had killed Ella, she and Henry were doing the opposite, spinning out more and more bad stories about the ways that humans, neurotypical or autistic, could be evil.

'Lois, pay attention,' Langham continued. 'Look at me so I can tell you can hear me.'

How could Langham imagine that Lois didn't hear her? Ada felt her shoulders tightening and she had to stop herself from doing the same thing that Lois was doing, turning away and trying to avoid eye contact. If neurotypical people wanted autistic people to make more eye contact, why didn't they do something to make it worthwhile to have an interaction with them?

'I'm going to have to dock you points for today,' Langham said. Her tone was matter-of-fact. There was nothing that anyone could point to that was inappropriate.

Still, Ada hated it. It made her feel like an elementary student all over again, in her sixth-grade classroom, with a teacher who insisted that she had to have her math book open during the class lecture time, even though she'd already finished all of the problems and could have done the lecture better herself than the teacher had done.

Ada felt Henry put a hand on the table, not touching her, but drawing her attention.

She looked just to the side of his face. His face looked . . . as it always looked. He was safety. He was familiar. He was the way things should be.

'Are you all right? Do you need to leave?' he mouthed to her.

Ada shook her head. She didn't like the idea that Langham was winning here. She was the one with power, not Lois. And Ada had to do something. She felt an urgency to stop Langham, to protect Lois, but she didn't know how. She hadn't been able to protect herself, or to advocate for herself when she was Lois. She had no degree in autism studies. She just knew it from the inside.

'No,' she mouthed to Henry.

'OK,' he said, giving her a thumbs up.

Langham continued. 'Thank you for looking at me, Lois. Now, let's continue our conversation. Each person should have a partner. You need to ask your three questions. Where they're from. What is their favorite band. And what is the last movie they saw.'

Stupid questions, Ada thought. How did those questions tell you anything that mattered about another person? Where they were born was a pure accident. What music they liked could tell you something about them, she supposed, but not from a question like that. And movies? Did people even watch movies anymore?

Ada couldn't remember the last time she'd seen a movie, not in a theater, anyway. All those people, all those faces, the weight of their physical presences. It was impossible to pay any attention to a movie when there were so many people around. All you could hear was the people noises.

Sneezing. Talking. Coughing. Wiggling. Shifting. Getting up and down. Voices hushed – or not hushed. Giggling. Crying. Slapping.

'I'll partner with Lois,' Henry offered.

'That's kind of you, Henry. Lois, Henry is going to be your partner, all right?' Langham said.

Ada could hear Lois ask Henry where he was from, and Henry answering.

'Ada, would you partner with Tomas here?' Langham asked, gesturing at the young man who was seated next to her.

Ada nodded. She hadn't noticed him before. He was small and held his body as if in a ball.

'Where are you from?' he asked.

She told him Wyoming.

He nodded.

She could see him making a note of it, to remember. Langham seemed to be preparing a test of some kind on the side, writing notes, so that she could see if her students got the right or wrong answers.

'What is your favorite band?'

Ada told him Kreator.

'What is the last movie you watched?'

Ada told him she didn't remember.

He nodded as if she'd told him a title.

There was a long silence.

'It's your turn now, Ada,' Langham said, making a motion with her hand.

So Ada asked Tomas the same questions. She was surprised when he told her that his favorite band was the Spice Girls, and that his favorite movie was *When Harry Met Sally*.

After a moment, she decided that he must have asked his mother what her answer to these questions was and had simply regurgitated her answers.

She didn't follow up with any other questions, and Tomas didn't look at her.

But when Henry and Lois finished, Langham demanded that Lois tell her what she'd learned about Henry.

Lois answered with her head down, except for when she spoke. Then she looked up briefly and looked back down.

'You didn't ask any follow-up questions. Go ahead and ask him now. Whatever follow-up question you want.'

It seemed that Langham had sent home these questions as homework and that the follow-up was a standard practice.

'What did you like most about the movie?' Lois asked.

'I liked that the characters were kind to each other. They didn't make cruel jokes or hurt each other just for the sake of feeling powerful for a few seconds,' Henry said.

Lois didn't understand the subtext of this. Ada wouldn't have at her age, either. But she did now.

She peeked at Langham, who didn't wince or show any reaction.

'Good work,' Langham said to Lois. 'All right, thank you all for participating. You're free to go now.'

Ada felt like the chance of her doing something was slipping away. Henry had helped Lois, but it hadn't been her. And she wanted it to be her, somehow.

'Excuse me. Why don't you ask the students to help make up the questions?' Ada put in, before they had actually left.

She could see the students stop moving. They didn't look at her, keeping their heads down.

'Of course I let the students suggest questions if they wish to do so,' Langham insisted. 'As long as they are questions that would help them in a normal social situation.'

Normal. Ada hated that word. It was always used to make autistic people feel like there was something wrong with them.

She said, 'Questions about music and movies don't make much sense for autistic students trying to socialize with each other. You should let them ask about hobbies, at least some of the time when they're relaxing at lunch.'

Langham waved a hand dismissively, and Ada wondered how much of the information the woman was trying to convey that way was missed by Ada and the autistic children. 'They talk about their own special interests all the time. They need to learn to talk about things they're not interested in. That's what social interaction at lunch is about. Being able to talk about topics that will help them in the real world.'

The real world. Another phrase Ada hated. Because, of course, autistic people weren't part of that.

'So what you're interested in matters and what they're interested in doesn't? Your interests are normal and theirs are "special interests"?' Ada asked.

She could hear that her voice was loud, and she supposed someone might say that she sounded angry, but she only felt full of energy that she needed to get out of her body before it exploded in some other way. She wondered if shouting at someone else would help her in other situations where she felt as though she might otherwise have a meltdown.

'We don't use loud voices in the cafeteria,' Langham said calmly. But her teeth were showing between her lips.

Ada thought that was less a smile than a warning sign, a threat like apes gave to each other before they attacked. Not that Langham would do anything as obvious as throw her physical weight into Ada's body and try to take her to the ground. That was what made people human, or so neurotypical people would say. The subtlety of the attack and the sheer unexpectedness of it.

'Ada,' Henry said. He was close to her, but still carefully not touching her. For once, she wished he would touch her, that some of his calmer energy would somehow transfer to her.

She could feel the staring eyes not of the students but of the other staff on her. An adult at every table was shushing the students and trying to get them not to watch her, though not for any kind reasons to protect Ada's privacy.

'Closing up the kitchen!' came Sylvia's call in the back of the room.

It was the perfect thing to break up the tension. It was normal, a part of the cafeteria schedule, and it triggered the scheduled response of the students.

'You're excused, students. Time to get back to your classrooms,' Langham said, clapping her hands.

The students all picked up their backpacks and began to move toward the doors. Langham did the same, though she waited there for Ada and Henry.

'Do you need to go back to the hotel?' Henry asked, as he motioned Ada to the side, so that her back was to the doors – and to Langham.

'No,' Ada said with as much strength as she could muster without sounding angry again. 'I want to talk to Langham again.'

'You can't think she's the murderer,' Henry said. 'I can't see that she has any motive. And she seems far too nice to kill a child and then hide it.'

Nice? Henry thought that Langham was nice?

Ada would never understand how it was that neurotypical men chose the women they had sexual interest in. Because Langham took care of her visual appearance, wore perfume, and did fake smiles a certain number of times an hour, Henry thought of her as 'nice.' Rex had thought Tomi was 'nice,' too. Well, maybe they were both nice, if nice meant that they were only concerned about how people perceived them.

Ada was convinced that Langham could well have a motive for murder. She showed no real warmth toward the autistic children. What would stop her from killing one who irritated her?

'She is awful,' Ada got out.

'Well, she has pushed your buttons, I can see that,' Henry said.

'She hates the students here. She hates all autists. That could make her a murderer,' Ada said. And even as she said it, she knew that she was missing something. She felt it somehow, without being able to articulate what the problem was.

Something about the photo was niggling at her, but she couldn't get her brain to spit out what it was. Whatever it was, it didn't fit with Langham. Which meant she and Henry had to go back to the office and talk to Director Sanchez.

TWENTY-THREE

'Do you need help getting back to the office?' Langham asked, gesturing down the hallway.

'No, thank you,' Ada said. She did not want any help from Langham, even of the most basic kind.

'You've been extremely helpful. We both understand the system here much better, and I want to say thank you for all you're doing for the children here, helping them to be able to interact at a more authentic level. That's the kind of practice that will help them move on to the real world as adults, so they can get jobs and become fully independent,' Henry said.

Ada stiffened at his words. She couldn't accept that he believed much of them, but she also didn't like the idea that he could lie so easily. And why? What was the point of making Langham think well of him?

'That is exactly what I'm doing here. Some autistic children are the brilliant exception, the Rain Man type who can find a way to be useful in specific situations that can earn them money. But most of them will need to learn to fit in to some degree, and even to disguise their difference when necessary,' Langham said.

She was looking at Ada the whole time she said this, not at Henry at all.

Ada had no wish to learn how to be more like Langham at meals. Then again, she didn't want to have meals with people like that or have any contact with them. And her life was livable now precisely because she had found a way that she didn't have to have contact with anyone that she didn't want to.

'Of course, we all wish that the world was a more tolerant place, but we have to be realistic. These children need to get jobs, and they will have to be able to pretend to be normal,' Langham said.

Ada cringed at the use of that word 'normal' again. She was tempted to give a lecture on the concept of mathematical norm.

But she resisted the impulse because she knew it would only make her seem less 'normal' to this woman.

'I hope that you learned something, as well,' Langham said, looking directly at Ada, holding her gaze in a very uncomfortable way.

Nonetheless, Ada refused to look away this time. She knew what looking away meant to someone like this. It meant that she agreed she was lesser, and she didn't agree to that. 'I'd like to know how you knew so much about me,' she said bluntly.

'So much about you?' Langham put a hand to her throat. 'I don't know what you mean. All I know is that you are here with Henry to investigate.'

'That is a lie,' Ada said, blunt again. 'You know that I had a physical altercation with Ella's mother two days ago. And you know that I am autistic.'

Langham stared at her. 'I don't know what—' she started to say.

'I just want to know who told you,' Ada insisted.

'Well, uh, Director Sanchez might have hinted at some things,' she said. 'That you were difficult and that your autism was why Mrs Kimball might have had trouble with you.'

Ada let out a long breath. 'Thank you,' she said.

'Is that all?' Langham asked coldly.

'Yes, that's all I wanted to know.'

There was an awkward silence as Langham continued to stare at Ada. 'Well, good luck with your investigation, Henry,' Langham said at last. She moved in to give him a quick embrace, and then kissed him on the cheek, as well. She did not look at or speak to Ada again. She simply went down the same hallway and turned through a door to the outside.

When Henry turned back to Ada, he had a hint of a smudge of a vibrant coral color on his cheek. Ada used to like that color. She would never see it again without thinking of Langham, that dreadful woman.

He rubbed at his face, looked down at his hands, and saw the color on them. 'Damn,' he said, and rubbed more vigorously. 'Is that gone now?' he asked.

Something about the color on his face reminded her of the photo. Something . . .

Henry went on, 'God, that woman was quite the performer. I can see why people hire her. And why she moves on from job to job quickly. She's been here since the start of the school year, but I imagine she'll leave as soon as she finds something that she thinks will make her look better.'

The photo, the color on Henry's face, Langham. Ada wanted to hit her head. She was so close to the final clue, but it was bouncing off the inside of her brain like a pinball in a machine, dancing away from her.

'Isn't that what all neurotypical people care about? Looking good for others? So that they can move up the proverbial social ladder until they get to the very top?' And then what? Ada hardly knew.

He tilted his head to consider the question. 'Well, in some ways, yes. I do consider what looks good. That's an important part of social interaction. It's not the only factor, to be sure. Sometimes I do things that don't make me look good at all, but I try to do them rarely. Only when they truly matter.'

Ada didn't feel as though she ever had a choice in the matter of looking good. 'How convenient for you.' She began to walk toward the office.

Henry came a few steps after her.

Before she opened the door, he caught up and then pulled ahead of her. He was standing in front of the door so that she couldn't reach the knob without touching him. She didn't want to do that, so she simply waited.

'You're angry at me,' Henry guessed.

'I'm angry,' Ada said. 'At many people and many things.'

'But at me, right now.'

Ada did not respond.

Henry continued, 'Yes, I let her think that I liked her. I let her kiss me. Sometimes that's necessary, to get people to trust you enough to give you a little more of the truth. Ada, it's how I was trained to do my job. I don't like it, but it's necessary.'

'Maybe you do like it. A little,' Ada said. She pointed at his cheek.

He sighed. 'I can't be like you, always telling the exact and whole truth. It's not the way it works in the real world. Certainly not in the FBI, when we're investigating murders.'

'So you think that she was right, that she's helping the children learn how the real world is?' Ada said. The niggling thing was still there, in the back of her mind. She had to trust that it would come out eventually, and it seemed that tugging at it wasn't helping. Her brain was something that she'd gotten used to over the years. It didn't always work in the way that made sense to other people, but it did make sense to her. It would make sense, eventually, if she waited for it.

Henry turned and opened the door. He held it open for Ada, and she walked in, hating the ridiculousness of this supposed act of chivalry, as if she could not open the door herself just as well.

'Maybe it is helpful. Maybe it helps them in the real world. I don't have to like it for that to be true,' Henry said in a low voice.

Right. And now Ada could let that go. She'd brought it up. She didn't lie or pretend. But she wasn't like a dog with a bone, no matter what Rex had said about her. She could let things go. She could, and she was doing it right now.

It didn't matter what Henry had done with Jennifer Langham. It didn't matter because she wasn't going to see Langham ever again, hopefully, and after this investigation was finished, she was unlikely to see Henry, either. So it didn't matter if he acted in ways she considered deceitful and immoral. Even if it was his job.

'I wanted to ask you about the staff you interviewed yesterday, when I stayed at the hotel,' Ada said as she sat down.

'The staff? I don't think they're important, but I can tell you about them if you'd like. The cook, Sylvia, you met in the cafeteria.'

'Who else?' Ada asked.

'There's the cleaner, Donna, and the woman who does the bookkeeping and scheduling, other administrative stuff for Director Sanchez. Mary.'

'What did you ask them?' Ada asked.

'Just standard questions,' Henry said. 'I asked them if they'd known Ella, what they thought of her, where they were when she died.'

'What did they think of her?'

'That she was a nice kid.' Henry shrugged. 'I don't think you need to worry about them. Maybe we should go out for a walk or something. Get out of here.' He gestured at the room.

'If I wanted to take a break, I'd go in the car and get out my face mask and earplugs. But that's not what I want right now,' Ada said.

She wanted it and she didn't want it. That was the central contradiction of her life, wanting things that she also didn't want because they were bad for her, because they would hurt her, or because she'd realize later that they didn't matter, and she'd wasted her time when it should have been spent working on important things. Like saving the planet and its inhabitants for the aliens who would, eventually, arrive. She hoped. Obviously, she couldn't know it for certain, especially not in her lifetime.

'OK, up to you. I don't think those interviews mattered,' Henry said.

'Why do you think that?'

'I . . . they aren't murderers. They're just ordinary women working ordinary jobs,' Henry said.

Yes, that was how they appeared. But they were every bit as likely to be murderers as anyone else, weren't they? If she looked at them clearly, without prejudice?

'Did you know that Sylvia has a brother with autism?' Ada asked. 'Or that she has to drive over an hour each way to get here because she isn't one of the teachers who get housing nearby?'

Henry hesitated. He rubbed a hand over his chin. 'Damn.'

'That means you didn't know that.'

'No, I didn't ask her any questions like that. But you surely don't think that Sylvia murdered Ella. What possible motive could she have to do that? She couldn't even have known her that well. She only saw her in the cafeteria.'

Ada wasn't at all sure that Sylvia had known Ella or the other students here any less because she worked in the cafeteria.

'Is it because you think she isn't smart enough?' Ada asked. She was asking the question out loud because she was trying to figure out if that was true of her own prejudice. Was that why she thought Sylvia couldn't have done it? Because the murder had been carefully done, planned in advance, and just as carefully disguised? Did Sylvia have anything to do with the niggle in her mind?

'I . . . maybe?' Henry said. 'I guess we should interview her again. And the other two.' He stood up.

Ada motioned him to sit back down. 'Just let me think here. And tell me about the other two. Donna and Mary. What did you ask them about? What do you remember about them?'

'You know, they teach you in the FBI to walk into investigations with no assumptions. They tell you to consider everyone as equally suspect. To look at all the information objectively.' He was shaking his head.

Ada was impatient. She snapped her fingers. 'You can judge yourself badly later. I want you to tell me what you remember right now. Donna. The cleaner. What did she look like? What was she wearing? How did she speak? What did you ask her?'

Henry waved a hand negligently. 'She was wearing . . . cleaning clothes. A loose top and a loose pair of pants. Like a uniform. She had on gloves, and one of those—' He touched his hair.

'A plastic hair cap,' Ada said.

'Yes, that. She was medium height. Medium weight. Brown hair. In her late thirties, maybe? Could have been younger, I guess. Or older.'

He hadn't really looked at her. She hadn't been a person to him. She'd been a role, a job. Ada pushed at the perception. It might have to do with the niggle, but she wasn't sure yet.

'What did you ask her?'

'I told you. The same questions as the others. What she thought of Ella and where she was at the time of death and what she did here at NAVITEK.'

'Did she seem to know Ella?' Ada asked.

Henry shook his head. 'I don't think so. Not very well. She said she cleaned the rooms when the students were in classes. She had a schedule. She said that a lot of the students didn't like a stranger going into their space, so she had to be careful to put things back exactly where they'd been before. Exactly.

'And she said that if beds weren't made, she'd been instructed not to make them. She dusted and swept and mopped, but she didn't do laundry unless it was in a basket for cleaning. And she folded things and put them in a basket at the end of each bed. She didn't put things back in drawers.'

'And was it the same for Ella? In her special room?' Ada asked.

'Why would it be different?' Henry asked.

'Because she has her own room. Because her parents are wealthier than the other parents. Because she was special. She was Ella Kimball,' Ada said.

'I–I don't know. I'll get her back in. We can talk to her together. Ask more questions if you want.'

It wasn't Donna, Ada was suddenly sure. She wasn't the missing piece. Or at least it didn't feel that way. So Ada asked her other questions. 'And what about Mary? The bookkeeper?'

Henry shook his head. His eyes looked – strange. Darker, somehow. Ada didn't know what that meant. She hated that she felt so stupid sometimes. Someone else could look at Henry's face right now and they'd think it was so obvious what his eyes were telling her, as obvious as a sign above his head, as obvious as him yelling at her with words. But it wasn't obvious at all.

'She was younger. In her twenties. Pretty. Slim. Dressed in a jumpsuit. With flowers on it.' He gestured at Ada, at her breasts.

'Were you attracted to her?' Ada asked. That had something to do with the murder. Why, she had no idea.

Henry reacted by yanking his head back. His eyes did something else, narrowing. 'What kind of a question is that?'

It was the kind of question that neurotypical people didn't like, even if it might be pertinent. 'I'm just asking for information. Was she attractive to you personally?' Ada asked.

'I . . . at first, maybe,' he said, and Ada wondered if he was trying to remember. Neurotypical people seemed to forget things so easily. Sometimes she was jealous of their ability to do that, to simply not remember. There were so many things Ada wished that she could forget, so many words thrown at her, so many failures.

'And then? Why did you stop being attracted to her?'

'I don't know. She wasn't a nice person. I asked her about Ella, and she said something about how spoiled she was – a spoiled little rich brat.'

'What else did she say?'

'That the school needed her parents' money. Without them, the school was going to have problems immediately paying bills and salaries, and even electricity, if it came down to it.'

'Why didn't you tell me any of that?' This could be important, but she still wasn't sure.

Henry let out a weird laughing sound, a sighing laugh. 'I thought she was exaggerating. Trying to act like she mattered. Handing out secrets or something. I told you, I didn't like her by then. I didn't trust what she said.'

'But you didn't think she could be the murderer?' Ada asked. She wanted to know why.

'No, I didn't think that she could be the murderer.' He gestured with his hands to the sides. 'Do you have some reason to think she is the murderer? I haven't heard anything to make me think that.'

'But you didn't think she could be. That's the problem. Only certain kinds of people can do certain things. Isn't that the prejudice that we're trying to fight against?' Ada asked. Her brain was buzzing, demanding she keep pressing Henry about this. Why? Why? Why? It hadn't told her.

'On a murder case? I thought we were trying to find the murderer, not fight prejudice.'

'We have to keep asking questions about Ella. About why she was the one who was killed,' she insisted. 'If her death means NAVITEK will close down, who wants the school to close down? Isn't that the way it works? Motive, means, and opportunity.' Her brain was still buzzing uncomfortably. She hadn't reached the geyser of truth yet, but it was bubbling somewhere there, beneath the surface.

Henry sighed and ran a hand through his hair. 'Ada, maybe it's time for us to accept that this wasn't a murder. Just a tragic accident.'

What? She gaped at him. She thought he believed her. Had it all been a lie?

He put out his hands as if to calm her. 'The photo was staged. I'm not saying it wasn't. It seems clear from what you said that it wasn't real. And there was the makeup. That girl didn't put it on herself. But what if the only crime here is someone making a dead body look better and taking a photo of it before contacting the authorities?'

Ada could barely hear Henry. His voice seemed tinny and far away, as if it were coming to her from through a tunnel. Something about what he'd said had made her brain explode with noise. Not real noise, just the sensation of pieces of a puzzle going together. But what picture did they make? That was still not clear.

'I don't know why anyone would have put makeup on a dead autistic girl, but it might have been a kindness to her. To make her look better,' Henry went on.

'Pink Cosmos,' Ada said out loud. 'Nuclear Pink.'

'What?' Henry asked.

'Ella was wearing Nuclear Pink on her lips. And the foundation was Starry Night, from my collection "Pink Cosmos".'

'I'm not following,' Henry said.

Her brain was so loud it was hard to hear Henry's voice over the sound inside. 'That's why Rex called me. Because he recognized the colors.'

'What? Still not following.' Was that concern on Henry's face? He was probably worried she was going to have another meltdown, but this was not a meltdown. This was the opposite. It was a melt-up. It was a revelation hitting her at last. It had been days in coming, but now she knew everything. Or everything that mattered, anyway.

'Orange Matter,' Ada said. 'Red Dwarf.'

'Ada, what is going on?' Henry asked.

'The colors of lipstick that Director Sanchez was wearing. The first day and today. I recognize the colors,' Ada said.

'OK,' Henry said, still clearly confused.

'They're from my first collection. When I founded Good Cosmetics. I called it "Pink Cosmos."'

'That's weird, I guess,' Henry said.

'Ella was wearing lipstick from that collection in the photo. The foundation she was wearing was from it, too. I think Sanchez wears the foundation, though it looks very different on her because her skin tone isn't at all the same.' Why hadn't she noticed that before?

'Surely that's a coincidence,' Henry said. And then he said some other things. She couldn't hear him, though.

'It's not a coincidence,' she tried to say. 'It was a very limited collection.' She couldn't hear her own voice, and she tried to talk up, but she still couldn't hear it. She could only feel the vocal cords vibrate in her throat when she put a hand up there.

Henry said something. She wasn't sure what. She tried to guess from the way his lips moved. Something about 'wrong.' What was wrong with her or what was wrong with the investigation?

Then there was a knock on the door.

'Here's the next interview,' Henry said. 'It's Indira Johnston, the nurse.'

Ada could hear him again. Her head was quieting down. The pressure had been relieved. It felt so much better. She knew the answer now. The mystery was solved. There were other questions to be answered, but they felt less important to Ada. Henry was slower, she knew. He needed her to fill in the gaps. He had always been like that. In high school, he had always needed more information than she did. He had been slow, and she had left him behind many times.

TWENTY-FOUR

A woman came into the room. She was unfamiliar, around forty years of age, with a round face and starting to go gray around the temples. She didn't wear any makeup, Ada noticed.

'Are you here to ask about my qualifications as a nurse? I can assure you I can deal with any medical problems your child may have,' the woman said.

'What? Oh, no, we're not parents of an autistic child. We're with the FBI, here to investigate Ella Kimball's death,' he said.

Johnston said, 'An investigation? But that was an accident. I saw her body just after it happened, and I explained it was an accident to the EMTs who came with the ambulance.'

'Who called you in?' Henry asked.

'Oh. That was the director,' Johnston said.

'Director Soledad Sanchez? Was she there when you arrived?' Henry asked again.

Ada's mind was whirling, trying to put all the pieces of this puzzle together.

'The director? No, I don't think she was there.' Johnston hesitated. 'At least, I didn't see her when I went in. Only Ella and Gavin.'

'Why would she have left?'

'I don't know,' Johnston admitted.

'Did you ask her about that later?' Henry asked.

'No, I didn't. I guess I was too upset about what had happened. I didn't think to ask about that.'

'Did she call you? Text you? How did she contact you?' Henry asked.

Johnston looked at her phone, then scrolled through it. 'I–I can't see any texts. She must have called me. But I don't remember it. I'm sorry.'

'Email?' Henry tried.

Johnston looked down at her phone again, scrolled, then shook her head. 'Maybe she came into my office?' She was asking, though, not sure.

Ada was trying to pay attention. She thought she already knew the answer. Her brain was dancing with the certainty that she was right. But she might not be right. She needed to be sure she was right first.

'What about the photograph? And the makeup on Ella?' Ada asked.

'What photograph? I think I saw she had makeup on, but I didn't think anything of that.' Johnston said.

'Did you ever see her wearing makeup before that?' Ada asked, just trying to make sure she wasn't wrong. It felt so good when the puzzle pieces went together, but there were so many pieces here.

'I don't remember her wearing makeup before, no,' Johnston said. 'But I didn't see her that often?'

The tone ended on a question. Ada couldn't find words to ask more questions. It all seemed so clear.

'Tell me what you saw when you were called in. Was Ella alive or dead?' Henry broke in. He didn't understand what had happened. He didn't read minds, especially not Ada's.

A long breath out. 'Sadly, she was already dead. I wish I'd gotten there earlier. Then I might have been able to save her. But she was already going cold. There was no point in trying to do chest compressions for CPR,' Johnston said.

'You found her cold? How long do you think it had been since she died?' Henry asked.

'At least an hour. I'm not a forensic pathologist or a medical examiner, of course, but that's my best guess,' Johnston said.

'What did you do next?' Henry asked.

'I called nine-one-one, of course. Not because I thought an ambulance would help the situation, but it was the best way to deal with an accidental death.'

'You mean, without contacting the police,' Henry put in.

'Yes,' she said faintly. 'The director wouldn't want that kind of publicity for the school.'

Of course the director wouldn't, Ada thought. That was the way all the pieces held together. With the director.

'What else did you see?' Henry asked, looking at Ada with a strange expression on his face. 'When you went to the room?'

'The room was vacuumed. No sign of any disarray,' Johnston said, her eyes narrowed as if she was rethinking whether that made sense.

'It didn't occur to you that someone had already disturbed the scene?' Henry asked.

'No,' Johnston said distantly.

'Do you know why there was such a delay in calling you?' Henry asked.

'I assumed it was because Gavin didn't realize that she was dead for so long. And he went non-verbal by the time I arrived.'

'So you accepted that Gavin had killed Ella? Accidentally?' Henry asked.

'I . . . yes. That is what I thought had happened.'

Henry didn't let that go. 'What aren't you telling us? You're obviously concealing something. Do you want to end up in court with charges against you for obstructing an investigation?'

Johnston put a hand to her chest. 'I didn't do anything wrong,' she insisted.

Henry's voice dropped to a lower, softer register. 'Then just tell us what you saw.' He glanced at Ada again, that expression on his face that looked happy. How could he be happy when he didn't know what she knew?

'It was Gavin,' Johnston said slowly, perhaps reluctantly. 'He had gouges all over his arms and stomach. Some on his legs and back, as well.'

'You think those were from Ella, as she was trying to escape from him holding her so hard she suffocated?' Henry asked, in that same soft, coaxing voice.

'I don't know when they happened. But there were too many of them and they were in too many places for them to be from that one instance of him holding her down,' Johnston admitted.

'And what else?' Henry asked.

'I–I can't say this for certain,' Johnston said. She looked at Ada rather than Henry as she spoke. 'I think there were older cuts on him, half healed. From several months ago, and maybe further back than that.'

It was another piece, Ada realized. She hadn't had all of it, not yet. The full picture kept growing. She had to be cautious here.

'You think that she had been hurting him for a long period of time. Abusing him,' Henry said.

Of course, Ada thought. Of course. They had been set up as a friendship pair for months, for the entire time that Ella had been here. Such good friends.

'I don't know what to call it. I don't know if she understood that she was hurting him any more than he understood that he was hurting her. But someone must have seen the cuts and bruises on him. Gouges like that – his mother . . .' She trailed off.

It was a bigger picture, but the center of it was still the same. Soledad Sanchez. The director had wanted to make sure that Ella stayed at the school for financial reasons. She'd been desperate to keep that money here, and so she had sacrificed her own son's well-being for that purpose. And when Ella died as a result, she'd felt enough guilt – or deceit – to try to make her body look beautiful. Or less terribly dead.

Ada felt a sudden sense of peace. It was done. All done now. Her mind felt sharp and clear at last.

'You said you hadn't seen Ella often. But that means you must have seen her before. When was that? What happened?' Henry asked.

Johnston swallowed hard and put a hand to her throat, but she admitted at last, 'She had hurt another child. Not like Gavin. She . . . poked at his eye, made it bleed. He had to go to an ophthalmologist for treatment. His parents took him out after that.'

Ada thought of what Sylvia had said about some autistic children being evil. Another piece, going into the right place.

'Do you think that Gavin and Ella were friends? We've heard them described that way by other staff here,' Henry said.

Johnston's lips pursed and then she sighed. 'I don't know. I can't see inside their heads. They spent a lot of time together. They were frequently assigned each other's company. I don't know who was behind that.'

'They had a shared special interest in frogs,' Ada said.

'What?' Johnston said, then waved a hand. 'Perhaps.'

Red
Is the color of

> Bleeding sunset.
> It hurts when you bleed.
> It hurts when things end.
> It hurts
> When yellow and green and black
> Turn red

Ada quoted Ella's poem back at Johnston, at Henry, at the universe. The little girl had been talking about her own death, predicting it perhaps, in that prescient way that autistic children sometimes had. But no, it wasn't really prescient. She had just been talking about her life, and the color of the blood that she drew from other children when she hurt them. It had all been literal, not poetic at all.

'You don't know a lot of things,' Henry said with a tone Ada knew was critical. 'It seems they are all things that only Director Sanchez could have been behind.'

Johnston wouldn't confirm it, but she didn't deny it, either. She just looked away.

TWENTY-FIVE

After Johnston left, they had another scheduled appointment, this one with the reading specialist, Dr Lorraine Berling. But Henry had already crumpled up the list of appointments and was moving toward the door.

'Well, come on,' he said.

'You know,' she said. Even though she hadn't told him directly.

'It wasn't a poem,' Henry said. 'It was a clue. Her telling us what she was doing. And why she was killed.'

'Yes,' Ada said.

'Maybe that was the most direct piece of information we've gotten in the three days we've been here. God knows Director Sanchez has done an excellent job for the last three days of misdirecting, manipulating, sidetracking, and delaying us. But the time for that is over. We need to interview her directly now, and with entirely different questions than before.'

Ada thought of Gavin, whom she had met. And Taylor, whom she hadn't. They were autistic children who needed their mother and the stability that Sanchez represented. What would happen to them if she went to prison for murder? What about all the other children here? If they were this desperate for one child's money, things had to be very bad. But if there was any chance for the school to be saved, that lay with Director Sanchez alone. No one else would do anything.

All the children here would be sent back home, to find their places in regular schools, if they could, or to go to other institutions which would surely treat them worse than here. They would be seen as defective, as less than, as not as valuable to society.

'Ada, she likely killed a child,' Henry said.

Yes, a cruel child who might or might not have understood what the red color of blood meant when she used her fingernails to pull it out of other children.

'She planned it in advance,' Henry added.

'Probably,' Ada said. 'How did you know? I figured it out, but I didn't tell you.'

'I'm not as stupid as you think,' Henry said with a very wide smile. He went to the door and held it open.

'It was the makeup,' Ada said.

'What? I don't understand.' Henry's head was tilted to the side, though he didn't accuse her of inventing facts, as Rex had last year.

'The color of the lipstick Ella was wearing in the photograph. It was from my set Pink Cosmos, and so was the foundation. The lipstick that the director has worn the two days I've seen her is from the same set.' When she said it out loud, it didn't sound so obvious.

Still, Henry didn't laugh. 'She is the one who has the motive. And the opportunity. She had to have called the nurse. No one said that, but it has to be her.'

So Henry had come here on an entirely different path. Strange. It happened that way sometimes, she supposed, with science.

'What if she lies?' Ada asked. 'She has every reason to lie again.' She wasn't sure that the pieces she saw together in her head counted as proof. What she saw so clearly wasn't always something she was able to make into sense for neurotypical people. She wasn't really a detective, just as she wasn't really an expert in autism. She just knew.

'We didn't have the right questions before now. And I will be watching her face to look for lies,' Henry assured her.

Ada had an impulse to walk out, now that she knew. Henry could do the rest surely.

But he looked at her with something – was that hope? – in his eyes. And she didn't run away, though she wanted to, though it would have been easier, though she didn't believe that she mattered here anymore.

'Come with me,' Henry said. His tone was gentle and soft, but there was still that hot energy in him.

'What if she did the right thing and killed someone who was hurting others? What if she's a good person who helps autistic children when no one else can or will?' Ada asked. This went beyond the puzzle pieces, beyond putting them together in the right way, to the reason that the puzzle existed, and even Ada did not know that.

'Then she will have to live with the consequences of her actions, Ada. But remember that Ella was autistic. She was a child. Children aren't evil. They can't be. They are simply immature, and unaware. If Ella was hurting other children, maybe even Gavin, she should have been stopped, yes. She should have been sent away from those she was hurting, even. But she didn't deserve to be killed. The sentence for children is never death.'

Ada wondered if her parents would have said the same thing. There had been two times in her childhood when she'd overheard her mother say that she wished Ada had never been born, that Ada would just disappear as if she'd never existed. That wasn't the same as saying she wanted her dead, or that she wanted to kill her with her own hands. But it had been something Ada had carried with her all her life. Her own mother hadn't wanted her to outlive her, though it was something that normal parents wished for all their normal children.

Ada walked with Henry down the hallway to the director's office. The door was closed, but Ada could see through the small window in the door that Sanchez was there, sitting at her desk. She looked to be staring at her computer screen, but she wasn't typing on the screen or moving the mouse. She wasn't moving at all, which was strange.

Henry knocked hard on the door.

The director looked up. She was wearing the bright Red Dwarf lipstick that Ada had created herself to look like colors of the cosmos. Now it just looked like blood. When Sanchez saw Ada and Henry, she stood and smoothed out her hair and her suit jacket and skirt. Then she finally came to the door. 'Come in,' she said. She looked at her watch. 'I thought you had one more appointment.'

'We don't need another appointment,' Henry said. 'We know what happened now. We have all the details necessary for an arrest and a conviction.'

'Oh? Really?' Sanchez didn't show any emotion. But she wasn't autistic.

'You lied to us,' Ada said. She felt angry about this betrayal, though she supposed she shouldn't. It kept happening, and at this point in her life, she should expect it to keep happening when it came to her relationships with neurotypical people.

'Yes, I did,' Sanchez said simply. 'I had to.'

'To protect Gavin, you mean. From Ella,' Henry said.

Somehow his slow speed of building up annoyed Ada. So she said, 'You killed Ella,' simply.

'She was a horrible child,' Sanchez said, not blinking an eye.

After a moment, Ada realized it was also not technically a confession. Of course, it couldn't be as simple as that, because Sanchez, for all that she insisted she understood autistic children, couldn't possibly just admit to what she'd done. It had to be the fault of someone else. Ella. Or Gavin, probably. Or Ella's parents. Or the other staff. Or the universe itself.

'Even if that is true, that is not an excuse for murdering a vulnerable child in your care,' Henry said.

Sanchez sat back in the chair behind her desk. She sat with dignity, not with any sense of defeat.

Even though Ada couldn't read her mind, she suspected, based on previous experience with neurotypical people, that Sanchez believed she still thought she could get away with this. She still thought that, tomorrow morning, she would come back here and sit in her chair behind that desk again. She thought she deserved to.

'If I showed you the marks on Gavin's torso and back, on his arms and legs, you wouldn't be so quick to say that she didn't deserve to be punished,' Sanchez said.

Yet Sanchez hadn't shown them any such thing. She'd done her best to make sure they never even found out about it.

'I can show you the list of other complaints. From students, from the staff, from the nurse on behalf of other students.' She started clicking on her computer and, after a moment, turned the screen around.

'There,' she said. 'You can see. There are over a hundred incidents from the time Ella Kimball was enrolled here. We reported the worst of them to her parents, but they refused to do anything. They said that it was our responsibility, because we'd agreed to the tuition they were paying for her. We were supposed to get her to stop, to behave better. We were supposed to provide autism-specific therapy for her so that she could work out her feelings in a healthier way.'

Ada listened to Sanchez as background noise while she read through the list of complaints.

Yanking hair out by the roots.
Slapping.
Throwing food.
Throwing feces.
Spitting.
Pinching hard enough to leave bruises.
Cursing.
Kicking.
Punching.
Peeing on one of the children in the other building while they slept.
Stealing food from other children.
Screaming for hours at night to keep others up.
Stealing food from the kitchen of the cafeteria at night.
Destroying furniture, in her room and in other rooms.
Destroying items from a staff member's purse.
Escaping the building and kicking in a headlight of a staff member's car.
Cutting apart a child's favorite stuffed animal and throwing the stuffing all around the room.
Tearing apart mattress in her own room and complaining that the school didn't provide her with a proper mattress to sleep on.
Cutting up her own clothing.
Carrying a pair of scissors concealed into classrooms to cut other students' clothing.
Carrying a knife out of the cafeteria into her own room and refusing to explain why.
Breaking windows and kicking the wood in doors.
Breaking plates and glasses, bending silverware until no longer usable.

'Did you ask her why she did these things?' Ada asked Sanchez.

Sanchez raised her eyebrows. 'Of course we asked. Sometimes she gave a reason. Sometimes she said it was because she wanted to. Or because God told her to. Or because her parents didn't love her.'

'Did you believe her reasons?' Ada asked. It wasn't impossible for an autistic child to hear voices as part of some complicated co-diagnosis. Ella could have had schizophrenia or other delusionary disorders. She could have some kind of religious OCD.

'At first, I thought she was trying to tell us her own truth, however inaccurate that might be,' Sanchez said.

'And then later?'

'Later, I didn't care what the reasons were. I just needed her to stop. The school couldn't continue to function with a child like that in it. All the other children were afraid. We were losing students and staff members because of Ella Kimball's very personal and unrelenting reign of terror.'

'And when she attacked Gavin again that night, it was the last straw for you, Director Sanchez,' Henry said.

Sanchez had been looking at Ada, but now she turned to Henry. 'He tried to endure her attack. That's his way. I tried to teach him how to fight back, but he wouldn't do it. He was just passive. He let her hurt him. He still thought she was a friend. He thought that he had to sit there and let her do that to him because that was what friendship meant to him.' Sanchez's voice broke on this last part.

Ada felt a wave of pity for the woman, but then reminded herself that this kind of show of emotion could well be used to manipulate. Just because she showed sadness didn't mean that was her primary motivation for killing Ella.

'Did you consider that her parents might have abused her?' Ada asked. 'That Ella was just doing to others what she had been taught was normal?'

Sanchez turned on her swiftly. Her sob turned into a laugh. 'Did I consider that? How could I not? She told us so many stories about what happened at home, but it wasn't possible they were all true. She was a liar who lied so often that she didn't know what was true anymore. I don't know if that's just how she was or if it was because of what her parents did to her. They are also terrible people, but they were not in my school, and they did not have access to my son.'

It was so strange for Ada to think about an autistic girl who had learned to lie after being lied to. She had instead grown a strict sense of the rules of honesty that she would never breach. Had her parents been better than Ella's? Perhaps they were. She had always thought the worst of them, but her parents had not sent her away. They had not made her into a monster, if that was what Ella's parents had done to her.

'And what difference did it make if they abused her, anyway? Her parents were paying the school enough to pay half the salaries all on their own. I couldn't send her away. It wasn't financially feasible. I had to keep her, had to work around the problems she caused as long as I possibly could. And I did that—' She stopped abruptly.

'Until you walked into that playroom and saw what she was doing to Gavin, and you snapped,' Henry said. 'Gavin didn't put his hands around her throat and choke her. That was you.'

TWENTY-SIX

Sanchez straightened and sat back in her chair. 'You have no legal proof of that. Whatever Gavin communicated to you wouldn't be admissible in court. And everything else is circumstantial. The makeup – Ella could have taken that from me. In fact, she did take it. She stole many things from the staff and students here.' Sanchez waved at the list of complaints.

'Gavin will become verbal again,' Ada said. 'And then he will be able to explain clearly that he never hurt Ella. That you did.' She was making a guess here that Gavin had been in the room when it happened, but she saw no reason to think that Sanchez would have sent him away. The director had too much confidence, and no remorse at all for what she had done.

Sanchez's face tightened. 'Maybe. Maybe not. Autistic children don't always regain their abilities after a trauma like that. And even if he is able to speak again, do you think a court will admit evidence by an underage child who is disabled and may or may not be able to sort out the truth from suggestion or imagination?'

She wasn't wrong. Ada felt sick at the realization. Gavin's mother could delay him regaining his speech. She was in a superb position to do so. His father was out of the picture and would do nothing to intervene. He wanted nothing to do with his autistic children. And Sanchez could poison any of Gavin's memories, even if he did regain them fully.

Autistic children were notoriously unreliable. Precisely because they were so easily manipulable.

The makeup evidence seemed clear to Ada, but what else did they really have against Sanchez?

'Nurse Johnston knows what happened,' Henry said.

Sanchez flicked a hand at Henry at that. 'She won't testify against me in court. And even if she did, she wasn't there when it happened. There were no cameras.'

'Why did you stage the photograph like that? Why take so much time before you called the nurse?' Henry asked.

It was what Ada wanted answered, too. The last tiny little piece in the grand picture that she had been putting together for three days now.

'Because once Ella was gone, I needed attention on the school. I needed more students to replace her. And that photograph has already brought us over a hundred new applications. It was necessary,' Sanchez said.

'And that's enough for you? You kill a child and let others mock her and your son online and it's enough if your school gets enough money?' Henry asked.

Ada put a hand to her head, trying to keep it from feeling as if it were flying away. Her makeup had been used for a marketing ad. On the face of a dead autistic girl. She couldn't imagine any nightmare worse, and Rex hadn't really had anything to do with it.

Sanchez turned the computer screen back around, her chin held high. 'I am the only person who can run this school. I alone can save it. Without me, these children will all go back to worse situations. Is that really the outcome you were looking for when you came here to investigate one girl's death? One girl against dozens?'

As if Ada could stand to leave other children under this woman's care, after she had not quite confessed to murdering Ella.

'Do you really think you are that important?' Henry asked. His voice sounded strange. Ada wasn't sure what it was. Some kind of surprise.

'Of course I am. There are very few autistic schools in this country, and none with the reputation we have. I'm here for a reason. I put together the team of staff that works here. I found this place and managed to talk the owners down in price because it was for the children – they have an autistic grandson, by the way. I get donors to contribute to our yearly fundraiser. And parents to pay tuition for their children. I find people to work for free to do our finances, our website, our marketing.' She was holding her head high, her nostrils flared, breathing heavily.

Ada knew that look. She'd seen it on Rex many times. And her mother. Her father once or twice, too. It was a look that neurotypical people had when they were explaining why they didn't follow the rules that they insisted were important for the rest of society. For the lower people. For people who didn't matter as much. The people who didn't understand that the rules were flexible.

Autistic people.

Sanchez went on. 'And it's worth it. All that time I've spent working till midnight, waking up at four or five a.m., before the boys do, so that I can work on a letter or a presentation in peace. The time I spend talking to the teachers and staff to make sure they know how to treat people who come in here for tours. Because those people ensure we keep going year after year.'

She thought she was a hero. Ada could hear Rex's voice in her head, when he told her he wanted her to give him the company. 'Everyone will be better if I'm in charge. You're too autistic to understand what a large portion of customers want. You started a company, but it will never grow if you stay. If you really care, you will leave.'

Ada's ears were still ringing with his voice, and Sanchez's.

'But—' Henry tried to interrupt.

Sanchez would have none of it. She kept barreling on. 'Have you seen our test scores? We are the number-one autistic school in the nation in reading and in math skills. We have moved up from number forty-five the first year we started. Steady progress year by year. Because of our donors. Because I make sure that we get the best materials available, the best staff, the most up-to-date research and training.

'My sons have a chance now. Even Taylor. He may have a real life someday. A job that pays him a living wage. He will have a chance to become independent. And Gavin, of course, as long as I make sure that he isn't convicted of any crime and there is no official record of this accident because he is a juvenile,' she went on. 'He won't fully remember what happened, I don't think. And if he does, I will remind him that I was protecting him. He will see that I did the right thing, the only thing.'

Henry coughed at this.

Ada felt her whole body begin to shake with anger. 'Gavin is better than you are by a thousand times. He will hate you.' She hoped Gavin would hate his mother. Or did she? For perhaps the first time since this had started, Ada was no longer sure what she thought the right outcome here was.

Sanchez went on, 'All the children here. Do you think that means nothing? That all the work I've done here should just be thrown away because one student couldn't listen and obey the simple rule not to hurt others? You think that she is more important than the rest of them, all of the ones who will come here and be helped by NAVITEK and by me?' She stood up, her hands firmly on the desk, her eyes flashing.

Ada didn't know how to respond, opening her mouth and closing it.

Henry was not nearly so stymied. He started clapping slowly, emphatically. 'Excellent. Well done. Good speech,' he said.

It took Ada a few moments to realize that he was being sarcastic. His tone didn't match the words at all. Yet more proof that Henry wasn't anyone she could trust. He was a liar. Maybe he didn't lie about the same things as Sanchez. Maybe he lied for good reasons. But still, the difference was a small one. And people could escalate their lying at any time. How could you know if they'd decide that another lie was a good reason, and another and another?

'Are you planning to use that in court? Or just on donors after you tell them that their children might also be murdered and then the murder covered up – if they aren't good enough for you and your standards here? Pass the tests and bring our average up, or you'll be dead in the morning. Guaranteed!' Henry said with his own style of acting.

'It was self-defense,' Sanchez said, changing her tone suddenly. She was tearful and sank back into her chair. She took off her jacket and unbuttoned her shirt sleeves slowly, then rolled them back. 'You see what she did to me?' On her arms were numerous marks of fingernails cutting into flesh, pinching and causing livid bruises, now several days old and turning the spectacular colors of green and blue and black as the blood settled.

'Nice try,' Henry said. 'You have no evidence that those marks were caused by Ella. You could just as easily have made them yourself, after you staged her body for those photographs. They could be fake, for all I know, something you put on with your own makeup this morning, just in case.'

She leaned over the desk and held her hands close to Henry's face. 'Touch them. You'll see they're real. They won't smear away.'

Henry didn't touch her.

She turned to Ada. 'Touch them!' she said again.

And for some reason, Ada did as she was told. She touched the bruises. Sanchez winced. And then slumped back into her chair.

'She could have killed me,' she said.

'A ten-year-old girl could have killed you? I doubt it very much. She hurt you, possibly. Too bad you didn't let Nurse Johnston see the marks on you when you called her to look at the body. How many hours did you wait? That doesn't look like the behavior of an innocent woman. It looks like someone who had time to make herself look however she thought would be best for her own defense,' Henry said.

'I was defending my son!' Sanchez shouted, energetic again. 'It was his life or Ella's. No mother should be placed in a situation like that, where she has to choose between her child and another child. But I did what I had to do. I don't think any jury in the country will convict me. Do you want to have another splashy case that doesn't even go to trial because the prosecutor decides not to move forward with the evidence you've collected so badly?'

Henry flinched, but Ada didn't understand. 'I see you've done your research on my recent past,' he said.

And Ada hadn't, she realized. It had never occurred to her to check up on Henry. Was this why he'd been so eager to investigate this case with her? Had it always been about redeeming himself? Nothing to do with helping vindicate her?

She should have known it was selfish. Everyone was selfish, in the end. Especially the people who claimed they weren't selfish.

Henry said, 'I am confident that no prosecutor would turn down this case. And that not a single person on a jury that heard the facts of this case would fail to convict you. You can pretend this was for your son, but he wasn't asking for your help. And even if he did ask, you were an adult, a trained educator and autism specialist, and after the girl was dead, you cleaned the room, put makeup on her, and took photographs to post online. That is not what an innocent woman does. That is what a guilty woman with a premeditated plan does to protect her reputation and her power.'

Ada felt a wave of cold run through her. Henry was right. It was all premeditated. Sanchez had left her son alone with Ella on purpose. Because she'd wanted to have this as a potential way to escape justice. She'd hoped to avoid an investigation in the first place, despite posting the photos for attention, but this was her backup plan.

'You don't know what happened. You don't know how unruly she was, like an animal. She was unstoppable. Once she'd started thrashing at me, I did the only thing I could do.' Sanchez waved at her computer. 'And her history of violence is well documented.'

'If only you'd told the truth in the first place,' Henry said. He sounded sad, but Ada didn't think he really was.

She was tired of this back and forth, the way that neurotypical people did it. As if it was all about who won this conversation and wasn't about the reality that this woman here, the mother of two autistic sons, and the director of an entire school for autism, had murdered an autistic child she couldn't control to her satisfaction.

'You hated her. That's all. This is a hate crime. You targeted a vulnerable autistic girl. You found a place where she had no one else to help her. And you put your hands around her neck and strangled her so she couldn't breathe. You kept doing it after she fell unconscious and was limp and unresponsive. You took photos of her so that the whole world would look at her and think her a monster because of her autism. You did it all out of hate. And you claim that you love your autistic sons?'

Ada could hear how her voice sounded. She'd been told many times that she sounded autistic, that her intonation was wrong, that she didn't do pauses right, that she breathed in the wrong places and spoke too fast, and that she didn't put emotion into her words. The emotion was in her heart, though. No one could deny that.

'Of course I love my sons. They are everything to me!' Sanchez said.

'No. Don't pretend that. Your husband left them, but you don't love them any more than he did.' Neurotypical people used the word 'love' to mean things it shouldn't mean. Dependence. Usefulness. Esteem. Admiration. Fawning. Manipulation.

'They are my life,' Sanchez insisted.

'Yes, they are your life. You need them to prop up in front of you so that you look good. You look like the long-suffering autistic mom who gives everything for her kids. And if one autistic child had to die, it wasn't going to be your son. Because you needed him to prop up your entire enterprise,' Ada said. She wasn't sure she'd ever felt like this before. She felt hot, but also light, as if she were floating above the ground, as if she didn't have a body at all anymore, but was pure energy.

'How dare you say that to me! After everything I've given up?'

'Given up? If you loved your sons, you would never say that. You wouldn't think of them as a burden, as people who are so, so difficult for you. Poor you, such a hard life you have because your children are different.'

'They are difficult. They are different. You have no idea what it's like. You don't have children, and like all autistic people, you can't see the world in any way other than your own,' Sanchez said. Her words were very precise.

'Gavin is a wonderful person. Not a difficult one. A beautiful person who deserves a mother, two parents actually, who see him as a full person in his own right, with his own desires and ambition, his own future where he becomes someone completely separate from you. I've never met Taylor, but he deserves that, too. Not for the two of them to be eternally dependent on you so that you can continue to use the label of autism mom to earn money and fame,' Ada continued. The words flowed out of her. She wasn't conscious of forming them at all. It felt like her mind was speaking aloud, not her tongue and lips and vocal cords.

'You have no idea what you're talking about. You don't know how many weekends I've spent with my sons, doing homework with them, trying to get them up to grade level, trying to make sure that they will have some kind of quality of life. You don't know what it's like to think about my retirement and to know that it will never be just me, that I have to plan for them living with me, too, and that I have to leave enough for their long-term care when I'm gone. When they will have to be cared for by people who don't love them like I do.' Sanchez's hands were shaking.

Henry looked at Ada silently.

She realized that he was waiting to see if she was done. She was not done yet. 'I hope that you go to prison and that your sons get a chance to be cared for by people who care about them as individuals, not as appendages. And I hope that someday they come to see you and tell you exactly what they think of you murdering another autistic kid while claiming that you did it for them. For this school. For all autistic children.'

TWENTY-SEVEN

This was the last straw for Sanchez. She scrambled over the top of her desk far more quickly and agilely than Ada had expected, or Henry had anticipated. In that moment, she had her hands around Ada's throat. Ada's body was flung back on the floor, the chair she'd been sitting on clunking to the side.

Ada was so stunned that she didn't fight back at all, not at first. She just lay there, in pain, feeling helpless to stop her own death. The sense of energy she'd felt before was gone now, replaced by the fiery sensation of agony in her throat. She couldn't breathe and she was gagging and fighting for air.

'Ada! Fight her! Kick her!' Henry shouted.

Ada could see his face just behind the reddened features of Sanchez, who was holding her breath such that her whole face seemed distorted and over-sized, like some cartoon version of an evil villain in a superhero cartoon. Henry had his hands around Sanchez's throat and he was trying to pull her off, but Ada was thinking about the physics of the angle he had her at, and it wasn't optimal. Sanchez's weight on top of her body, on the other hand, was far better placed to resist.

Sanchez was going to win. She was going to murder again.

One part of Ada's strange, slowed-down and time-altered brain thought that this was just what she should have been trying to do. This proved in real time that Sanchez was capable of murder. Henry could be a witness at the trial, state that he'd seen her kill Ada, too. And even if they couldn't prove that she'd killed Ella, Ada's own murder would be an easy case to prosecute.

Yes, Ada would be dead, but that didn't seem to matter much. As the world appeared to grow dark in her vision, shrinking to the space of Henry's head shouting something at her that she couldn't hear and certainly couldn't understand, she thought that at least she'd done something that mattered. It wasn't what she'd always wanted to do, contact aliens, but it was more than most people did. It was more than her parents might have ever believed she could do. It was certainly more than Rex would have thought she could do.

Somehow she managed to make her legs move, even though she couldn't see anything at all anymore. She knew where Sanchez's body was because it was on top of her. One of her legs was cooler than the other. That one wasn't trapped by Sanchez's warmth. Ada moved it swiftly to kick at Sanchez's stomach.

A moment of breath, sweet and clean and fresh.

Then pain and gagging again.

Henry's face visible, his lips moving.

He wasn't the worst neurotypical person she'd ever known. He was a liar, yes, but he did try to lie for good reasons.

Hen wanted her to stay alive.

Hen needed her. Without her, he'd never have found the murderer in this case. He'd never even have investigated it. At least, not until Sanchez killed again. And she would have killed again. That was . . .

Ada kicked a second time.

No air that time.

Her legs felt numb. Her whole body felt heavy, sleepy. She usually liked it when her body felt like that. She didn't like to be trapped inside a body. That was another reason she'd always wanted to contact aliens. Surely aliens that advanced would have to know how to translate a mind into something that wasn't so . . . squishy and messy and wet and warm and fragile.

Ada kicked one last time.

She heard a noise. It sounded like the squeak of a mouse.

She hated mice. She was terrified of mice. If she hadn't been so limp, she would have jumped up on Sanchez's desk and shrieked about the mouse. It was very unscientific, and she would have been very embarrassed for Henry to see her like that.

It was her. She was the mouse.

'Ada, are you all right?'

She could hear Henry's voice now, though his face was fuzzy above hers. He was holding Sanchez's arms behind her back and cuffed her. Her face was bleeding from a cut below her left eye. Ada wondered if her leg had done that or if Henry had done it.

She found out later, from Henry, that it was all her. Her feet, still in the sensible, thick shoes that she always wore.

'Thank God you weren't wearing some ballet slippers or something,' he said.

But before then, he read Sanchez her rights.

And Ada sat on the floor, realizing she wasn't going to die after all. Which meant she still had a chance to contact those aliens. There had to be aliens out there. There were too many stars, too many planets, too many possibilities. As long as she was alive, there was still hope.

TWENTY-EIGHT

Before they left NAVITEK, Ada insisted that she wanted to go see Gavin one last time.

Sanchez was more subdued by then. She had a dark expression, but Ada didn't try to parse what it meant. She didn't have to waste any more time on figuring out that face. She'd done it already. She was the one who had understood what all the pieces in the puzzle meant. She had done it without all the tools that neurotypical people said were so important. She had her own tools.

'I can take her to the car and wait for you there,' Henry offered.

'No. I want Sanchez to be there,' Ada said. She wasn't sure why she wanted it, but she did. Maybe something about proving her value to her parents, even if they'd never know.

Henry didn't argue with her. He got Sanchez to her feet and maneuvered her from behind. She didn't resist him anymore. The energy had gone out of her.

They walked down to the room with the window in the door that Gavin had been in when they met with him the day before yesterday, but it was empty. Ada checked her watch. It was about three p.m., and she wasn't sure if that meant school was out for the day or not.

'He's in his reading class,' Sanchez provided. 'He'll be here soon.'

That was when Ada realized that Sanchez had her own reasons for wanting this meeting. Sanchez wanted to see him again, maybe for the last time before she went to prison for murder.

So they waited there, in silence.

When Gavin finally arrived with Tamsin, he saw his mother and said, 'Mama,' out loud, and put his hands out as if for a hug.

Sanchez said, 'No touching now.'

That was enough for Gavin to stop moving forward and drop his arms. He was wearing a skirt today, with purple bows and lace. On his feet, he wore dark red sneakers. His hair was still long, and it had been pulled back into a ponytail that wisps had fallen out of, so that he looked a bit like a scarecrow, wearing clothes that belonged to someone else.

Ada wondered if Gavin was trying to wear clothes like the ones Ella wore when she was still alive. It was a common autistic trait to mimic others, down to specific clothes. Ella's parents had packed up all her things, and Ada had only gotten a glimpse, but she thought Ella had worn very feminine clothes, mostly dresses.

'Hello?' Tamsin said, looking from Sanchez to Henry and then Ada, then back to Sanchez.

'It's all right. They just have some follow-up questions,' Sanchez said calmly.

'Do you need anything, Director?' Tamsin asked.

'No, no. Go on and do your lesson,' Sanchez said.

There was something in her body language that was off, Ada guessed, though she couldn't quite see what it was. Maybe it was just the fact that she wasn't using her hands and they weren't at her sides, as they normally would be. Or maybe it was something about the way Henry was standing. He seemed to Ada to be more alert than he usually was, his eyes darting this way and that more often than when he wasn't trying to keep a criminal from escaping.

'These are friends, Gavin. Remember, friends?' Tamsin said.

'Friends,' Gavin repeated.

Ada thought that his language was already getting better. But who knew if that would continue if his mother was removed? And his brother, as well. Whatever placement they found for the two autistic boys, it was unlikely that they would be together. One autistic child was hard enough to find a placement for, let alone two.

Ada remembered her mother telling her once that her parents had sat down together after her diagnosis and considered whether she might be better off living with another family. That was what she had called it. 'Someone who wouldn't be so frustrated with your strange ways.'

'Another family?' Ada had said, her whole body tensing. She felt very close to vomiting, though that was the bodily response she most hated in herself. She hated how it felt when the acidic liquid came back up her throat, hated even more the look of it once it was out. A reminder of how disgusting her body was, how parts of it were not part of her at all.

'But they told us that it's impossible to find placement for a child like you, an autistic child, so quickly. It could be years, in fact. They said they'd keep us on the list, but for now, you have to stay here.'

She hadn't said 'stay at home.'

It was years before Ada found out that her parents had taken her off that list. During all that time, she had been trying so hard to make sure that she did well enough that they didn't send her away. She had to prove to them she was worth keeping as their daughter.

Maybe she did and maybe she didn't. Looking back now, Ada thought that her parents might have simply been more embarrassed at being thought the kinds of parents who gave their child up to the state to be raised than they were embarrassed about what Ada did at school.

'Let's leave Ada and Gavin alone now,' Henry said, putting a visible hand on Sanchez's back.

Sanchez glanced at Gavin, and then added, 'Mama loves Gavin.'

Gavin made the sign language symbol for 'I love you,' and then waited for Sanchez to sign it back to him, which she obviously could not do because of the handcuffs.

'Go on,' Sanchez said again, and used her head to motion toward the door.

Gavin went in with Tamsin, and Ada followed.

'Ella,' Gavin said, his hands flapping as he sat down on the floor, amidst several boxed containers of the toys Ada had seen him playing with before.

Tamsin didn't open any of the toys. 'Do you plan to stay long?' she asked.

'No. I just wanted to ask Gavin about Ella again.'

'Ella,' Gavin repeated. 'Ella, Ella, Ella, Ella, Ella.'

Tamsin put a hand on his shoulder and pinched it. Ada didn't think it was hard, but it was apparently an ingrained response because Gavin stopped saying the name over and over again.

'I wanted Gavin to know that we found who killed Ella,' Ada said. She watched Gavin very closely. An autistic child didn't have the same expression that a neurotypical child did, but she thought she could read him a little better for all that his face was more muted.

'Ella,' Gavin said again, and this time instead of repeating the name, he pulled at his shirt sleeves.

'Did Ella hurt you?' Ada asked, bracing herself to see the marks that Sanchez had told her about. 'Before, when she was still alive?'

'Who told you that?' Tamsin asked, glancing toward the door.

'You don't have to hide it anymore. Ella is dead now,' Ada said. 'But if Gavin doesn't mind, I'd like to see his arms.'

Gavin had apparently been raised to obey, because as soon as Ada asked, he began to pull his sleeves up more.

Ada got a good glimpse then of the healing scars on his body. There were dozens and dozens of marks, some red, some black, some purple. Some had crusted over with scabs, but others hadn't bled. There were just so many of them, and to see them all like that was very painful to Ada. She'd dealt with animal dissection in high school just fine, because they were animals and they were already dead. But Gavin was still alive, and he winced as he pulled his sleeves back down.

'The nurse saw him and he's getting treatment,' Tamsin put in. 'He'll be fine.'

'Did you know about Ella's hurting him?' Ada asked directly.

'I–I'd seen some signs of her treatment, but not this bad, no.'

'Did you ever see similar scars on Ella herself?' Ada still wondered if the autistic girl had been abused at home, but it seemed useless to try to prove that now. It wouldn't make things better for Sanchez, and Ada didn't want that, anyway.

'No.'

Ada turned back to Gavin. 'You liked Ella, didn't you? She was your friend.'

'Friend,' Gavin repeated, smiling one of those odd smiles that to Ada didn't look real somehow. It seemed too happy.

'Gavin, did your mother make you play with Ella? Did you wish you didn't have to play with her?' Ada asked. As soon as she said it, she knew that this wasn't something Gavin was going to be able to answer.

Gavin bent down to pick up one of the figures he'd used to

communicate with Ada before. 'Ella,' he said, holding one. Then, 'Gavin,' he said, holding the other. He had them dancing in his hands, and Ella bumped into Gavin a lot. 'Friends,' he said.

Ada wanted more than that. She wanted Sanchez, watching from the window, to see what she had done to her son. But that wasn't happening here.

'What about your brother Taylor?' Ada asked. 'Is he your friend?'

Gavin dropped the Ella figure and picked up another one. 'Taylor,' he said. 'Gavin,' he said, naming the other one. He had the two figures dancing, but they didn't touch each other.

'Brothers,' he said.

'Brothers aren't the same as friends, are they?' Ada said. She'd never had a sibling. She would never know what that was like.

'Taylor needs Gavin. Gavin needs Taylor,' Gavin said. It was the closest to full speech he'd gotten since Ada had known him.

'That's right,' Ada said.

'Are you done now?' Tamsin asked.

Ada wasn't finished. She wanted to stay. She wanted to watch Tamsin and Gavin interact. She wanted to stay at this school for days yet, to see what an autistic childhood could be like in the best of circumstances.

But then again, Ella was dead, so there was that.

TWENTY-NINE

Ada stood up. 'Yes, I'm done. Thank you.' She took a few steps away before she was caught from behind by a hug from Gavin.

'Love,' Gavin said.

Ada didn't know if the hug was meant for her or for Sanchez, but she hugged him back. She felt tears prick at her eyes and couldn't remember the last time she'd cried. Even when Rex had left her, even when she realized how much he'd stolen from her. She'd shaken all over, she'd been unable to sleep, but the tears had never come.

She got to the door, opened it, and then leaned against it, breathing in and out.

'Gavin is a very loving child,' Sanchez said. 'He is good for his brother.'

'This doesn't change our minds. We're not going to walk away from this and just let you go,' Henry said.

'It's not just the school you're going to destroy. That little boy will never be the same again. Look at his innocent face. Think about his brother and how they may never see each other for the rest of their lives. Can you live with that?' Sanchez asked.

Ada felt sick again at how cold-bloodedly Sanchez was using her son's pain to try to escape justice for herself.

'Do you know how many criminals try to make it the fault of the people in law enforcement that there are consequences of their actions?' Henry asked.

'Ah, but those law enforcement officers are officially on duty. You aren't officially on duty, are you, Henry Bloodstone?' Sanchez asked.

'What?' Ada said, her attention jerking back to Sanchez and Henry, away from the window where Gavin sat playing with Tamsin.

'Henry isn't on duty. He's not here in any official capacity. I contacted the FBI about him when he first asked to come interview my staff about Ella's death,' Sanchez said.

Ada's hearing felt as if it had gotten too loud. The sound of Sanchez's voice hurt her, and she winced at every word as if they were blows.

'If you knew that, then why did you let us interview everyone?' Henry asked.

Sanchez said nothing, though her face twisted.

'It's because you were so sure that we wouldn't find anything. You were so arrogant that you thought you would walk away from this. Well, too bad for you,' Henry said.

'I talked to the FBI about your history. Your last case went badly, didn't it? After that, they decided that you needed more time off to grieve your wife's death. You were demoted to desk duty. Until you got information about Ella Kimball's death, and you brought it to your supervisor, and he told you that it wasn't an FBI matter. So you asked for leave for two weeks, and you didn't say where you were going or what your plans were.'

'Henry?' Ada asked. She tried to find his eyes, but she couldn't focus on them.

'I have all the evidence I need for when I take you back. My supervisor will believe me now. They'll be happy to have such an easy conviction.'

'But you don't have to do it. You could go back in a week, and no one would ever know,' Sanchez said.

Ada wished more than ever that she could read Henry's expression. Was he actually considering betraying all these children – and her – because he hadn't gotten permission for this? And why had he lied to her in the first place? She tried to think back to what he had said. Had he told her that the investigation was authorized? That he was working as an active FBI agent? She couldn't remember his exact words anymore, but he surely knew that he had given her the impression that this was an official FBI murder case and that he was in charge of it.

'Why would I do that?' Henry asked.

No, no, no, Ada's brain screamed. This wasn't possible. After all the work she'd done, Henry couldn't let this go.

'Because you have no idea what will happen if you take me in. They might discipline you and throw you out of the FBI entirely. They certainly won't let you continue on this case.

Someone else will be put in charge, and you'll be back on desk duty for who knows how long,' Sanchez insisted.

Ada hated her now. She wished she'd done a better job when they were grappling physically. She'd had a chance then to make sure she gave as good as she got. That was what one of her counselors in high school had suggested years ago, though she'd only meant it about verbal taunts from other students. She'd even tried to coach Ada about specific things she might try to say if another student said this or that.

'You're the ugly one.'

'I don't smell bad, just normal.'

'I like my clothes. They're comfortable.'

'Well, I care about other people, not just about myself.'

'I might be awkward, but you're mean.'

She'd tried a couple of them, but they'd never made any difference. They just made people laugh at her more.

She'd never gotten into a physical fight with anyone until Sanchez, but she thought she finally understood the appeal of it. It had made her feel alive in a way she hadn't before. Her heart pumping, her throat choking, her whole body filled with cortisol.

'I'm not particularly afraid of returning to a desk job. If I leave you here, then that's what will happen anyway. Bringing you in is a gamble, but it's worth the risk to me.'

'Is it? Remember, I'm a powerful person. I have connections in government. Our donors are people who could make life difficult for you if you ever tried to rise higher than a mere agent in the bureau. Don't you think about the future?'

Henry didn't glance at Ada once during all of this. He kept his attention focused completely on Sanchez. 'You think that your connections are going to want to offer favors once they find out the truth about Ella's murder?'

Sanchez flushed. Her hands shook until she held them tightly against her backside.

Ada recognized how it felt to be afraid. That was how her body reacted, too.

'No, they probably won't. And all of the power I might wield on your behalf will be destroyed. It doesn't have to be that way, though.' Her voice was mostly steady, but Ada wondered how hard she might be working to keep it like that.

If she were in handcuffs, Ada thought that she would be having a meltdown. She'd flop on to the ground and try to roll herself into a ball, try to protect her brain from any more sensory input. But Sanchez wasn't autistic. She was a neurotypical person who was still able to use the power of persuasion to try to get out of a murder charge.

'You could be my ally – is that what you're saying? If I let you off on this charge, then you'll help me. Tit for tat?'

'Well, you don't have to put it as crudely as that. You must know about making friends in high places and how important that is for your career. You're not autistic.' She laughed a little at this. 'You have a sense of self-preservation. Maybe even an idea of compromise. You have to have seen a bit of how the sausage is made inside of the FBI. It can't be that different from the rest of the government.'

'So you're offering me help in the future if I help you now?' Henry said.

Sanchez bit her lower lip. 'I can offer more than that if you want,' she said quietly.

'And what's that?' Henry asked.

Ada wanted to leave. She felt dirty even hearing this conversation. She thought about how many television shows and movies and books she'd had to stop enjoying because the people in them were disgustingly amoral. They only cared about themselves in the end, even if they'd initially been presented as heroes. Neurotypical people were never heroes. They couldn't be, constitutionally. It was an impairment.

And they thought that autistic people were the ones who were 'deficient' in some way. That was just to disguise how morally bankrupt they were. They covered it all with other words. 'Compromise' and 'nuance' and 'realism.' But it was the same thing. It was selfishness.

'I have money. A lot of it. I could give you a half million dollars,' Sanchez offered.

She didn't sound like she was lying, but Ada didn't trust herself to tell the difference there.

'Why should I believe you have anything like that amount of money?'

'You think I've been running this school the last several years and only paying myself the salary that's listed on the books?' she asked. 'I'm not a fool.'

'So Ella's parents weren't your only source of income?'

'Of course not. That would be stupid, wouldn't it?'

'And if you walked away from this, the school would keep on running anyway?' Henry asked.

'It would if I helped it along with the funds I've hidden away.'

Henry hesitated. He got out the key to the handcuffs. Then, to Ada's astonishment, he used it and released Sanchez.

She sagged forward and just barely managed not to hit the ground. Then she pulled her arms forward and started rubbing them together. She made a sound of distress at the pain.

It was all Ada could do not to feel sorry for her.

'I can give you a million dollars, then. But no more than that,' Sanchez said.

Henry handed Sanchez her phone. 'Show me,' he said. 'Send it to me right now.'

She blustered a bit. 'I don't know if I have it all in cash. It might take a few days.'

'You don't have a few days,' Henry said. He looked at his watch. 'You have six minutes.'

Sanchez's hands worked clumsily on her phone, as she tried to alternately rub blood flow back into them and type. 'There,' she said after only a few minutes had passed. 'It's right there. Just give me your account information and you'll have it.'

That was when Henry finally looked at Ada. She thought his expression was kind, and a little sad, but if it was supposed to mean something more than that, she didn't get it.

'Thank you very much,' he said, and snatched the phone away from her. He held it above his head as he threw the key to the handcuffs to Ada.

She caught it and then lunged for the handcuffs that he'd let fall to the floor.

Sanchez was a little slow, and that gave Ada the extra three seconds she needed to put one handcuff around Sanchez's left wrist and then yank it back with full force until Sanchez let out a cry of pain and fell to her knees.

After that, Henry handed Ada the phone. 'Can you memorize all that information?' he asked, nodding at the screen, as he made sure that the other handcuff was put around Sanchez's other wrist and then locked in place.

Ada heard the snicking sound with a sense of relief. But mostly she used her brain to memorize numbers. She'd always been very, very good at that. Maybe that was the only real reason Henry had wanted her here today, for any of this. Just for this one last moment.

'How did you know that I had money?'

'I've arrested people for murder before. They usually have other reasons. And usually those reasons are money,' Henry said to Sanchez, as he helped her to her feet.

She was shaking worse than ever now and had to lean on him physically to stay upright. 'But you did come here without permission,' she said. 'You could still be in trouble when you go back.'

'I took a chance,' Henry said, answering Sanchez but looking still at Ada with some expression that made her want to turn around and see what it was that was behind her that he was looking at so intently. 'I bet on someone I've always known tells the truth, no matter what. I still think that was a good bet.'

THIRTY

After that, Henry and Ada walked out to the car. Sanchez got into the back, and Henry cuffed her to a barrier Ada hadn't noticed before.

'So that she can't try to get at us,' he explained.

'You lied to me,' Ada said, almost a whisper, after Henry had closed the door behind her and climbed into the driver's side himself.

'I'm sorry. I kept thinking I would tell you the truth, and then it just got away from me. I know how much you hate lies, even ones for a good reason. And I'd already done it. I just . . . I just wanted to spend a little more time with you. Every day, I kept thinking that.'

'Why?' Ada asked, bewildered.

Sanchez barked laughter. 'You really don't know, do you?' she asked. 'You poor oblivious autistic woman.'

'Why?' Ada asked again.

'Because I think you're about the most amazing person I've ever met, and I couldn't miss the opportunity to see you again, to help you. And to just watch you do your amazing thing,' Henry said.

Ada thought about this for several minutes. By the time she spoke to Henry again, he had already driven out past the school, down the road, and on to the county highway. They had arrived at a gas station, and he'd stopped there to fill the car up with gas.

'You want anything to drink?' he asked Ada.

'No, thank you,' she said automatically. She was still thinking.

'I'd like a latte,' Sanchez said.

Henry didn't respond to this, but to Ada's surprise, he did come back with a latte for Sanchez and one for himself.

'This gas station has pretty good lattes,' Sanchez said, as she sipped it. The fight seemed to have gone out of her, but Ada didn't trust someone like Sanchez. She was good at pretending, so she figured she and Henry had to be ready for another attack.

'I can't tell when you're lying to me and when you're telling me the truth,' Ada said at last, when they were back on the road.

'What?' Henry said.

'When you say nice things to me, I can't tell if it's a lie or the truth,' Ada tried to explain.

'Why don't you give me the benefit of the doubt and accept that I'm telling you the truth? What harm is there in that?' Henry asked.

Ada had to try not to react angrily. But it seemed a stupid question. 'Do you not have any idea how many people have lied to me? In school, to try to get me to do their assignments for them? In business, to try to guilt me into giving them money. My ex-husband. And even you. You tell me what you want me to know, not what is true. So how can I ever trust you?'

Sanchez made a noise behind them, but Ada tried hard to ignore it.

'Do you really not believe that anyone could think you're amazing?' Henry asked.

'Of course not. Why would anyone think I'm amazing? I'm autistic,' Ada said. 'The first time they told me what I was, I knew it was a bad thing, and no one has ever made me believe any differently. This whole . . .' She waved back toward the school. 'It hasn't changed my mind in the least. Autistic children are always lied to. For their own good. No one trusts them enough to tell them the truth. Even though autistic children are the only people you can always trust to understand the truth.'

This time, Sanchez's snorted response was louder. 'Autistic children want to know the truth? What ridiculousness. They can't handle the truth. They least of all. Some of them don't even know their diagnosis. Their parents haven't told them yet. And we have to find some way to explain why they're at a special school when their parents insist we still not tell them that they're autistic.'

Ada didn't say anything else for the rest of the drive, and Henry didn't, either. It was several hours to her apartment complex.

When Henry pulled into a parking spot, she opened the door immediately. He hopped out with her, and she thought he was going to leave Sanchez alone in the car, which she was going to tell him was a very bad idea, handcuffed or not.

But he thought better of it and closed the door behind him, then locked it with his key fob. 'I want to talk to you about all this later, if that's all right? When she isn't here to interrupt us. And when the case is all finished.'

'When will you find out if you're still in the FBI?' Ada asked.

Henry looked as if he'd swallowed something too big to go down his throat. 'I . . . in a few days, probably.'

'Call me then,' she said, and walked away from him and back into her own home.

THIRTY-ONE

It was strange, walking into her apartment after a few days away. It felt strange, but also familiar. How was that possible?
    She sat on her couch and stared at the colors of the walls. Did she still like them? She wasn't sure.

She went to the fridge, only to find that the few things in it had gone rotten, probably even before she left with Henry. She got out some crackers and a box of juice. Whenever she bought those juices, the shopper who delivered them to her house would usually leave a message about hoping that her kids enjoyed their snacks. A lot of the food Ada ate was considered child food. She didn't care about that.

After her snack, she cleaned out the fridge and put everything out in the big trash container in the parking area.

Then she went straight to bed. She was exhausted and didn't think to check the time.

She woke to the sound of her phone ringing. It wasn't a number she recognized, so she sent it to voicemail. She tried to go back to sleep and failed.

Then her phone rang again. Another unknown caller, also sent to voicemail.

When she got six more calls in a row, she turned off her phone and looked at the voicemail message. The transcripts told her that they were all from news outlets, trying to get her opinion on the story of Director Sanchez of the NAVITEK school for autistic children and the murder charges that had been brought against her by the FBI. She was listed as a consultant on the case, it seemed.

After looking through several news articles online, she watched a short clip with Director Sanchez, who insisted that she was not guilty and that she was the subject of a 'deranged autistic woman's revenge fantasy.'

A text popped up on her phone a few minutes later, from an old high school acquaintance she hadn't talked to forever.

Are you OK? Have you seen the news?

Ada had no interest in texting the woman, so she ignored that. She tried to ignore her phone as much as possible, but she kept scrolling the news feeds for more information.

Later that afternoon, there was a clip with Henry, who was wearing an FBI badge, which seemed to indicate that he hadn't been fired. 'When all the evidence has been presented in court, the director's guilt will be clear. She is a woman who had care of dozens of the most vulnerable children in this country, and almost total control over them. The fact that she killed one of them and then covered it up must be disturbing to every parent out there, whether they have an autistic child or not. The autistic community deserves better treatment than this, and the FBI is going to make sure they have justice.'

Henry was red-faced, and Ada thought that he was spitting as he spoke. She was glad she wasn't standing in front of him like the reporter who was recording him.

She thought he was telling the truth, but how could she ever be sure with him again? He could turn it off and on, his telling the truth. It was so easy for him, and so difficult for her.

When her grocery delivery came just before her usual dinner time, she opened the door without any particular care. She didn't realize there were a dozen or so news people standing outside her door, waiting for her. It hadn't occurred to her to check before she went out. They got images of her in her pajamas, which she had put on only when she woke up because she'd been too tired to put them on the night before. Her hair was standing up in bits and pieces because she hadn't combed it.

She stared at the images on the internet where she saw them just a few minutes later. The news people were shouting questions at her, but she thought she looked a bit like a frightened, feral dog, as she grabbed at her bags of groceries and scurried back inside.

The next day, there was a new story about her. 'New information about the autism expert who was called in by the FBI to consult on the murder investigation at the NAVITEK school for autism. Her name is Ada, and she is best known for her work in inventing new products in the cosmetic industry, including a line of environmentally friendly products under the brand name "Pink

Cosmos" that was enormously popular, though other products by her company Good Cosmetics have not been as popular. Her business and personal partner, Rex Friendly, now ex-husband, has this to say about her.'

And then Ada had to look at Rex talking about her to the whole world. She'd somehow imagined she'd never have to see him again, and that he would never have reason to criticize her. But she'd been wrong.

'Ada is definitely autistic. Whether she's an expert on autism is another question.' His head was tilted to the side and his eyebrow quirked up. She'd learned what that expression meant: high skepticism, usually reserved for claims about contacting aliens.

'She has frequent meltdowns in public, though she is mostly a shut-in these days, rarely leaving her apartment if she can avoid it. She's difficult to speak to and incredibly rigid in her thinking. There is only a right and a wrong, and she is always the one who is right.'

'Can you tell us about your brief relationship with her and about the cosmetics business you formed together?' the reporter, who was off-screen, asked.

Founded together? Who had told the reporter that?

Rex said, 'Well, I initially felt sorry for her. I suppose that began a habit of making excuses for her odd behavior. I also thought that her autism made her a kind of savant. She has an active imagination, and she had a thousand different ideas for Good Cosmetics. Her initial ideas were good, but she couldn't sustain them.

'Of course, as an autistic woman, she can't really understand the social element of fashion, and her sense of beauty is, at best, diminished. But once she removed herself from the company, our business has increased exponentially. See our new product line now on our website.' Rex flashed a smile at the camera, and Ada's stomach dropped.

That was why he'd sent her the link to Ella's picture. He wanted to use all of this as free publicity for the company. He wanted to sell the new line of cosmetics he and Tomi had developed.

The screen flashed several of the new sets of colors that Ada hated. Rex cleverly avoided mentioning how the original Pink Cosmos line was connected to the murder. That wouldn't be good publicity, of course. So he lied. Or failed to tell the full truth, as he would put it – just another kind of neurotypical lie.

'You must understand that once she signed the company and all its products over to me, after our divorce was finalized, she told me that her main goal now was to contact aliens that she believes are just days or weeks away from Earth. She actually believes that they can come to save humanity, if only she can speak to them.' He rolled his eyes.

Ada's hands clenched. She knew she should turn this off, but she couldn't.

The reporter said, 'There are photos of Ada in high school that indicate that she was involved in some kind of romantic relationship with the lead FBI investigator on this case, Henry Bloodstone. Do you know anything about that?'

Ada saw a blurry image probably from the yearbook she had never looked through, of her and Henry together in front of the bus. That wasn't a date, she wanted to explain. It was a school competition. They hadn't dated. Not ever. She would never have dated Henry.

She did finally turn off her computer and turned on her heavy metal music from Kreator. It was loud enough to keep out the sound of the frequent doorbell rings.

The good thing about having private meltdowns in her own apartment was that she didn't have to go anywhere. And she already had all she needed to deal with them. The meds were in her cabinet in the bathroom, and no one had to help her get off the floor. She'd made sure that the carpet was double-padded here when she moved in. Just in case.

THIRTY-TWO

It was a week later when her phone buzzed at her, and she looked at it in confusion. Hadn't she turned that all off?

Whoever this was, her phone listed the call as 'Emergency,' and so Ada answered it.

'Hello?'

A tired and familiar voice responded. 'Ada, it's Henry. Can you come let me in?'

'You're here?' Ada asked, standing up so fast she almost vomited. She'd been lying down for forty hours straight.

It occurred to her on the way to the door that she hadn't showered in several days – she couldn't remember exactly when her last shower was. She must stink. Her hair would look terrible. These would all be problems if she cared what Henry thought of her or if she were a neurotypical woman who wanted his romantic interest.

There were several camera flashes as soon as Ada opened the door. Henry bustled in quickly and then locked the door behind him.

'Sorry about all that,' he said, waving behind him.

'I'm not interested in you romantically,' Ada said, staring at him directly in a way she rarely did. It was important that he understood this was not a joke.

'Yes, Ada, I know that. You've made it exceedingly clear.'

'I never felt romantically toward you before, and this case was not about us. It was about the school and about the director. About the murder.'

'Yes, Ada, I understand all that.' Henry looked like he'd lost weight. His skin looked as if he hadn't put any good lotion on it for quite some time. His hair had grown longer and was falling over his left ear in a childlike way.

Not that she cared about how he looked. That wasn't what made for a viable relationship. She'd made a mistake about physical attraction meaning something it didn't once before, with Rex. She wouldn't make that mistake again.

'Then why are you here?' Ada asked.

'I . . . thought you might like to know what was going on with the case. Now that things have settled down and we're moving toward trial.'

'Oh. Yes, thank you.' She gestured to her couch. 'Do you want to sit down?'

Henry hesitated a moment, but eventually sat. When she sat down on the other end, he moved to the very edge of the couch, just like she did, her arm over the covered wood, holding her position tightly.

'Director Sanchez is being charged with first-degree murder. With additional hate crime stipulations added. What she did was specific to an autistic child, as you know.'

'Good,' Ada said. 'Does that mean she'll be in prison for the rest of her life?'

Henry tugged his hair behind his left ear. 'I don't know if I can promise that, but it will be a long time.'

'What about Gavin? And Taylor?' Ada asked.

'We've found them a good foster home, together. Their father was contacted, but he wasn't interested in taking custody.'

'I see.' Some people were like that. In the end, Ada couldn't really think worse of him than of their mother, who had used them while she pretended to protect and love them. Better for someone to walk away if they didn't truly love you.

'Gavin has asked about you, apparently. The foster parents would welcome you if you want to go visit him at any time. Just let me know and I can arrange it. It's about an hour's drive. I can take you there or you can go with another FBI agent. Their location has to be kept secret in the circumstances, you understand.'

Ada nodded. She understood. She wasn't sure she was ready to make a decision about going to see Gavin. She was grateful that Henry had offered the possibility without pressuring her.

'The prosecution would like to interview you at some point before the trial to decide if they want to add you to the witness list,' Henry continued.

'I see,' Ada said. She was thinking about the likelihood that she'd have a meltdown on the witness stand and if that would make the case more difficult to prosecute. She didn't want to be responsible for making it easier for Sanchez to get off.

'We'd make sure that accommodations are offered. You could testify by video, if necessary, to ensure you are comfortable.'

'Thank you,' Ada said. She folded her hands in her lap, assuming that Henry had delivered all the information he had come for, and that he would be leaving now. He'd said he understood she didn't want a romantic relationship with him.

'Do you have any questions for me?' Henry asked.

He didn't look at her, but at her left shoulder. She appreciated that.

'Did you intend to lie to me when you came the first time?' Ada asked.

Henry's eyes fluttered wider. He hadn't expected that, it seemed. 'I . . . no. I didn't set out with any specific intention, really. I came because I was curious, and I wanted to talk to you again. And then the more I talked to you, the more I believed that there truly had been a murder.'

'And that was when you decided to lie to me,' Ada said.

Henry sighed. 'It wasn't like that. At least, not in my head. But yes, I suppose that was when I decided to lie to you. I thought that, given our previous connection, I was the best person to pair with you in the investigation, and I knew that I wouldn't be assigned to the case if I brought it back to the FBI. I was also pretty sure you'd be cut out. So I lied to you, and to other people, that I was officially investigating as an active agent of the FBI.'

'I won't ever be able to trust you not to lie to me again,' Ada said.

Now Henry did look at her in the eyes, if only for a moment. 'I know that. And I'm sorry.'

'But it was what had to be done, to get justice for Ella. Is that what you're going to say?' Ada asked.

'I . . . maybe it was necessary. I guess we'll never know for sure. I thought it was what had to be done. But my judgment might have been clouded.' He grimaced.

Ada waited for him to stand up and leave. When he didn't, she said, 'I hate that photograph from high school.'

He laughed loudly at that. 'Yes, that was a terrible one. Blurry and not very flattering of either of us.'

'It makes me feel . . . naked,' Ada said. 'People looking into my past like that. Sorting through all the pieces to find the one that looks worst.'

'Yes, I know what you mean. Hmm.' He tapped a finger on his knee.

It was the most obvious of all signals of body language, but it still took a moment for Ada to interpret it as him wanting to say one more thing before he left.

'I won't say what Sanchez tried to force you into doing,' Ada offered. 'If that's what you're worried about?'

'What?' His face jerked up again. 'No, no. Don't worry about that. Tell them everything you want about that part. It will just make things worse for her. I've already fully disclosed everything that she said anyway. It's probably impossible to hide it, and the defense will surely try to use it against us. So we have to be upfront about it.'

'So what is it? Your tapping – you want to say something else?'

Henry stopped his fingers from tapping on his knee. 'You know, for all you claim to not notice tells, to not see the obvious things, you sure seem to read people well.'

'I don't see the obvious things. I see the details. I live in an upside-down world where everything that matters is opaque and everything that doesn't matter is glaringly obvious.'

'Yes, well, that is what I wanted to talk to you about. I wanted to know . . .' He trailed off again.

'Just say it. You don't need to massage it for me. I like it better when it's plain and simple,' Ada said.

'Right, well, I was going to ask if you might be interested in working on other cases with me. Where I think you might be useful.'

Ada was stunned into silence.

Henry stood up then, brushing off his pants even though nothing was on them. 'I don't want you to think that I imagine our relationship would be anything other than professional. I'm not trying to trap you. I just saw how you work, and I think you'd be an asset.'

Ada still didn't know how to respond. This was such a surprise to her, another reason why she hated how bad she was at guessing the thoughts of neurotypical people.

'Or, if you'd rather, I could find another agent who could work with you. I mean, if you're too uncomfortable around me,' Henry said.

Ada finally found some words to respond. 'I will consider it. If I have time, and if the case interests me. But not with another agent.'

Henry let out a breath of apparent relief. 'All right, then. Good. Thank you. I mean, I'm glad you don't hate me after all this.'

'My feelings toward you are neutral,' Ada said. 'Which is good. Most neurotypical people who have lied to me don't get all the way back to neutral, and certainly not so quickly.'

Henry gave a half-smile and a bit of a bow. 'Well, thank you. I'll take that as a compliment. And once this case is finished, I'll be looking out for other chances to collaborate with you.'

'When I'm not busy trying to contact aliens,' Ada said.

Henry turned back from his exit, and he seemed unsure of what response to give to this.

So Ada helped him out and laughed. 'That was a joke,' she said.

'Ah, yes. An Ada joke,' he said, and laughed with her.

And that was that.